DARK PRINCE'S MATE

A REALM OF DRAGONS & SCROLLS 2

ANNA ZAIRES

CHARMAINE PAULS

GREY EAGLE PUBLICATIONS

This is a work of fiction. Names, characters, places, and incidents are either the product of the author's imagination or are used fictitiously, and any resemblance to actual persons, living or dead, business establishments, events, or locales is purely coincidental.

Published by Grey Eagle Publications
www.greyeaglepublications.com

Cover by Alex McLaughlin

ISBN: 978-1-64366-914-4
Print ISBN: 978-1-64366-915-1

CHAPTER 1
ELSIE

The warmth of the soft sand beneath my back is welcome in the cool, dry air. The weather isn't warm and humid like I've grown used to in Lona, and instead of smelling like moss and flowers, the breeze carries a stale, salty scent.

Goosebumps run over my arms under the light fabric of my shirt. I stretch out to better soak up the pleasant heat from the sunbaked beach. Squinting at the misty glare of the white sun, I study the colorless sky. There's not a pterosaur or cloud in sight.

I'm lying on the shore of a small silver lake with gargantuan trees all around it. The star-shaped leaves are so delicate they're almost transparent. They catch the pale light twinkling on the branches and sparkling in the reflection of the water. The fallen leaves glitter like a lacy carpet of cobwebs on the ground. The lake isn't deep because the same trees dot the surface, standing up to their knobby roots in the water.

Betty, my quetzalcoatlus friend, sits close by in the shade of a palm tree, which is such a deep green it almost looks black. She watches me sulkily, her gaze flitting between my face and the weird tadpole-ish thing she's plucked from the water and tossed next to me. It looks like a giant sperm with catfish barbels and two disproportionately miniscule lizard feet at the front.

"Nope," I tell Betty. "I'm not going to eat that."

She extends her giraffe-like neck and pokes the beige-brown, slimy glob with her beak. It wobbles like jelly.

Eww. And I'm definitely not eating it raw.

The tadpole hisses and slashes its tail viciously through the air, kicking up sand as it hits the ground.

"You'd better throw it back in the water." At the almost dejected way in which Betty hangs her head, I add quickly, "But thanks for wanting to feed me. I appreciate it all the same."

She lifts her long lashes, blinks innocently with those soft, big eyes, and unceremoniously gobbles up the tadpole.

Gross.

I suppress a shudder as she tucks her head beneath a wing to doze off in the hollow she's scrubbed for herself in the sand. After a moment, I follow her example and interlink my fingers behind my head to make myself more comfortable and finally process what has happened.

I flew.

I freaking flew.

On a dinosaur's back, no less.

The knowledge is so unreal and exhilarating that it still feels like a dream.

How much distance did we cover? I have no idea. I only know we were in the air for a long time. The landscape changed from stark iron-blue cliffs and foamy white-capped seas to rolling hills of succulent grass and tree-studded lakes. The vegetation slowly grew denser and darker until it turned into a jungle. We landed in a small clearing next to the water so that Betty could eat and drink. I sensed she was getting tired.

If anyone back home had told me I'd fly across a strange world on a quetzalcoatlus's back, I would've laughed in their faces. How is this even possible? All I had to do to steer Betty in a specific direction was to think where I wanted her to go. Back at the palace, I only had to reach out to her with my mind, and there she was, landing on the balcony.

The strange power zapping like currents of electricity under my skin is responsible for this ability. It's hard to believe that a short while ago, I lay in a hospital bed in Cleveland, Ohio, while my parents grieved in a corner as a doctor told me I was dying. Just as I was mourning my impending mortality, a circle of lights appeared, and I was sucked onto a different planet, an Earth-like world in what I figure must be a parallel universe. A world where lizard people would've gang-raped me and sold me as a slave if a darkly handsome prince with a terrible power hadn't saved me, claiming that I was his mate.

I take a deep breath and slowly let it out. I've been too preoccupied with staying on Betty's back to dwell on what happened with Aruan, but now I can't help myself.

We had sex. He took my V-card, only to treat me with a cold, cruel indifference in the aftermath.

My chest tightens as I relive those terrible moments.

He must've hated the sex.

For all his claims that I'm fated to be his, we're clearly not compatible as mates.

At the time, I was too overwhelmed to think clearly. I simply had to get away. What I've done only hits me now.

I escaped.

Holy fuck.

I actually did it.

This is what I wanted. This is what I set out to do from the moment I arrived on Zerra and doubly so when I found out that my presence could be dangerous for this strange, beautiful world. So why do I feel so down, so disturbingly… forlorn at the thought of putting distance between me and Aruan? Sure, we had sex. But it wasn't like we made love. It was more like "let's rip each other's clothes off and just get it over with."

No, that's not true. Aruan did take his time with foreplay. I can't fault him for that. He ensured my pleasure, even if the act was painful at first. He'd vowed that I'd enjoy it, and although I have to admit so begrudgingly, he kept his promise.

An involuntary sigh falls from my lips.

A certain something, a feeling I can't place, is growing inside me, and it's not a pleasant sensation. I feel as if I'm out of sync with myself, as if I'm somewhere I'm not supposed to be. It's as if I'm… incomplete. Yet at the same time, I feel good in my own skin. This weird power that has taken over my mind has settled inside me with the ease of something that has always belonged there. But there's also something amiss. With the distance from Aruan, the pull toward him is stronger. Which is stupid. And silly. And doesn't make sense. Especially seeing how he treated me. He even told me our mating wasn't complete, so there's no reason for me to feel so dejected.

No, it's better like this.

I'm not pining for a man I slept with once. I'm just a bit out of sorts, seeing that it was my first time. Besides, Aruan's power is far too dangerous, and he's demonstrated on multiple occasions how easily he loses control of it when he thinks the safety of his mate —a.k.a. me—is at stake. I can't shake the memory of those strange scrolls and their prophecy, the warning that a powerful prince will destroy Zerra because of his mate.

Aruan is certainly powerful. The man can set off a nuclear explosion, for crying out loud. And he is a prince.

Yeah. I'm not superstitious or into prophecies, but I'm not willing to take that risk. It's better for everyone that I left—for Aruan, who was clearly disappointed with our sex, for me, and for Zerra.

I made the right decision. I'm sure of it. Yet when I push onto my elbows with newfound determination, the heaviness doesn't lift from my chest, and the illogical sense of loss only worsens when I get to my feet and command Betty with my mind.

"Let's go, girl."

Betty lifts her head and shakes out her feather tuft. I climb onto her back and hold on tightly to her neck, knowing the take-off is going to be bumpy.

She leaps into the air with a powerful thrust of her legs, spreads her wings, and takes off over the water. Once we're high enough, she picks up speed.

I try to enjoy the wind in my hair and the incredible feeling of freedom I experienced earlier, but I fail to rekindle those thrilling sensations. There's a heavy stone in my stomach, my chest tight with a peculiar sadness.

Wiggling my shoulders as if I could physically dispel those feelings, I focus on the landscape instead.

A black lake stretches out to the left. My pulse jumps. I recognize that gray, windswept shore. That was where the Phaelix almost loaded me on their slave boat.

A shiver of repulsion runs over me.

They brought me here, so they must know how to create a portal to send me back to Earth. My poor parents must be worried sick about me. I don't even want to think about what's going through their minds. They must expect the worst. Their only child—a dying child—disappeared from the hospital where they'd left her. A cult could've kidnapped me to use me as a demonic sacrifice. A shady organization that supplies dead bodies for people wanting to fake their own deaths could've stolen me. Maybe Mom and Dad have started preparations for a funeral, but they won't even have that closure if they don't have a body.

I can just imagine them grieving while looking for me everywhere. Knowing them, they would employ private investigators. Mom would make posters and put them up on lamp posts. She would post on social media and on all her local app groups. Dad would be driving the streets around the hospital, showing everyone a photo of me and asking if they've seen the woman in the picture. In my mind's eye, I see him sitting hunched over his steering wheel and squinting in the darkness as he searches for me until late in the night.

My chest clenches painfully.

"I'm coming, Mom and Dad," I whisper. "I'm so sorry."

The water seems to go on forever. The sky is even paler here, almost white. With the flat, black surface reflecting the washed-out light, it's a bleak portrait.

Just when I'm about to give up hope of ever seeing land again, the opposite shore appears in the distance. Humongous palm trees fringe the narrow beach.

Beyond the trees, a jungle stretches to an indigo mountain, and there, at the foot of a hill, a thin ribbon of smoke curls into the air.

My heart jolts.

Fire.

That means there's life.

I steer Betty that way. As we circle over the hilltop, I suck in a breath. A village of crude wooden houses on stilts stands in a clearing, their scrawny thatch roofs like cone beacons in the midst of the jungle. Meat skewered onto sticks is roasting over a fire in the center of the space. The smell of barbecued chicken reaches my nostrils, reminding me of the meal my kidnappers fed me after abducting me.

Five Phaelix sit around the fire, poking at the coals with sticks. They look up when Betty crosses the clearing, their bulging eyes narrowed. Jumping to their feet, they speak excitedly in their guttural language, but I have no idea what they're saying. They can't see me because they're looking directly up. All that should be visible to them is the underside of Betty's belly.

One of them bends down and picks up a long stick with a spiked end. He holds it in the air, ready to launch it, but we're too high for Betty to get hit.

Okay, so I need some kind of leverage or bribe to convince these dudes to portal me back to Earth. I have to think about that.

Just as I'm about to fly us out of here, I spot movement on one of the decks of the stilted houses. The door opens, and a Phaelix with a basket in his arms steps out. Another with a spiked stick exits. He turns back toward the door and shouts in an angry tone while waving at the clearing with his stick and slicing his hand through the air as if he's telling someone to hurry up.

The two Phaelix on the deck steal glances at Betty. A third appears at the doorstep, holding something that resembles a slingshot in one hand and a big rock in the other.

They must think Betty is circling them to pick one of them off the ground as a meal, and that slingshot is their best chance at protecting themselves. A hit to the head could be fatal.

I'm about to hightail it to safety when someone else stumbles through the door, someone with blond hair.

Holy cow.

It's not a Phaelix. It's a woman. She screams and hangs back, trying to duck into the house, but the Phaelix with the stick grabs her wrist and pulls her roughly onto the deck before pushing her toward a rope ladder. She screams again, lifting her dirt-streaked face toward the sky. Her clothes are in tatters, and her arms and legs are so filthy they look brown.

Hold on.

I know that face.

Oh, my god.

It's the woman from the slave barge, the one who spoke to me in English with a British accent.

The Phaelix leading the party drops his basket to the ground. It lands with a thud, sending a cloud of dust into the air. He barks out something to the others before climbing swiftly down the ropes. The Phaelix with the stick shoves the woman toward the ladder, inviting even louder screams. The one with the slingshot takes up a position on the deck and fixes a menacing gaze on Betty.

The leader snatches up his basket and turns it over next to the fire. A heap of rocks falls at his feet. Ammunition. It looks as if they may try to stone poor Betty to death if they can't get her with a single rock from the slingshot.

By now, the woman and the Phaelix with the stick have also climbed down the ladder. The Phaelix grips the woman's arm and drags her a short distance away before forcing her onto her knees. Her sobs and pleas have no effect on him as he points the stick at her and tells her in his rough accent, "Shut up, slave."

It's a trap. They're using the woman as bait to lure Betty closer. They have no qualms about sacrificing a slave, turning her into dinosaur meat to save their own skins, or I should say, scales.

Bastards.

I steer off to the right and land behind a hill where we're hidden from sight.

"Go home," I tell Betty, giving her a quick hug before clambering off her back and jumping to the ground.

There's no way I'm allowing them to hurt her. I also don't want to give Betty a chance to be tempted by the human meat waiting for her in the clearing. She may be as tame as a poodle with me, but I haven't had a chance to test the extent of my power yet. Betty remains a wild animal, and a dangerous, giant predator at that.

She tilts her head.

"Go on," I urge.

She's hesitant, but I can always call her back if I need her. However, if my plan works, I'll be on Earth before sunset.

Fuck.

I may never see Betty again.

I won't be able to explore this parallel world and its dinosaurs.

I'll never see Aruan again.

The notion hurts with unexpected force, but I push it down. I need to focus. I need to think about Mom and Dad.

Putting everything else from my mind, I run to the foot of the hill. When I look back over my shoulder, Betty is hovering in the long, fatty blades of swaying grass, following my movements with unblinking eyes.

"Go," I say again, trying hard to speak normally when my voice is close to breaking. "Go home before it gets dark."

It's not until I'm halfway up the hill that Betty finally lunges into the air. I stop, shading my face with my hand. She circles me once, twice, and then flies back in the direction from which we came.

"This was awesome," I whisper. "I'll never forget it."

Tears burn at the backs of my eyes, but I blink them away and carry on climbing until I reach the summit.

The village is visible from the top of the hill. I can make out the activity that, now that the threat of a "dragon" attack is over, is focused on preparing dinner. The blond woman is no longer kneeling on the ground but setting out wooden bowls on a flattened log. Another woman with red hair, whose face I recognize from the barge, is throwing logs on the fire.

How many human slaves do the Phaelix keep at the site?

I must get them out of here. Once I've freed them, I can force the Phaelix to take us back to Earth via the same way they brought us here. The question is, how? We've already established I'm no match for them in strength. I had a few cracked ribs and two missing teeth to show for my efforts, until Aruan's brother healed me. But that was before my Alit superpower made itself known.

Glancing around, I look for signs of animal or insect life. When the Phaelix brought me to Zerra, there wasn't a shortage of big, scary creepy crawlies in the jungle. True to my expectation, a line of giant ant-like insects with lobster-sized pinchers climbs up the trunk of a blue rubbery tree. They're so big I can clearly make out their compound eyes, elbowed antennae, and powerful jaws. Their hairy, scissored back feet resemble those of crickets. With their bright orange bodies and brownish-red heads, they look like enormous Parktown prawns.

I skirt around a purple fern the size of a bus with leaves like octopus tentacles to get a better look. The prawn-like insects form a steady line to the top of the tree where some weird teardrop-shaped cocoons hang from the branches. They deftly cut one open with their pinchers, exposing a fat, ash-gray larva as long as my arm.

The larva starts to wiggle, sticking its black, horned head outside, but the prawn-ants are on it before it has a chance to escape. They strike from all sides, cutting their prey to pieces with their gigantic pinchers. The larva lets out a high, shrill sound—almost like the whistle of a kettle—as the insects quickly chop it up.

Before I can blink, the army of alien prawns has cut open all the cocoons and is making minced meat of the larvae. Poor larvae. I feel bad for them, but I don't dare interfere in the cycle of nature or the natural food chain of this world. Who knows what disastrous ecological effects my meddling may have? As sorry as I am for the larvae, I have to admit that the prawns are impressive. They'd be lethal if they attacked in thousands.

A piercing cry comes from the Phaelix settlement. I swing around, just in time to see the group of Phaelix holding the redhead face-down on the ground. From the angry red forked dicks that slither from their groins toward her, there's no question about their intentions. I have to act quickly.

A single thought from me sends the prawns back down the tree and across the jungle toward the clearing. One of the Phaelix cackle-laughs as he hooks what's left of the woman's torn dress in a claw and pulls it up over her waist. All the while, those snake-like, dripping dicks are moving closer to her naked butt while she screams murder.

'*Faster*!' I command the prawns.

Their speed and agility are astounding. As they advance, their number grows. Hundreds of prawns pour from small craters in the ground to march with the rest in the direction I'm sending them.

By the time the prawns reach the village, they're a sea of orange that quickly swallows up every other color. The only sound that gives warning of their approach is the rustling of the vegetation they traverse.

They catch the Phaelix with their dicks hanging out off-guard. By the time the lizards see the insects, they're surrounded. The prawns are all over them in a second. The Phaelix jump up and down and grope for their pointed spear-like sticks that lie next to them on the ground, but in another beat, not a single green scale is visible beneath the crawling, pinching mountain of dirt-brown heads, bright orange bodies, and the pinkish red of the insects' undersides.

The chilling shrieks attract the attention of others Phaelix who pour from the jungle with fishing nets in their claws. At the sight that greets them, they drop their nets and run yelling for their houses, but the prawns cut them off from every angle. Soon, they, too, are drowning in the orange sea.

The redhead has scurried to her feet and is clinging to the blonde next to the fire, both of them sobbing uncontrollably. I command the prawns to move around them. The patch of mud in which they stand barefoot is like an island in a squirming saffron-colored sea.

Green goo and glob cover the soil as the prawns make steak of the lizards. I try to block out the horrific screams of the Phaelix. It's like an Alfred Hitchcock movie with prawns instead of birds. I still need some of the Phaelix alive if the humans and I are to make it out of here, so I command the prawns to back three of the Phaelix up against a tree before encircling them. One of the three is the guy who called the shots when Betty and I arrived on the scene, whom I presume to be their leader.

When all the lizards except for those three are dead, I clear out the prawns but leave the ones guarding my prisoners. The insects quickly disappear. I don't waste time in getting to the clearing.

The women stare at me with terrified, pasty faces while the Phaelix shout something in their language that sounds like insults.

"You're Elsie," the blonde exclaims. "Elsie from Cleveland. I remember you!"

I grin. "Fancy running into you again."

"What arc you doing here?" she asks with a slack jaw.

"Looking for a way back to Earth."

She continues in a daze as she looks around. "What happened? Where did these insects come from, and why didn't they attack us?"

"There'll be time for questions later." I point at the Phaelix. "Do you speak their language?"

She rubs her dirty arms, shivering as she gazes at the treetops nervously. "A little. Be careful. There may be more of them. They live in treehouses."

I glance over my shoulder at the makeshift bungalows on stilts. "Do you mean those aren't their homes?"

"Those are the prisons," the redhead says. "They're for us."

I take in her bony frame and the ribs protruding from underneath her threadbare dress. Bruises cover her arms and legs. Those lizards did a number on me too when I first arrived, so I have no doubt about who put those marks on her. They didn't starve me, but maybe they were just fattening me up before they intended to sell me. Yeah, no. I don't find any compassion in my heart for the dead lizards.

"How many humans are here?" I ask.

"Six, including us." The redhead's green eyes flash. "We were twelve, but Penny and Sabrina got sick and died. The other four guys were killed when they tried to overpower our captors."

Fuck. "We need to grab the others and get out of here." I turn to the blonde. "Ask them who can create a portal to Earth."

She opens her mouth, but instead of speaking, she lets out a scream as she fixes her gaze on something behind me.

I twirl around to see at least a dozen Phaelix swinging down on ropes from the thick foliage of the trees.

Before I have time to even think "prawns," a Phaelix jumps right in front of me, clutching a branch like a baseball bat.

Forget the prawns. There's no time. Think lizards.

I focus hard on the Phaelix surrounding me, commanding them to knock each other out with those bats they're waving around, but they only snarl and snap their shark-like teeth.

Oh, fuck.

My power doesn't work on the lizards. I guess I can't command intelligent species. I should've kept the prawns around, but it's too late to rectify that oversight.

Both the blonde and the redhead scream at the top of their lungs. I'm screaming too. Or I think I am, but maybe I just want to and never get a chance because even as I make a beeline for the jungle, something hits me so hard on the head that my brain rattles in my skull.

I'm trying to think of dinosaurs, but my mind is fuzzy, and my vision goes out of focus.

As I go down, the strange world with its vivid reds, yellows, purples, and oranges turns black.

CHAPTER 2
ELSIE

I wake up in a fetal position on a cold, hard surface. My head is pounding, and my mouth is so dry my tongue sticks to my palate. The rattling of my bones as I shiver convulsively doesn't help my headache. Wherever I am, it's like a fucking freezer in here.

Something sharp digs into my cheek. I turn onto my back and dust off the grit that sticks to the side of my face. With the splitting headache that hammers in my temples, the smallest movement hurts. I grind my teeth against the pain, crunching sand between my molars.

Where the fuck am I?

I peel open my eyelids and scan my surroundings. The darkness is so thick I can't see a thing. A dull ache pulses at the back of my skull. I brush my hand over the spot and hiss when I press on a huge egg.

Ouch.

My fingers come away wet and sticky. I bring them to my nose and inhale the metallic scent of blood.

The bastard who hit me most likely gave me a concussion with his makeshift baseball bat.

Groaning, I sit up carefully. "Fuck." That hurts.

"Quiet," a woman whispers in a strained tone. "You don't want to let them know you're awake."

I recognize that British accent. "Where am I?"

"In one of the cells."

Sniffling comes from the corner.

"Hush, Maeva," the British woman says. "Try to get some sleep."

Sleeping in the bitter cold and in the harrowing situation we find ourselves in is out of the question. I get onto my hands and knees, almost puking from the pain that increases with the minor effort, and test my balance before pushing to my feet.

Swallowing down bile, I feel my way through the darkness with my arms stretched out in front of me. All the while, I fight the dizziness that threatens to claim me. I take tiny steps, cautiously putting one foot in front of the other until I hit a barrier. I sweep my palms over the surface. The wall appears to be made of vertical poles that are covered with scratchy fabric.

I walk along the length, searching until I find the edge of the rough cloth, and pull it aside. The rudimentary drape acts as a curtain. Behind it is a wall crudely fabricated of branches that act as prison bars. A soft glow spills through the narrow gaps between the bars. The light comes from a fire that burns on the ground below. The smell of the smoke is thick outside. It seeps inside, already clinging to my clothes and hair. The silhouettes of the stilted houses are visible around the clearing. The sky is scattered with stars but moonless, leaving the landscape dark beyond the border of the trees.

When I turn my gaze back to the room, a circle of pale faces are staring wide-eyed at me. The group is a mix of different ages. I count one man and five women.

"What are you doing?" one of them whispers. "They'll punish you."

I snort. "They can try."

"They're forever punishing us," someone else replies wryly. "We don't even know why, so what difference does it make?"

I bundle the cloth between two bars to keep a corner open for a bit of light and slide down to the dirt floor. This way, I can also keep an eye on the clearing and on the Phaelix when they return. Bracing my back against one of the branches, I wrap my arms around my knees to maintain some warmth.

A woman creeps closer and sits down in front of me. Her golden-blond hair catches the light. I recognize her from earlier.

"I'm Sandy," she says, keeping her voice down.

I lean my head against the pillar and swallow more bile. Nausea is definitely a symptom of a concussion.

She studies me with a curious expression. "What happened to you? How did you end up here after that Alit took you away?"

I sigh. "It's a long story. In short, I escaped. What about you? I thought you'd gotten away with the barge. I hoped you'd found a portal to take you back to Earth."

"We did get away." She snickers. "I did some sailing in my day."

The man shuffles toward us on his knees. "We ran into slavers while crossing the jungle." His accent is Germanic. "The bastards got us again." A long, unkempt beard matches the chestnut color of his shoulder-length hair. "We didn't stand a chance." He holds out a hand. "I'm Karl, by the way."

I shake his hand, wincing at how thin and bony his fingers feel in my palm.

The woman called Maeva whimpers louder in her corner.

"Shh." A willowy woman with platinum-blond hair throws an arm around Maeva's shoulder. "There now, *dorogaya*. I've got you."

"Maeva wasn't with us." Sandy sneers as she juts her chin toward the clearing. "Those dogs already had her when they intercepted the rest of us. Who knows what they've done to her? She never speaks." She taps her temple. "She's fragile up here."

"We've all been here for different lengths of time," the redhead says, moving toward our circle. "But Maeva seems to have had it the worst."

"What about you?" I ask Sandy. "How long have you been here?"

She squares her shoulders. "Longer than the others,

but I'm strong. It'll take those motherfuckers a hell of a lot more to break me."

I look around the room. "How did you all end up on this planet?"

"The same way," Karl says. "The last thing each of us remembers was being sucked through a circle of colorful lights. There's no regularity to the abductions. We come from different backgrounds and places."

"I was taken from Central Park where I was jogging early in the morning," the redhead says. "Alexa." She gives a little wave. "Pleased to meet you. I wish it was under more pleasant circumstances."

"I'm Irina," the platinum blonde says in a strong Russian accent. "I was walking home from work in Moscow."

"What about you?" Sandy asks. "What were you doing in Cleveland when they took you?"

"I was in the hospital." I bite my lower lip as I consider if there could be a pattern to the kidnappings. "I wonder how they choose their targets?"

"From what we could figure out, the abductions are random," Alexa says. "We're from different countries around the world, including Germany, Kenya, the USA, the UK, and Russia. We're not sure where Maeva is from, but I think she could be either from Canada or France because she sometimes mutters in French in her sleep." She averts her eyes. "The others who didn't make it were from China, Belgium, Spain, and other countries in Europe and Asia. Most of them only spoke a few words of English."

I look around the group. The same air of despondency surrounds each of them. They're dirty and undernourished, which worries me. Even more concerning is the scene I witnessed when the Phaelix pushed Alexa down on the ground.

Lifting my head, I clear my throat. "Are we slaves as in forced, unpaid labor, or are we sex slaves?"

"So far, they've only used us to cook and clean for them," Sandy says. "But I overheard them talking about a slave auction that's happening soon." She bares her teeth. "I bet that's when we'll truly find out."

Maeva utters a high-pitched cry.

"Shh, *dorogaya,*" Irina says, pulling Maeva's head onto her shoulder.

I catch Alexa's gaze. "That's not what it looked like earlier."

"That was a first," she says, quivering while rubbing her arms. "They got really worked up about the dinosaur that circled over the huts. They call them dragons. I don't know what got into them, but you don't want to unleash their violence. It seems that danger and fighting make them fucking horny."

"Bastards," Karl bites out.

I think about my own near-rape experience and suppress a shudder.

"Have you tried to escape?" I ask.

"Impossible," Sandy says. "They always keep watch. Even now, one of them is guarding the area from their outlook decks in the trees." She turns her face to Irina. "And we all know what happens when you try."

Irina drops the sleeve of her blouse and shows me half of her back. Long slashes crisscross her shoulder blade. "They did this with a thorny branch. I'm lucky it healed without getting infected."

Fuck.

Alexa leans closer. "If you don't do what they say, they drop a slug-like leech into your ear." She points at a woman with cherub cheeks that sits in the center of the floor. "That's how Eucabeth went deaf. From how she screamed, it must've been agonizing."

Cruel fuckers. They'll get what they deserve. Too bad we need some of them alive to get off this planet.

"Have you found out anything about the portals?" I ask. "Those lizards brought us here. Some of them must be able to create portals that can take us back."

Sandy shakes her head. "They don't even discuss it among themselves when they think we're not listening, and they're aware that I'm the only one who understands a little of their language. It must be a tightly guarded secret."

If only I could connect with the prawns, but my head is hurting too much. It feels as if my brain has been through a blender. I can hardly think, let alone concentrate on using my power.

I rub my aching temples. The pain is getting worse instead of better, which isn't a good sign.

Sandy observes me with a pinched brow. "You don't look good."

My chuckle is wry. "One of you don't happen to have painkillers, do you?"

I try to keep a sense of humor, but if moving hurts, laughing is pure torture.

She sighs. "Medicine is a luxury the slavers never allow. I don't even think they know the concept."

In that case, I may end up dead after all. Unless I make it back to Earth in time.

Sandy studies me with a curious light burning in her blue eyes. "What happened at the beach? What did that Alit want with you? He looked downright scary."

"This is going to sound weird."

Sandy chuckles. "Believe me, hun, nothing can sound weird to me anymore."

Point taken. "He's an Alit prince, and he thought I was his mate."

I expect them to burst out laughing, but they only stare at me with owl-sized eyes.

"But..." Sandy frowns. "I've picked up a few things since arriving here, and from what I've gathered, the Alit don't mate with humans."

I consider telling them the truth, that I discovered I'm an Alit myself, but I decide against it. I'm not sure how they'd feel about me if they learned I'm not a born-and-bred Earthling, and it's too cumbersome to explain the whole history. Besides, I don't understand everything myself yet. Nor do I want to dwell on what happened between Aruan and me, especially the fact that a part of me already misses him. So I shrug and settle for, "He was wrong."

I'm not his mate. We did the whole consummation

thing and all the hotness that went with the act, and then he told me our mating had failed.

"Wait," I say as I remember something. "He spoke to you in his language, and you understood him."

"I've picked up a few words." Sandy hugs her knees to her chest. "I'm a fast learner, and I've always had a good ear for languages."

I sit up straighter and immediately regret the sudden movement when pain lances into my brain. "That means you've met some Alit."

"Only one, and I never formally met him. He always came to see the Phaelix after dark, and he wore a cloak that hid his face. He obviously didn't want to be seen. He brought a Phaelix with him who spoke his Alit language and who could interpret for them. When they'd come, I'd keep quiet and still, trying to become invisible in whatever corner they'd tied me up in for the night. But the man hasn't been back for a while now."

"What did they talk about?"

"I couldn't make out all of it." She rocks back and forth, appearing thoughtful. "They were obviously negotiating because they mentioned debts and payments. The Phaelix said something about slaves. That's when the man said the Alit only mated with their own kind."

I think about that. "Do you think the Phaelix wanted to sell him a slave?"

"Maybe." She pulls her shoulders up to her ears. "Who knows? All I know is that the Alit must be dangerous because the Phaelix were scared of him, and they're not scared of anything. They acted cocky in front of him, but they were nervous before he came, and they were certainly edgy when he left."

"Did you get a name?"

"No." She stops rocking and swats at a huge fly that buzzes past. "How about your guy? I suppose communication wasn't easy."

I don't tell her that Aruan's brother, Kian, gave me the ability to understand and speak their language. I'm too busy contemplating something I've wondered about since the incident when Aruan saved me from the slave traders. "What did he say to you that made you go so quiet?"

"That day on the barge?" Sandy asks with big eyes. "He told me to leave you alone unless I wanted to end up as ashes, and to go back to where we came from. I assumed he meant Earth." She snort-laughs. "After what he did to those slavers, I wasn't going to argue with the man. Anyway, from the way he clutched you like a wild dog that had just found his favorite bone, I assumed you knew each other."

"Nope," I say, leaving the explanation at that. "We need to figure out which ones of these lizard dudes make portals. Do you have any idea who they may be?"

Alexa makes a face. "They all look more or less the same, and they don't have names, at least not any we're aware of."

I can see how that's going to be a problem.

"We'd better catch some sleep while we can," Sandy,

who seems to have taken up a leadership position in the group, says. "They'll wake us before sunrise to fetch water and cook their breakfast."

At the word "breakfast," my stomach grumbles, reminding me it's empty. Although I'm not sure I'd be able to keep food down. From the way I'm feeling now, I'll probably be sick if I eat.

The women settle down, huddling together to keep warm. Karl lies down too. I remain in my spot, set on keeping watch. When the Phaelix show themselves, I can try to overpower them with some giant jungle critters, but I'd better make sure they let us out of here first. There's no point in killing them and then dying of starvation in our prison. Unless I can command a dinosaur to snap the branches in two and break down the wall.

I focus hard on Betty, willing her to come, but as the hours drag on, nothing happens. I have to admit that my concentration is iffy. Did the knock on my head damage my power?

When the sun finally peeks through the branches, the Phaelix descend on ropes from the trees. In the daylight, I can make out the wooden decks and thatch roofs in the treetops that peek through the leaves. You wouldn't notice those well-hidden treehouses unless you looked up and knew what to search for.

While the people stir awake around me, I scout for animal life. Finally spotting a line of giant hairy ant-like spiders scurrying across the clearing, I perk up. The arthropods may not be venomous, and I have no idea if they're dangerous, but if all else fails, I can smother the Phaelix under a mountain of ant-spiders. I just need one of those dudes to unlock our cage first.

As I hoped, a Phaelix heads straight for our prison, already shouting unintelligible orders from a distance. Karl and the women scurry to their feet. When I stand, my stomach convulses. I double over, retching as spasms rack my body, but only bile comes out.

Sandy walks to the exit when the Phaelix opens the gate. She says something in his language while pointing at me. I'm too busy surviving the pain that's like an axe splitting my cranium to care about the exchange. All she gets for her effort is a slap across the face that makes her head jerk to the side.

Wiping a trickle of blood from the corner of her mouth, she gives the Phaelix a cutting look before walking onto the deck. The rest of the slaves follow. Alexa takes my arm and helps me outside.

Strangely enough, I feel a little better after emptying my already-empty stomach, but my thoughts still don't have any effect on the spiders. The last one disappears into the thick undergrowth by the time we reach the clearing. My knees wobble beneath my weight. If Alexa weren't supporting me, I would've collapsed in a heap on the ground.

A bustling of activity follows as the Phaelix shout orders, and the slaves jump into action. Karl grabs a broom and sweeps the clearing while Irina piles twigs into Maeva's trembling arms. Sandy is already building a fire. Alexa, Eucabeth, and I follow a footpath to a lake. A few Phaelix guard us, one walking in the front and another at the back. The bright, violet, tube-shaped worms that wiggle on the ground with gaping jaws and saliva dripping from their fangs make me grateful for my boots, but I worry about the other women who are barefoot.

It quickly becomes clear that the Phaelix are not only with us to make sure we don't escape but also to keep the creepy-crawlies at bay and prevent them from stinging or eating us.

A few wooden buckets with rope handles hang on the branches of the trees that grow on the shore. Alexa and Eucabeth take them down and wade into the water.

The Phaelix who took the lead points at my boots and puts his face in mine while yelling something. I reel from the stink of his rotten breath.

Haven't they invented the toothbrush here? Another pang hits me from nowhere when I think about the comfortable cleansing room in Aruan's palace and the sweet-tasting paste that left my teeth clean and sparkly white.

The Phaelix raises his arm and makes a fist with his hand.

"Okay." I duck and almost faint from the movement. "Fuck. Ouch. Calm down, dude. I get it. You want me to fetch water."

He grabs a bucket and shoves it into my arms. I turn the bucket upside down, sit down on my improvised stool to remove my boots, and make a humongous effort not to keel over when I get up again. He stands over me, watching me with narrowed eyes as I roll Aruan's pants up to my knees before taking the bucket and padding into the water.

Fuck. It's freezing cold. The muddy sand pushes between my toes. Something slimy brushes against my calf. I yelp and jump to the side, only to almost pass out again.

"Stay in front of me so they can't see you're not working," Alexa says through the side of her mouth. "I'll fill your bucket."

Fill my bucket? What she means becomes clear when I look at Eucabeth. She's not scooping up water but digging with sticks in the sand. Every now and then, she throws down her stick and dunks her arms up to the elbows into the water before pulling out one of those giant sperm tadpoles that Betty had caught. It takes both Alexa and Eucabeth to lift the tadpole out of the water. One holds it around the middle and the other grabs its tail, preventing it from lashing out or biting them.

When the buckets are full, we drag them out of the water onto the shore. I'm dismayed to find my boots gone. Our guards must've confiscated them. Damn. I really liked those boots.

The buckets are too heavy for even two of us to carry, so the Phaelix take the buckets while we gather firewood on the way back.

When we return, the clearing is swept, and a huge cauldron of water is boiling over the fire. The Phaelix dump the buckets on the ground and shout more demands.

Moving closer to Sandy, I ask, "What are they saying?"

"They're planning on feeding us," she says with a concerned expression.

"That's good, right?"

"Not necessarily," she whispers. "They never do anything without a good reason. They've got something up their sleeves."

"Why do they starve you?" I ask, suddenly furious, which also doesn't help to diminish the pulsing pain in my skull.

"I don't think they do it intentionally. The food they eat doesn't always agree with our stomachs, and sometimes, we get sick from it. They mostly give us fruit and roots that we dig up and boil in water, but they keep the meat for themselves. Unless…" She bites off the rest of her sentence as she glances at Maeva, who's kneeling next to the fire.

Unless they're selling us today. They want to make sure we're not going to faint from hunger. That's why they fed me when they first brought me here.

My stomach roils at the thought. And now my power is useless. I won't even be able to save us. For all I know, I've sustained brain damage, and my power is permanently gone.

A Phaelix pushes me roughly, causing me to fall to my knees. He dumps a bucket full of wiggling tadpoles in front of me and screams loud enough to make my ears ring. Wiping away his spittle that landed on my face, I look at the other women for a clue of what I'm supposed to do, and then I almost vomit again.

They're using flat stones to crush the heads of the tadpoles before gripping the top and bottom jaws and turning them inside out. The thick leathery skin of the tadpole detaches easily from the slippery body, allowing the women to skin the fishy sperm effortlessly.

I watch in horror as a Phaelix rips the skinned tadpoles into pieces between his sharp teeth before spitting the morsels into a bucket. Karl takes the pieces from the bucket and skewers the meat onto a stick that he hands to a trembling Maeva who roasts the meat over the fire.

Soon, the smell of barbecued chicken fills the air.

Oh, my god.

That's what they fed me on the night they abducted me? Giant sperm toads?

The Phaelix eat first. When Sandy hands out the leftover meat to the humans, I consider giving my ration a pass, but I need my strength. Only, when I swallow my first bite of juicy meat, it comes straight up again.

The Phaelix sitting closest to me isn't happy. He waves the pointed stick in his hand at the undigested meat on the ground and throws what sounds like a string of accusations at me. I pick up the meat, dust it off, and pretend to eat, but when he's not looking, I throw it in the fire.

As soon as breakfast is over, we're shooed into the bushes to relieve ourselves while two Phaelix stand guard. The fire is quickly put out and the clearing covered with branches, presumably to hide it. Then we take off along the same path to the lake.

Instead of crossing the water in a barge as I was expecting, we walk along the shore to the other side before cutting through the jungle. Yellow, red, and blue flowers with glittery anthers grow everywhere, competing for space with black, spongy ferns.

A rocky mountain leers up in front of us. A broad river divides the landscape. A barge similar to the one from before waits in the water. Once we're all inside, two Phaelix row us downstream with paddles. At the mouth of the river, we enter a lake. The mountain rises from the water with a halo of smoke hanging over the top.

Holy cow.

It's a live volcano.

At the foot of the mountain, we enter a cave with a ceiling that's so low we have to lie flat in the barge to prevent our heads from bumping on the rock ceiling.

On the other side, the cave opens onto a tropical beach in the middle of the mountain. Cliff walls surround the beach from all sides, cutting us off from visibility. It's a brilliant hideout. Under different circumstances, I'd call this secret beach in the hollow of a volcano paradise.

A big wooden platform stands in the middle of the

beach. The circular stone benches surrounding the stage are packed with Phaelix.

Oh, shit.

A Phaelix runs up to pull our barge onto the sand. We're promptly escorted off the barge and lined up behind the stage.

"This is it," Sandy says, spitting on the sand. "We're being auctioned."

"What are they going to do with us?" Alexa asks in an unsteady voice.

"Your guess is as good as mine, hun," Sandy says.

The Phaelix who brought us here are on the stage, making some kind of speech while the crowd goes crazy. It all happens in a haze. I blame it on my concussion, not quite realizing what's going on when a Phaelix shoves me between the shoulder blades and orders something I don't understand.

I look at the other women and Karl. They're all naked. We're definitely not being sold to work. Well, not only. If these assholes want to glare at the goods, it can only mean one thing. They intend to rape us.

When I don't move, the Phaelix grabs my shirt and tears it down the middle. There's a flash of claws, and then I'm naked too.

Maeva is the first one to be manhandled onto the stage. Strangely enough, she's not crying but only staring vacantly in front of her.

The other women are shivering on the wet sand, looking on with terrified expressions. Karl stands helplessly, his jaw bunched in powerless anger. My turn is next. I stumble, nearly going down onto my knees. I sway on my feet in the center of the stage, barely hanging on to consciousness. I don't want to pass out now. Who knows what these fuckers are going to do to me? If only my power would return... Unfortunately, I'm as powerless as the day I arrived on Zerra.

Someone calls out something from the audience. I turn my face toward the sound.

What the...?

I blink twice to make sure I'm seeing right.

Shit.

Not all Phaelix look alike, after all. The one who's standing, pointing a flabby arm adorned with shiny bangles at me, is enormous. His head is the size of a yoga ball, and his red glowing eyes are bulging out of his head. The folds under his chin wobble as he says something.

The Phaelix on the stage, who's digging his claws into my arm, calls something back. The Phaelix in the audience laughs so hard his big stomach shakes. He lifts the folds that hide his groin in both hands to reveal a red tongue-shaped dick with a forked end snaking from somewhere. With all those scaly layers, it's impossible to tell where it's attached to his body. He makes a vulgar thrusting gesture with his hips, causing raucous laughter to break out in the crowd.

I can only imagine what he's saying, but I'm not staying to find out. Concussion or not, one look at that dick dripping with sticky, green goo is enough to propel me into action.

I jam an elbow into the ribs of the Phaelix holding me, catching him by surprise. He lets my wrist go and utters a cry of pain. I kick him between the legs for good measure, taking no small satisfaction in how his eyes cross as he cups his groin and goes down on his knees.

My best bet is the water. I'm sprinting for the side of the stage, knowing that with my head injury, the jump has a good chance of killing me, but I'd rather die with my face in the sand than between that Phaelix's legs. Or worse, with that red dick down my throat.

I'm almost at the edge when my run is broken violently. A claw locks around my ankle, plucking my feet from under me. My wind is knocked out when I hit the wooden surface.

For a moment, I can't breathe. All I see are fireflies. They're everywhere—on the beach, in the sky, and behind my eyelids. I'm blinking through the fog, trying to clear my head when the big Phaelix drops the folds around his middle and raises his arm triumphantly in the air.

A chorus of cheers rises among the Phaelix.

Oh, fuck.

I think I've just been sold.

CHAPTER 3
ARUAN

"Find her," I command my mother through clenched teeth as I pace in front of the window in her quarters.

Sweat beads on her brow. "I'm trying."

"She's too weak." My father hands her a cup of wine. "The Phaelix attack drained what little strength she'd recovered."

"Gaia!" I call loud enough to be heard in all the corners of the palace.

My father's tone is stern, but the look he gives me is wary. "Calm down, Aruan."

Because losing control means unleashing my power, and we've all seen how that turns out.

My mother collapses on a chair. "I can't carry on. I have to stop for a while."

I pause in front of the window and grip the ledge hard. Elsie vanished not minutes ago, and already, it feels like forever. Too long.

I left her in my quarters to confront my mother, and the next moment, a dragon landed on my balcony and carried away my mate. I saw it happen through this very window, and I was powerless to stop them. Elsie flew away on the dragon before I had time to portal myself there.

It wasn't just any dragon, either. I recognized the tear in its wing. It was the dragon Elsie begged me not to kill at the lake, the one she called Betty. Since that encounter, we discovered that my mate has control over the mind of not only that dragon but also of small insects like water dragons and all the pets in the palace. I have no doubt Elsie summoned Betty so she could escape, something she'd wanted to do from the moment her feet had touched the ground in Lona.

Who knows where she's headed? She couldn't have reached another kingdom yet, not even at the speed a dragon flies. The kingdoms are too vast. But every minute we waste is a minute she's moving farther from me. I can feel her presence just like I did when she first appeared on Zerra, so she must be only a local portal away.

Gaia should be able to find her, but if we don't act fast, the distance may become too far for my sister to handle, and then only my mother will be able to help me. However, in the queen's current state, she may not be of much help.

I hate to admit it, but my father is right. My mother is still too weak after being poisoned and then wearing herself out by using her power extensively during the attack. It takes an immense amount of strength and energy to create portals, especially the powerful ones my mother is capable of making.

I spin away from the window. "Where the dragon is Gaia?"

"I'm here," my sister says, hurrying through the archway. "I came as soon as I heard. Is it true? Did Elsie fly away on a dragon's back?"

I curl my fingers into fists. As always, the gossip spreads fast. "Find her. She's still within our kingdom."

Gaia sits down on the daybed and gets to work. My father urges my mother to drink some honey wine to recover her strength, and with his help, she manages to take a few sips.

While Gaia opens portal after portal in various locations, my mother drifts off into a fretful sleep. That she does so is evidence of how worn out she must be. Normally, she abhors napping and never sleeps during the day. In all my life, I've never seen her doze off sitting up in a chair. My mother is much too regal to indulge in a practice she considers to be a weakness, not to mention a display of bad manners in the presence of company.

The sun is already low when Gaia finally begs for a break. I look at my mother, but my father discourages me from waking her with a shake of his head.

"Let her sleep a bit longer," he says. "She'll be better able to help you if she's regained her strength. There's no point in disrupting her rest before she's recovered sufficiently. We'll only prolong the search if she's not strong enough to wield her power."

The compulsion to find Elsie is overpowering, but I recognize that my father is once again right. What he says makes sense, not only in my mother's case but also in my sister's, so I fill a goblet with water from the decanter on the stone table and hand it to Gaia.

While she drinks and takes a moment to catch her breath, I stalk to the window and peer at the horizon.

The sky remains clear. There's not a dragon in sight. Not that I expect Elsie to return. Why would she? She made it clear she doesn't want the bond that ties mates together for life.

Her rejection is nothing new, but it cuts that much deeper now that we've mated. After I claimed her, I had to leave right away, and not just because I was impatient to question my mother about how Elsie ended up on Earth. I needed a moment to deal with Elsie's reaction. Once the uncontrollable mating heat had dissipated, she regretted letting me fuck her. The dismay was written all over her face. And even if it hadn't been, the mere fact that our mating bond didn't strengthen as it should've told me how she felt about me. About us.

And then she escaped. Left me.

She ran the moment I turned my back.

This is so wrong. It's not the way it's supposed to be.

The sex was explosive. The intensity and pleasure I had with Elsie were unlike anything I've experienced.

However, the bond was incomplete. *Is* incomplete. The mental and emotional tie that should've connected us irrevocably is the same as it was before the mating. In the hollow of my chest where I can only ever sense the thoughts and feelings of one woman, our connection remains unchanged, weak.

Where did I fail?

What went wrong?

It doesn't make sense.

Taunted by the emptiness of the sky, I turn away from the window. "Ready to continue, Gaia?"

My heart is like a live volcano in my chest, about to spew liquid fire.

"I need another minute," she says, wiping sweat from her brow with her sleeve.

Why the dragon must this take so long?

We carry on through the night, my mother and Gaia taking turns to open portals but with no success. Eventually, my mother catches a few hours of sleep while my father keeps watch at her bed, and Gaia is forced to continue the search.

As the day breaks and time rolls on, my despondency grows. The memory of the last time I saw Elsie invades my mind. Reliving that moment is the cruelest torture, but I can't stop punishing myself with those images that will haunt me for the rest of my life. I see everything clearly, as if it's happening right now.

The dragon leaps off the balcony, shaking the ledge. Flakes of brick sealer and stone chips rain to the ground. The beast spreads its wings and dives down toward the cliffs before rising almost straight up. Elsie clings to its neck as it levels out close to the clifftop. The dragon makes a circle over the palace, and then it takes off in flight, heading south.

An invisible crack stretches between us. It grows and grows, ripping my heart straight down the middle and tearing out my soul. It gets bigger and bigger, reaching all the way to my bones.

As the dragon flies away with Elsie, ice settles in my chest, and everything inside me turns to stone.

Gone. What was always meant to be mine has been ripped from me not once but twice.

My ears start ringing. It takes a beat to realize the noise comes from within my head. As that roar gets louder, the ground shakes beneath my feet, and fissures snake up the walls.

"Aruan."

The sound of my name reaches me through the haze that has taken over my reason.

"Aruan."

My mother.

She's awake.

I come back to my senses, calming myself with great effort. My mother sits upright in her chair with one arm stretched out and her fingers splayed. A circle of colorful lights dances in front of her.

Keeping the portal open, she says, "I found her."

CHAPTER 4
ARUAN

The sight that greets me when I exit the portal in the center of a volcano makes me see red. Elsie is lying face-down on a platform, her delicate ankle clasped in the clutch of a Phaelix who's sprawled out on his stomach behind her.

Killing rage blasts through my veins. Fury boils my blood. Another male is touching my mate. *Hurting* my mate. The blood that has dried in her hair at the back of her head makes my vision fray around the edges.

In a wink, my power fires through me with such force that it feels as if my skin is aflame. I'm blind to everything but Elsie and the male who threatens her. The offense tastes sharp and bitter on my tongue. He dared to lay his dirty claws on what belongs to me. He drew blood. My mate's blood.

He's dead.

I'll make that scaly piece of filth wish he was never hatched.

Targeting on the male the rage that continues to build like an earthquake inside me, I take great satisfaction from his screams as I dissolve him from his feet up.

At the first screams, Elsie stops struggling and whips her head to the side. Her lips part as our gazes collide.

The Phaelix lets go of Elsie's leg, withering and yelling until there's nothing left of him, but I'm no longer paying him attention. All my focus is trained on the small, fragile woman with hair the color of a pale sunset and eyes like the turquoise sea.

Mine.

Forever.

No one touches her and lives to see another day.

A single glance conveys those notions rushing through my head and beating in my chest. Only she can read my thoughts. And she does. I feel it. I also feel her relief as well as her dread.

Locked in that stare, we're frozen in the moment. Everything else falls away. Nothing exists but Elsie.

When reality finally returns, I register the chaos that has broken out around us. Phaelix are tripping over benches and stepping on those who have fallen to reach barges beached on the sand. After seeing what has happened to their friend, they know what's in store for them, and they think they can escape my wrath.

With a flick of my hand, I knit the rock mass in front of the cave together and seal off the exit. The Phaelix who were headed in that direction stop in their tracks and spin on their heels to run in the opposite direction. Some of them are trying to scale the steep cliffs, using their claws to climb up the almost vertical drop.

"Aruan."

The sound of my name on Elsie's lips is like a siren to my senses. Her voice pulls me. Her call is undeniable, impossible to ignore.

I look at her. She's gotten onto all fours and is regarding me as if I'm both her downfall and her salvation.

I make it to her in a few long strides and lift her into my arms. "I've got you, my sweet. You're safe now."

She trembles from head to toe. "Aruan! The mountain… It's going to blow."

I hardly pay the groaning soil and roaring volcano any notice. "You're hurt." I hug her tighter to me while examining her body with a practiced eye. "You're bleeding." My anger reaches a new level. "What have they done to you?"

"It's just my head." She grasps my shoulders. "If this volcano is going to erupt, we'll have bigger problems to worry about."

It *is* going to erupt. I don't bother reining in my power. This place needs to be razed to the ground. Any fool can see what's been going on here. I've just walked into the secret location the Phaelix have been using as a slave market. We've been searching for it for many moon cycles. My father delegated the task of eradicating the slave trading operation to me, and as fate would have it, the opportunity has fallen into my lap.

"Don't worry," I say. "The portal is open. I'll get you out of here."

"We have to take them with us," she cries out when I start moving, pointing at a row of naked people lined up behind the platform whom I haven't noticed.

The humans are smaller than the average Alit, but it's not only their meager height that gives them away. Their features are distinctly Earth-like with daintier bone structures and more sharply defined lines. I recognize a few of those faces from the barge. They're the ones I sent on their way when I first found Elsie. Back then, I was too consumed with having found my allegedly dead mate to worry too much about how they'd get back to Earth. They study me now much like they had on that first day, looking as petrified as the Phaelix.

I don't like to deny Elsie. Of course I won't leave them here to die. However, a group of humans will cause havoc at the palace. The scrolls forbid all contact with Earth, and I don't want it to be known that someone besides my mother can open portals to that world. The believers—and there are many—will consider these humans to be violating one of the principal laws of their doctrine. The result will be chaos. Plus, on a diplomatic level, it will be difficult to explain their presence without coming clean about the slave trading, which we've suspected for a while. The objective of letting me deal with the issue quietly was to avoid pandemonium in the kingdom. Bringing these unfortunate humans back with us will have the opposite effect.

I purse my lips. "I'm sorry, Elsie."

A piercing shriek rips through the sky as a Phaelix loses his footing and tumbles to his death. The others climb faster, but the cliff face is too steep. A cruel smile curves my lips. Considering what awaits them, the one who fell was lucky. At least he died quickly.

When I look back at Elsie, she's glaring at me. "You're not suggesting that we leave them behind?"

"I'll bring them to safety and set them free, but it'll cause nothing short of a rebellion among the followers of the scrolls if I bring them to Lona."

"Your mother can send them back to Earth," she exclaims. "Why would you deny them that?"

"I won't be able to keep their presence a secret at the palace. There are too many eyes and ears in that place."

She crosses her arms and lifts her chin. "I'm not going without them."

I narrow my eyes. "You're making the mistake of thinking I'm giving you a choice."

Panic flashes through her beautiful eyes. They glitter like gemstones as she cuts me to pieces with her angry gaze. "All right." She clenches her dainty jaw. "Name your price."

I turn toward the portal, tightening my arms around her. The portal has been open for long enough as it is. I don't know how much longer my mother will be able to hold it.

"Wait!" Elsie says, glancing over her shoulder at the humans who stand uncertainly in place. "Aruan, please. I beg you. Stop."

Dragons. I can't deny her when she's begging me. I pause to look down at her gorgeous face. Her cheeks are streaked with dirt, and her bloodied hair stands up in all directions, but she's the most beautiful woman I've seen.

"If you take them with us…" she starts hesitantly. "I'll…" The column of her neck bobs with a delicate movement as she swallows.

My curiosity is piqued. I arch a brow. "You'll what?"

"I'll mate with you willingly," she declares in a rush.

I go still.

"Anytime and anywhere you want," she adds. "I won't be difficult or resist." She takes on a pleading expression. "I'll learn. I'll try harder to please you." She continues with darkening cheeks. "I'll do my best to give you what you want in bed."

Her offer stuns me. She *is* everything I want in bed. But her willingness to please me does something to my cock. It rises eagerly to the occasion. Albeit… "Did you just offer me sex in exchange for saving these wretches?"

The pink stains on her cheeks turn bright red, but the tilt of her chin is as stubborn as ever. "If that's what it takes."

"You're willing to stay and never run away again for the sake of these humans?"

"I didn't say that."

Huge rocks are breaking loose from the summit of the mountain and flattening the palm trees on the island. The world is literally falling to pieces around us, but I can't help the smile that tugs at my lips. Elsie is always feisty and full of surprises. Not a single moment with her is boring. I could never grow tired of spending time with her.

"You'll stay," I say. "In my bed, where you belong. Promise me, and we have a deal."

Her actions have consequences, but we'll talk about her escape at home. The subject still makes me too volatile.

"Fine," she mumbles under her breath.

"Come again?" I bring my ear to her delectable mouth. "I'm not sure I heard you."

"I promise to stay where I belong," she bites out a little louder. "Happy?"

"Very." I flash her a dark smile. "But don't think for a moment that will exempt you from your punishment."

The blush vanishes from her cheeks, leaving them ashen. "Punishment?"

"We'll worry about that later. Now hold on tightly, my sweet."

"What about the Phaelix?" she asks, looking around. "They're pretty much trapped in here."

The violence that churns inside me carries on my

voice. "Don't worry about them." Turning to the same woman I addressed the last time, the one who seemed to have understood me, I say in a tone that's not entirely hospitable, "Come."

You'd think they'd jump at the chance to leave with us. Instead, the flaxen-haired woman grabs the ones next to her and hangs back.

"It's all right, Sandy," Elsie calls to her. "Aruan is going to help you. We'll get you back to Earth."

At that, the woman relaxes her tight hold on her friends a tad. After a hesitant beat, she takes a step forward.

I head for the portal. "You have one beat to make up your minds. Once I've gone through, the portal will close behind me."

"He's going to destroy the island," Elsie says, struggling in my arms. "Please, Sandy. Bring the others. Quickly."

Seemingly coming to a decision, Sandy takes the hands of the women closest to her and pulls them to the platform. When she's helped everyone up, they run toward us. Stopping in front of me, they avert their gazes, not daring to meet mine.

"Go on," I order in a clipped tone. "I'll follow when everyone has gone through safely."

The humans shoot questioning glances at Sandy.

"You heard Elsie," Sandy says. "If we stay here, we're dead."

The island is fast disintegrating. Long cracks run through the ground, and the mountain is shaking.

Phaelix hang like green fungus on the sides of the cliff, using any pair of legs dangling above them to pull themselves higher with no regard for the others they pull off, who plunge to their deaths on beach.

Sandy is the last woman to leave. When she's entered the portal, I pull up a fraction of my power when all I want to do is to let it run wild. But I don't know what will happen if I do, so I contend myself with only using a small portion of my talents.

Just before I leave with Elsie, I enjoy a moment of uninhibited freedom as I unchain my power and unleash my rage. The mountain blows in a massive spray of fire and sparks, burying the slave traders and their buyers under rivers of glowing red lava.

CHAPTER 5
ARUAN

The moment I enter my mother's quarters with Elsie in my arms, my father's ire rains down on me.

Red-faced, he waves a hand at the trembling humans who are doing their best to make themselves small behind a table. "What in the name of dragons is the meaning of this?"

They're all wearing simple robes, except for the man who's dressed in pants and a tunic, which either my mother or father could've fabricated to cover their nakedness. I do the same for Elsie even though I'm shielding her from any invasive stares in my arms. It's easy enough to disintegrate the cloth that covers the table and reassemble it in a soft, warm gown straight on her body.

Elsie gives a start as she takes in the dress she's suddenly wearing, but with the palpable strained atmosphere in the room, she doesn't make a squeak.

I look around. "Where's mother and Gaia?"

"Your mother is consulting her secretary," my father says. "Despite my order to rest." He extends his arm toward the man and women again. "All because of this. Of *them*. I sent Gaia to fetch my advisor. We need to figure out a strategy."

My tone is dry. "Thank you for asking about the welfare of my mate."

He barely glances at Elsie. "I can see that she's safe."

"Your concern is heartwarming," I mutter.

"Your careless action breaks the first and foremost commandment of the scrolls," he says in a harsher tone. "How am I to appease the followers? How am I supposed to justify their future ruler, who should be setting an example, breaking the rules?"

"You know I'm not a believer."

"That's beside the point. What matters is that most of the people and the royals are. What in Zerra were you thinking, bringing them here?"

"Would you rather I left them to die?"

"You should've left them somewhere else until we've figured out a way to deal with the problem, not flaunted them under the noses of every Alit in Lona."

"It's my fault," Elsie says. "Don't blame Aruan. I told him I wouldn't return unless he brought them with us."

My chest swells at the fact that Elsie is defending me, but I won't allow her to fight my wars, especially not with my family.

"They're victims of the slave trade," I say. "I'll go

into the details later. For now, I have to take care of Elsie. She's injured."

"What about them?" my father calls, gesticulating at the humans as I turn for the archway.

"Put them up in the empty quarters. Mother will send them back to Earth when she's recovered enough."

"You know any contact with Earth is forbidden," he says through gritted teeth. "Opening a portal there even more so."

"We'll have to find a way around it."

I don't wait for my father's reply. I make it back to my quarters in record time, tapping into Kian's mind on the way. Usually, I don't let my brother anywhere near my thoughts, but the situation calls for desperate measures.

Kian acknowledges my request immediately. Once he's taken note of what I need, I close off my mind, making sure he can't use the opportunity to dig deeper into my head.

Inside my quarters, I make quick work of stripping Elsie and inspecting her injuries. Through it all, she doesn't say a word, which is very unlike her.

"Does it hurt?" Cupping her face, I ask, "How do you feel?"

Her chuckle is meek. "Terrible, actually. It feels as if my head is going to explode. I think I have a concussion."

I don't know what that word means, but she definitely has a head injury. She sucks in air through her teeth when, after gently parting her hair, I accidentally touch a big bruise on the back of her head. My fury ignites in a flash again. It's a good thing the Phaelix who did this to her is dead, or I would've taken great pleasure in torturing him to his last breath.

"I think I'm going to be sick," she says, sounding as miserable as she looks.

"Dragons, Elsie." Anguish follows hot on the heels of my rage. "Hold on, my sweet." I lift her into my arms and carry her to the cleansing room. "Vitai is on his way."

"Remind me to never take on a gang of Phaelix again."

Stopping dead, I narrow my eyes. "What did you say?"

"They were going to rape Alexa." She rubs her temples. "I had to do something."

"What exactly did that *something* entail?" I ask with equal amounts of anger and dread. How dare she put herself in such a vulnerable position?

"I sent a swarm of prawns to, um…" She clears her throat. "To get rid of the Phaelix."

I frown. "Prawns?"

"Huge, orange-brown insects with mean pinchers and hairy back legs. Unfortunately, when I sent them away after clearing the area, I didn't know that the Phaelix live in treehouses and will jump on me from the sky."

I grind my teeth together so hard I feel the crunch

in my jaw. "If you ever do anything so dangerous again—"

"I should've kept the prawns around." She rolls her eyes. "Yes, I know. It was stupid to let them go immediately. In my defense, I'm new to all this fighting."

I'm having a hard time keeping my voice even and not showing her just how much I'm fuming inside. "You're not listening to me, Elsie. You'll never—"

"Don't worry. I can't try something like that again even if I wanted to. My power is gone. It seems the Phaelix who hit me destroyed it when he gave me the blow on the head."

The scenarios she's describing are enough to drive me to madness. It's difficult to cling to reason through the haze of red that invades my vision.

"I'm kind of sad about it," she says in a small voice. "I mean, about having lost my power. It was cool."

Just like that, my anger vanishes, and my heart softens. A need to soothe her compels me to say, "Maybe it's temporary."

"Have you seen Betty?" she asks with sudden alarm.

I grit my teeth and remind myself that the priority is healing her.

"Aruan?" she says when I continue on my way to the cleansing room.

"No," I say through a clenched jaw.

She searches my eyes as I climb down the steps and lower us into the water. "You're still angry."

Angry doesn't come close to describing what I'm

feeling. I sit down on the reclining bench, bend my knees, and settle her between my legs. "Lean back. I'll take care of you."

She does so reluctantly and gasps when the water washes over the back of her head.

"Sore?" I ask, gently scooping water over her wound.

"It burns like a bitch," she hisses.

Holding her in my arms has a profound calming effect on me. As the knowledge that she's safe takes root, the anger and tension flow from my muscles, aided by the salts I added into the water.

I even manage a smile as she tilts her head back and gazes up at me.

"You have a strange way of expressing yourself," I say. "I've never heard that saying, burning 'like a bitch.'"

"Earth lingo." She grins and then sucks in a breath. "Ouch."

"Easy, my sweet." I brush a hand over her hair, avoiding the bruise. "You'll feel better in a bit. I promise."

"Why don't you undress when you get into the water?"

I arch a brow. "Do you want me to undress?"

"Don't put words in my mouth. You know what I mean."

"I was in too much of a rush. Besides, it's easy enough for me to dry my clothes. It only takes a moment."

She perks up a little. "How do you do that?"

My smile stretches. My little inquisitive mate. "The same way I fabricate water from the air but just the reverse."

"You're awesome," she says, already sounding sleepy.

Grinning, I tighten my arms around her to prevent her from slipping down. "Am I, now?"

She tries to wave my remark away, but she doesn't manage to lift her hand from the water. "You're making fun of me."

"Never," I tease.

The calming effect of the water is not only making her tired but is also loosening her tongue. I haven't added sleeping salts to knock her out cold this time, but I instructed a maid to mix a little potion with a numbing effect into the water. The remedy numbs both the body, to relieve pain, and the mind.

"I mean," she continues, slurring a little, "your power is awesome."

"Most people will disagree with you."

"Who cares about what they think?" she says, yawning. "Mm, I already feel better."

"That's good, my sweet. You can relax. I won't let you go."

I mean it in more ways than one, but I don't know if she catches that. Her eyes droop, her long, sunset-colored lashes brushing her soft, pink cheeks, and still, she fights the sleep that's stealing over her.

"I'm not falling," she says in wonder. "Just… floating."

"You fell?"

She tries to nod, but instead, her head lolls to the side and comes to rest on my shoulder. "Oh, yes. The first time in this pool. It was awful. I thought you were drowning me."

"I'd never harm you, Elsie. You're my mate. It's my duty to protect you."

"Duty." She scoffs before adding sarcastically, "I'm sorry to be so much trouble."

"Trouble? It's my honor."

"Honor. Duty." She sniffs. "Aren't you supposed to be doing these things because you *like* me?"

"Like you?"

What kind of a statement is this? I think about that for a moment. By dragons… she wants me to feel something for her. The unexpected notion warms me. If she cares about what I feel for her, it must mean she's not completely immune to me.

Of course I like her. I more than like her. I find her irresistible, and I don't mean only her body. I enjoy her sharp mind, and I admire her strength and determination.

She'll make an outstanding queen one day.

I open my mouth to tell her that, but her eyes are already closed, and she's breathing evenly. So I just kiss the top of her head. "Sleep and heal, my pretty little rebellious mate."

I make quick work of cleaning her and washing the blood from her hair. I've barely dried us and tucked her into my bed when Kian enters.

He sounds surprised. "You found her."

Irritation gets the better of me. "Of course I did." I'll always find her, even if I have to go to Earth to do so. "What took you so long?"

"Mother heard about Elsie's power. Tarix told her when she consulted him about a sensitive issue." He flashes me a knowing smile. "Which turned out to be the humans you brought to the palace."

Kian no doubt found out about that by reading our parents' minds, and now he's taking pleasure in letting me know *he* knows, which is just his way of rubbing my so-called *mistake* in my face.

"That's what took you so long?" I ask with a growl that quickly sobers him.

"Father summoned me. He and Mother wanted details about Elsie's power. Her ability is potentially dangerous. You can understand why they're concerned."

I glance at Elsie, who's sleeping soundly, looking small and lost on my large bed. "I need you to find Vitai and tell him to come immediately. Elsie is hurt, and it's serious." I look at Kian. "She sustained a head injury. Her power is gone."

He reels. "That's unfortunate. Maybe it'll return when she's healed."

I cross my arms. "That's what I'm hoping."

He scrutinizes me. "You weren't keen on your mate developing her power when you first found out about it."

"You saw for yourself what she is capable of doing with that power."

"Running from you," he says, not trying to hide his smirk or the fact that he's enjoying my anguish. "What changed? Aren't you happy she lost it? At least she won't fly off on a dragon's back again."

"She won't regardless," I say in a harsh voice. Making an effort to calm myself, I continue. "An Alit is incomplete without his power. That's not what I want for Elsie."

"I see," he says, more surprise flickering in his silver eyes. "You actually care about her."

"She's my mate." I drop my arms to my sides and walk to him. "Of course I care. But enough of the chit-chatting. We're wasting time. Where's Vitai?"

"Last I saw him, he was going fishing. Let me see." Kian closes his eyes and opens them half a beat later. "He's by the lake. I've summoned him."

I nod my gratitude. It's quicker to use Kian's mind-reading ability to reach out to our brother than to go through a dozen or more portals opened by my sister. "I need you to do something else for me."

"Yes," he drawls. "The Earthlings. I already gathered that from when you opened your mind to me."

"Father would've arranged for them to be taken to an available quarter. Make sure they're fed and treated for injuries."

"What's the plan?" he asks, his usual disinterested manner back in place.

"The plan is for Mother to send them back to where they came from."

"Tricky," he muses. "Opening portals to Earth is forbidden."

"We don't have a choice."

"I don't envy you," he says with a chuckle on his way out. "Luckily for me, I was born second. Just as well I don't have to deal with these sticky issues."

I sit down on the bed when he's gone, taking Elsie's hand in mine. Vitai arrives a short while later, wearing water boots and a commoner's tunic. His shoulder-length hair is untamed and tussled from the wind. Mud mars his arms where his sleeves are folded back. A few muddy stripes are painted across his tunic. He resembles a pond lily hunter or a plough hand on the fields.

I look him up and down. "If Mother sees you like that…"

He dismisses me with a shrug and walks to the bed. "What happened to her?"

"A Phaelix hit her on the head." I suppress the anger that simmers beneath the surface of my calm. "The blow must've been hard. It broke skin." I hesitate. "She said she's lost her power."

Shock washes over his expression. "That's a first."

"I know," I say, my mood dark. "Will her power return when you've healed her?"

"There's only one way to find out," he says, stepping closer.

I give him space, letting him work, but I hover close

by in case Elsie wakes up. It's impossible to stay too far away, especially after almost losing her a second time.

The healing takes a while. Sweat drips from Vitai's face when he's done. I dismiss him with an inadequate and hurried thank-you, wanting nothing more than to finally be alone with Elsie.

"Let me know about her power when she wakes up," he says as he turns to leave.

Once he's gone, I seal the exit.

On cue, Elsie's lashes lift, and then I'm staring into those arresting blue-green pools.

"How do you feel now?" I ask in a voice gruff from uncharacteristic tenderness.

"Like my old self," she says with a small smile. "Thank you."

"Of course. You didn't think I'd let you suffer?"

"Not only for healing me."

"For what else?"

"For saving me." She looks away and says under her breath, "Again."

She doesn't sound entirely pleased about that.

I climb onto the bed and, stretching out on top of her, keep my weight on one arm while gripping her chin in my free hand to turn her face toward me. "Why did you run away, Elsie?"

She purses her lips.

I search her eyes. "Did I not give you pleasure? Did you hate it that much?"

"You did," she admits, averting her gaze. "I didn't hate it. But you were disappointed."

"I was."

Her mouth drops open as her gaze snaps back to mine. She tries to pull free, but I hold fast.

"I was disappointed that the bond hadn't been completed. You clearly rejected me."

"Oh! Oh—" she splutters, fighting me harder. "Are you saying it's my fault?"

Gripping her wrists in one hand, I pin them above her head. "Calm down, Elsie." I make my voice hard. "I wasn't the one who had a problem with accepting our bond."

She arches her back, writhing beneath me. "Last time I checked, you came inside me. You said consummating the mating would secure the bond, and it was fucking consummated." Animosity glows in her eyes. "There was no resistance from my side, you know that. Well, not at the crucial point." She stops her futile efforts to escape and says through gritted teeth, "Let me go."

"Never." Never again.

Her chest moves with rapid breaths. She's not shouting, but the soft words she throws at me have a more potent effect than any outburst could've. "I hate you."

My smile is sardonic. "And there you have it."

"Go to hell," she spits out. "Maybe you should look inside yourself before pointing a finger at me."

"I don't hate you."

"Why should you?" Her face twists. "You're not the one who was stolen from your home."

"This *is* your home."

"You really have a way of making me feel welcome."

I'm fast reaching the limit of my patience. "What's that supposed to mean?"

"For crying out loud, Aruan. A glacier has more warmth than what you projected after fucking me."

My frustration mounts. "I wasn't cold toward you. I needed a few moments to think, and you made it obvious that you didn't want me around. What did you expect after showing your regret so openly?"

"I regretted having sex with you because of the way you behaved afterward." Her voice rises. "You made no secret of the fact that the sex didn't please you, and then you walked away and left me cold."

"I never said the sex didn't please me."

"Oh, come on." She utters a laugh. "You didn't have to. It was written all over your face."

"Sex with you was an incandescent experience, Elsie." I tilt my hips, pressing the tormenting hardness of my cock against that enticing soft spot between her legs. "I have a feeling that's not going to change. I can prove it if you don't believe me."

She bucks and twists her hips, rubbing herself in the process over my cock and only aggravating my need with her struggling.

"Keep still," I warn. "Or don't hold me accountable for the consequences."

She goes quiet at that, staring at me with all the hatred she proclaimed not a moment ago. Yet her body isn't unwilling. I can hear the wild rhythm of her heartbeat. My enhanced senses allow me to smell the sweet scent of her arousal. I can feel her wetness through the layers of my clothes and the sheet that covers her. Her nipples are hard little pebbles that poke my chest. And it's all I can do not to rip apart the fabric preventing our naked bodies from touching and my cock from sinking into the welcome heat of her pussy.

The thought alone sets my body on fire. Sparks sizzle beneath my skin. My intention changes from talking this through to something entirely different. I can't control the all-consuming lust. I can't hold back.

She opens her mouth, but before she can protest, I press my lips to hers. Her mouth tastes like honey. Her lips are soft and pliable, a gift for my taking. And I take. I steal inside her mouth with my tongue and tease hers into doing this dance with me.

At first, despite her promise, she's resistant, pushing on my shoulders to put distance between us. But as every successive sweep of my tongue explores a little deeper, a little longer, the tension in her muscles eases. I cup her face and keep her in place while eating those lips that are the most delicious treat ever created.

By the time I bring the kiss to a slow halt, she reverses the roles by snaking her arms around my neck and refusing to let go. A protest escapes her mouth when I tear my lips from hers, but the sound quickly changes to a throaty moan as I glide a hand over the silky sheet to explore her naked body underneath.

I lean on one elbow to study her exquisite shape. The sheet draws her naked curves in a thin, shiny fabric spun from the silver silk of the rarest silkworms, creating a stunning picture that's even more erotic than if she were naked. Her small breasts are firm and pert, her nipples extending beneath the teasing strokes I administer with my palms. The dip of her stomach is a beautiful valley that leads to the small mound of her pelvis. I take my time to memorize her contours with my gaze and to learn her shape with my hand, and then, finally, I slide my fingers to the prize between her thighs.

The caress is light, but her breath catches, showing me the effect my touch has on her body. I reverse my path, getting reacquainted with all her pretty curves by using my fingertips like the brush of a painter to outline her shape. I start at the hollow of her throat and her collarbone before tracing my way down to her breasts, her nipples, her navel, and the junction of her legs.

Her breathing turns labored when I draw light patterns over the silk that covers the most intimate part of her. She moans again, gripping my wrist when I circle her clit in a touch that's barely there, but she doesn't push me away, so I increase the pressure and rub the button at the apex of her sex with the heel of my palm.

"Aruan." She digs her nails into my skin. "Please."

I trace her slit with the flat end of my hand, watching as the action dips the silk between her folds. "Who do you belong to, Elsie?"

She throws back her head and presses her thighs together. "Ah."

The thin fabric clings to her wet pussy, the sight driving me wild. Pushing down my own need so that I can take care of her pleasure first, I massage her clit in circles through the smooth fabric. I slide that slippery silk over her swollen flesh until she begs me again.

"Say after me." I let her pleasure build faster, not sparing her any longer. Just as her body draws tight like a bow, I stop. "I belong to Aruan, my mate."

"Aruan," she cries out.

"Say it, Elsie."

"I—" She whimpers. "Oh, my god."

"Say it."

"I… I belong—"

She swallows the rest of her words as I take her over the edge. Her climax is a powerful aphrodisiac. Her pleasure is my greatest accomplishment and my biggest trigger. Yet I don't rush. I continue to ignore the need firing through my body, a need that demands I claim her and ease the ache in my loins.

Wanting the moment to last, I unwrap her slowly. I draw the sheet down little by little, exposing the perfect canvas of her naked body. All for my taking. Mine. Mine alone.

"You belong to me," I say with a growl reverberating in my chest as I lean down and suck a hard little nipple deep into my mouth.

She grabs the sides of my tunic and tugs impatiently. I smile around the curve I'm devouring, loving it when she makes her own demands and takes what she needs. I sit back on my heels, straddling her thighs, and lift my arms to make it easier for her.

As soon as she's pulled the garment over my head, she reaches for the button of my waistband. I clench my hands into fists, summoning every fraction of willpower I possess to refrain from touching her when all I want to do is pounce, submit, and claim.

I let her undress me as far as she can, and then I get off the bed with every intention of removing my boots and the rest of my clothes.

To dragons with that.

I'm too impatient to bother.

Elsie's eyes flare as I disintegrate my clothes in a flash, but it's not only the use of my power that elicits her reaction. As she trails a gaze over my naked body, I can't help but enjoy the way in which she's watching and unconsciously wetting her lips. I climb back onto the bed and kneel in front of her, one thought running through my head and ruling my actions.

I need to taste her.

Now.

"Lie back," I say, the command almost sounding animalistic. "Open your legs for me."

Instead of obeying like a good mate, she gets onto her knees and pushes me back with her hands on my shoulders. Every part of me is eager to take her, to hunt her down and to put my mark on her, but I'm curious about what she has in mind, so I force myself to let her have this moment.

When I'm sitting on my heels, she kneels between my spread legs. My cock juts out between us, painfully hard and throbbing with need. The sac at the root is heavy with the seed meant to fill her. The sensitive flesh contracts, eager to expel its load into the warm body that was created to receive my seed alone.

She fixes her gaze on the precum leaking from the tip of my cock, her cheeks flushing with a need that reflects my own. When she lowers her head, it takes everything I've got and then some not to combust on the spot and climax before she's even touched me.

The halfmoons of my nails dig into my palms as I clench my fists harder, fighting the urge to reach for her like I've never fought anything in my life. A lightning bolt rips through me when she locks her hand around the base of my cock. Her fingers brand my flesh where they touch my skin. Heat rushes to my groin when she moves another fraction closer, and then flames erupt in my gut when she finally presses her lips on the crest.

Holding my gaze, she laps up the drop of precum designed to ease my possession of her body. She hums her approval, stoking the fire that tears through my insides and sizzles in every extremity of my body. The lips she presses on the crown are like the branding of white-hot metal. Her kiss burns with the sweetest agony.

Clenching my teeth, I endure the torture as she uses both hands to guide my cock to her mouth before sucking me deep. Her lips stretch wide to accommodate my girth, her struggle to swallow me only turning me on more because she wants to please me.

And please me she does, almost too much when she pulls back and swirls her tongue around the crown before sliding her lips over my length again with her tongue flattened on the underside. I will myself not to come, but it takes tremendous self-control not to empty myself in her mouth when I hit the back of her throat.

She pulls away to breathe, her turquoise eyes glittering from tearing up. Then she sucks me into her mouth again, making greedy little noises as she battles to take me.

It's too much. Despite my steely willpower, I snap. The man vanishes, and in his place emerges a beast ruled by the basest of instincts. He's driven by one purpose only—to claim and mark his mate. To fill her with his seed.

Cupping her head between my hands, I prevent her from escaping while driving my cock through those soft, lush lips. It's pain and pleasure simultaneously, the pleasure excruciating and the need to come painful.

Mindful of her small frame, I barely manage enough self-control to keep my thrusts shallow. Tears run over her cheeks, and saliva drips down her chin. I hit the back of her throat again, pull out to let her breathe, and push straight back in with a wild, uncontrollable frenzy to finish what she's started.

She drops her hands to my thighs, holding on as I

fuck her lips and make her swallow as much as she can. The untamed creature inside me roars in victory when the scent of her arousal grows stronger in the room. Weaving my fingers through her short hair, I close them in a fist to keep her where I need her while slipping my other hand between her legs.

A growl tears from my chest. She's soaking wet. She likes this. Sucking me off turns her on. I part her folds and sink a finger inside her, stretching her to prepare her for what's to follow. She moans around my cock while grinding herself on my hand.

"Dragons, Elsie," I bite out, her needy little sounds making me burn hotter.

When her inner muscles soften, I add another finger. She cries out, swallowing those sexy moans with my cock when I rub circles around her clit with my thumb. She's such a pretty sight naked and panting between my knees with her mouth stretched wide around my cock. The image alone is enough to send me over. I move my fingers hard enough inside her to spank her pussy with every thrust. When her muscles clench around me, I let go.

I shove one more time, hitting deep, and come. Spasms of painful ecstasy lock my body in a vise while heat burns through my cock and erupts in ribbons of cum. I pump myself empty, making her take every drop. Only when I'm practically dry-humping Elsie's throat do I pull out.

She takes a deep, shuddering breath, her chest heaving with the effort of dragging in air. She's a beautiful, disheveled sight. I reach out and wipe a drop of cum from her chin. The tender kiss I press on her lips is in direct contrast to the urgency with which I grip her hips and lift her onto my lap with her thighs straddling mine.

I just came, but I'm already hard for her again. It should be impossible, but I'm fast learning that she has an effect on me like none other. Not in my wildest dreams could I have known how intense fucking her would be or the havoc she'd wreak on my body.

The only warning I give her as I grab the root of my cock is, "Hold on."

She barely has time to curl her fingers around my shoulders before I impale her on my cock in a single thrust. Her pussy is warm and inviting, but she's so tight.

"Relax," I coax, kissing her neck and nipping the curve where it meets her shoulder.

She gasps when I start to move. "Aruan."

"I know, my sweet." I kiss her lips again. "I'll make it better."

"Wait," she says, her eyes growing round. "Protection."

In the heat of the moment, I forgot she doesn't want to conceive. She told me she doesn't want children, or maybe she doesn't want *my* children.

The notion stings. It aggravates the beast who wants her to carry his babies. But I force myself to push down those instincts. I'm too far gone to stop, though. As I hadn't planned this, I don't have a potion at hand that will prevent her from conceiving.

Instead, going against every grain of my nature, I make her a promise. "I won't come inside you."

"Are you sure?" She sounds uncertain. "You won't lose control?"

Her trust is important to me. If I make an oath, I'll keep it, no matter how difficult it is. "Yes, I'm sure, and no, I won't lose control."

She relaxes a little, giving me her trust, and the sweetness of that gift takes some of the bitter edge off her refusal to birth my babies.

I move slowly, giving her time to adjust, and when her inner muscles turn soft around me, I don't hold back any longer. I bounce her in my lap, making her ride my cock while giving her as much as I'm taking. Soon, she's moving to my rhythm, arching her back and giving me a stunning view of her perfect body.

If anything, the sight makes me harder. Around her, my cock is permanently hard. As long as I'm inside her, it feels as if it'll stay hard forever.

I nuzzle her temple. "Elsie."

"I'm close," she says, locking her arms around my neck and flattening her breasts against my chest. "Again."

"Come," I order, watching her face transform with ecstasy as she gives me her pleasure like an obedient mate.

Dragons, I love that look on her. In her moment of abandon, her eyes are hazy and her expression soft and dreamlike. There's nothing of the reservations and walls she puts up when she's with me outside of bed.

I bask in the feeling of connectedness as I hold her while she rides out her climax. Shortly after, I find my own. Like I promised, I pull out, painting her breasts and stomach with hot jets of cum.

We rest in each other's arms, holding one another like lovers but not like mates. And for all my good intentions, I can't ignore the raging disappointment that's like a snake nipping at my heels.

Because once again, where the connection is supposed to grow between us, there's only a cold, gaping void.

CHAPTER 6
ELSIE

I'm draped over Aruan's naked lap with my ankles crossed behind his back while he holds me in a possessive embrace. My skin is flushed with heat, and my inner muscles ache deep inside. His cum covers my breasts and my stomach, making me sticky all over, yet I can't bring myself to move. Instead, I lean my head on his shoulder and soak up the welcome heat of his body.

I can't believe how quickly I fell back into his bed. My eagerness should appall me. Where is my self-preservation and control? Every time he touches me, my mind recedes to a distant corner of my being, and my body takes over my actions. Yes, I promised I wouldn't deny him—not that this strange, unignorable physical attraction makes a shred of resistance possible. However, this time, I took things much further than not resisting him.

He initiated the kiss, but I instigated the rest. I just

couldn't help myself. I simply had to taste him. How can I fight the urge when that switch between my logical mind and my traitorous body is flipped every time he strips naked? He's built like a gladiator. A girl has to be blind not to appreciate his hard-cut perfection, and he's not making it easy for me to put up my defenses. He knows exactly how he affects me.

Of course, the sex was hot. I liked what we did. A lot. But even now as he's holding me in the warmth of his strong arms, coldness bleeds into the gaping hole that rips into my heart. Despite the warm, fuzzy orgasmic afterglow that leaves me lethargic with a delicious feeling of utter relaxation, I can't ignore the bitter disappointment that reflects inside me. The feeling isn't my own but my so-called mate's.

He kisses my neck and untangles himself from me gently. "Shall we get cleaned up? As much as I regret leaving my bed when I have you in it, an important matter is awaiting our attention."

That matter would be the humans we brought with us. Yes, I understand, but I still don't like it when he severs our physical contact and gets off the bed. As before, I feel colder and emptier without him.

He offers me a hand and helps me to my feet before leading me to the cleansing room. After draining the water in the pool and letting it auto-clean, he fills it with fresh water that he heats with his mind while testing the temperature by dipping his hand inside.

We're quiet as he takes care of me by washing my hair and my body. He's exceptionally gentle. Yet wherever he trails his hands over my skin, no matter how innocent the touch, he rekindles the lust that refuses to abate. If he picks up on the quickening of my breathing and the acceleration of my heartbeat, he doesn't acknowledge it, so I bite my lip and force myself to ignore the tormenting need already building in my core again.

After washing himself quickly, he pauses for a moment, watching me with a serious light in his mercury-colored eyes.

I swallow as I take in his devastatingly handsome face. I'll never grow used to how beautiful he is. Every time I see him is like the first time all over.

"What?" I ask after a couple of seconds, his intense stare making me self-conscious.

He sits on the bench and leans against the side. Drops of water roll off his chiseled chest, drawing a stunning picture of pure, unadulterated male virility.

He drags his hands over his wet hair, brushing the dark strands back without breaking our eye contact. "What were you going to do after flying off from here, Elsie?"

I have no reason to lie about what my intentions were. "I was going to find a way to go back to Earth."

He pins me with a dark look. "How?"

I take a seat on the opposite bench so that my breasts are submerged under the water. Being naked makes me feel more vulnerable, especially while having this conversation.

"At first, I just flew. I have no idea for how long or

how far Betty and I went, but eventually, I recognized the lake where you intervened when the Phaelix had taken me. Then I saw smoke and followed it to a Phaelix settlement. I reckoned as they'd brought me to Zerra, they'd be able to take me back to Earth. But then I saw the human slaves."

"Let me guess." His voice is devoid of emotion, but I can feel his anger. "You decided to free them."

"I couldn't just leave them."

He inhales with flaring nostrils, taking a moment before continuing. "What happened then?"

"I brought in the prawns that chopped the Phaelix into small pieces." I shudder at the memory. "And then the Phaelix descended from the trees and caught me unawares. Next thing I knew, I woke up in a prison cell. The following morning, they took us to the slave market, and then you arrived on the scene."

He leans over and grips my chin between a thumb and a forefinger. "Taking the Phaelix on alone was an unwise and dangerous thing to do."

"I handled it, didn't I?" At the look of calculation that comes over his face, I add, "Although I admit I shouldn't have been so quick to lower my guard."

"You're never to take such a risk again." His gaze drills into mine. "Do you have any idea what could've happened to you?"

I want to argue, but I remember the last thought that went through my mind at the slave market only too well. When I realized I'd been sold, all I wanted was to be back here in the safety of Aruan's arms. More than that, I missed Aruan. I just didn't want to admit that to myself at the time.

"Did I make myself clear?" he asks, his eyes tightening in the corners.

I promised not to resist his advances and to do my best to please him in bed, which I did just a few minutes ago. Although, honestly, I was doing that more for my own pleasure than for his, seeing that my knees go weak whenever his clothes come off, and I can't seem to help myself. I even promised that I'd stay where Aruan believes I belong—in his bed. But I never said I wouldn't try to escape again, and I'm not going to lie to him. For some reason, I can't bring myself to do that. The thought of deceiving him hurts me. My stupid weakness for this man won't allow me to do anything that will cause him concern or pain. Which is really inconvenient because escaping will do just that.

Shit, I'm so fucked.

He loosens his grip on my chin and traces my jaw with his thumb. "Why are you running so hard from a destiny neither of us can change?"

"I was angry," I admit. "I felt cheated, as if I didn't have a choice because of the damn mating heat."

Letting me go, he gives me a strangely sympathetic look. "We don't have a choice. Nature decided for us. How we deal with it is up to us. I told you already, you don't have to make this difficult for yourself."

"I didn't like the way you treated me."

"It won't happen again."

"But you're still disappointed."

"Not in you or in our physical bonding."

The tightness in my chest gives a little. So he didn't hate the sex. In that case… "You really want our bond to be complete, don't you?"

He doesn't reply, which makes me realize something.

"You think it's my fault," I say, watching him intently.

"I don't know why our mating is unsuccessful. To the best of my knowledge, a similar case doesn't exist." His expression turns blank. "It doesn't matter. Nothing will change the fact that we're mates."

But it does matter. It matters to him. He can't hide that from me, regardless of how hard he's trying.

He stands and holds out his hand. "We'd better go see how your friends are doing."

Ashamed that I didn't give them even a fleeting thought while my brain was drugged with lust, I put my hand in his and let him pull me to my feet. He leads me to a bench where bath sheets and clothes are put out and uses one of the sheets to pat me dry. I wonder why he doesn't just use an evaporation trick. I suspect it's just an excuse to touch me, but I'm not complaining. His broad, warm palms on my body are soothing, and the subtle vibration of his power that's like a static hum in the air calms me.

When we've dressed—I in a pale-yellow gown with matching slippers and Aruan in a white tunic with black pants—he guides me to the room adjoining to his bedroom.

Food has been set out on the table next to the window. Someone must've brought it while we were dressing.

"Shouldn't we go check on Karl and the women first?" I ask.

"Kian is taking care of them. I can feel your hunger, mate. Filling your empty stomach is more important." He takes my hands and kisses them before ushering me into a chair. "I beg your forgiveness for my negligence. I should've fed you before attending to other needs." His smile is wolfish. "I tend to get sidetracked when you're naked in my bed."

The heat in my cheeks is more from self-loathing than embarrassment. That makes two of us.

Admittedly, I'm starving, and when I take in the food, gratitude warms my chest. Aruan made sure all my favorite dishes were served.

My stomach growls. Now that I'm no longer nauseated from the concussion, my hunger has returned with a vengeance.

He pulls closer a small box decorated with shiny shells that sits on the corner of the table. Curious, I watch as he flips back the lid to reveal a necklace with a silver chain and a glowing red oval stone pendant. He lifts the necklace from the box and moves behind me to fasten it around my neck.

I'm not a jewelry kind of girl, but the fact that Aruan is the bearer of the gift makes the gesture seem hot. Suddenly, I understand why some women find it romantic when guys give them bling.

Surprised and touched, I lay a hand over the pendant that lies just below the hollow of my throat. "You got me a gift?"

He comes around the table and takes the seat opposite me. "It's more of a practicality, but now that I know you like gifts, I'll rectify that neglect on my side too."

I can feel myself blushing furiously as I realize my mistake. His crooked smile only makes my humiliation worse.

"The stone is very rare," he says, mercifully not commenting further on my assumption that he got me a gift like a boyfriend who cares. "It turns black in the presence of poison."

The reason for the "practicality" becomes clear. Someone in the palace tried to poison me. Although he doesn't mention the incident outright, the threat hangs all too real and dark between us in the air.

"I didn't oversee the cooking myself," he explains. "I'm not taking any risks."

I swallow away the sudden tightness of my throat. "Where did you find the stone?"

"I commissioned Kian with the task." His lips quirk. "He has valuable contacts when it comes to stone trading."

He serves a generous helping of each dish on a plate and places it in front of me.

I look down. The ruby-red stone continues pulsing gently with an inner light.

No poison here. Which is a relief, both for obvious

reasons and because I would hate for this delectable-looking food to go to waste.

Despite the unpleasant memory of our mating ceremony, during which someone slipped a deadly substance into my drink, my curiosity gets the better of me. "How does it work? I mean, how does it really work when you break it down to science?"

He arches a brow. "To science?"

"To a logical explanation of its inner workings."

"Ah. No one knows. Like the scrolls, it's a mystery."

A faint scratching noise on the other side of the wall that separates the bedroom from the hallway draws my attention. I prick up my ears.

"What's the matter?" he asks, his relaxed features setting into concern in a heartbeat.

"I heard something. I think it's a spiked pet."

"They're always on the prowl for food. If there are a few crumbs to be scavenged somewhere, you can count on finding them under the table."

More than hearing the tuatara, I can feel it. At first, the connection is faint, but then it slowly grows in my chest, the presence of not only the tuatara but also of other living beings filling me until the feeling bleeds out to every cell of my body.

My heart lurches. Could my power be back? I'm afraid to find out. What if my ability to connect with animals is gone for good?

Aruan reaches over the table and takes my hand. "What is it, Elsie?"

"My power," I whisper. "I think I feel something."

He gives my fingers a squeeze. "Like Vitai said when he healed you, there's only one way we'll know."

The first thought that pops into my head is Betty. I'm frantic to know if she made it home in one piece. I'm holding my breath, my face trained toward the window, when a piercing cry rips through the sky. I sit like a statue, unable to speak or move as I wait for the verdict. And then she dives straight up out of nowhere in front of the window and lands with a thud that shakes the balcony.

I'm on my feet and in front of the window in a blink, opening the latch with laughter bubbling from my lips. From somewhere behind me Aruan is calling my name, but I'm too ecstatic to acknowledge anything but the fact that Betty is here, safe and sound.

I make a beeline for the predator, who lowers her long neck to put her head at my eye level.

"Good girl," I say, scratching her chin.

"Elsie," Aruan says, this time with more warning than caution.

I turn around to face him like a giddy child, unable to squash my happiness and excitement.

"It's back," I cry out. "My power is back. Betty is safe."

He holds out a hand, his arm stretched out toward me with the palm facing up. "Come to me, Elsie. Now."

Understanding dawns. He thinks I'm going to fly off again.

He continues grimly. "Step away from that dragon—"

I narrow my eyes. "Do not say 'or,' Aruan, not if you want whatever we're trying to do here to work. I won't allow you to threaten Betty or give me ultimatums."

A muscle ticks in his temple. "You're testing my patience, mate."

"I can't live with you if you threaten the animals I love."

"You neglected to mention that detail of your terms when you negotiated the safety of your friends on the island. You should've thought about making a list of your requirements before you offered me a deal."

My joy turns to anger. "Don't be like that."

"Like what?" He drops his arm and comes closer. "Honest? You obviously care more for the dragons than for your own mate."

"Are you jealous of *Betty*?"

The floor starts shaking, huge cracks that have nothing to do with Betty's weight running up the walls.

"I just got you back, and I'm not losing you again," he bites out.

"I'm not going anywhere." To prove the point, I take a step toward him. "I just wanted to say hello to her. That's all. Calm down, Aruan. Please."

It takes a moment before the earthquake he brought on with his power passes, but it doesn't completely stop until I place my hand in his. His grip around my fingers is almost painful.

I glance over my shoulder at Betty.

Catch you later, girl.

She takes off into the air with a screech, once more quaking the rock face of the palace.

"Come to the table," Aruan says, pulling my attention back to him. "You have to eat."

My hunger is all but forgotten. Giving my power a last test-drive, just to be sure, I reach out in my thoughts to Pip, the cute little anurognathus.

Aruan seats me at the table and pours water in my glass. Not a moment later, Pip plunges through the air and darts into the room through the open window. I squeal in delight when he perches on the edge of the table next to my place setting, eyeing the food on my plate with greedy little beady eyes.

"You did it," Aruan says. "You summoned that pixie dragon."

I meet his gaze, expecting an accusation there but only finding relief and pride.

"It seems the head injury only temporarily impaired your ability to use your power."

I'm more relieved about that than disappointed that my plan to return to Earth failed. And that makes me a selfish jerk because what I should be doing is thinking about my parents. I mean, I am. I'm worried sick about them. Of course I still want to see them. I haven't lost sight of that goal. The thought sobers me, putting a damper on my excitement, and as if reading my mood, Aruan turns broody.

We finish our meal in silence with me feeding bits and pieces of my food to Pip, who gobbles everything up before licking his paws and cleaning his whiskers like a cat. I dare to stroke his head and get away with petting him with all my fingers intact.

Once I've satisfied my hunger and thirst, I assure Aruan that I can't take another bite, and then we walk to the quarters in the west wing of the palace.

Aruan stops at the end of a long hallway. The stones sealing an archway vanish to reveal a room that resembles Aruan's, only bigger. Instead of one big sunken bed, several daybeds are lined up against the wall. Stone benches with padded cushions run along the other walls. An arched window with pink glass panes looks out over fields. The haphazard roofs of a village are visible on top of a hill in the distance.

Sandy and the rest of the women sit huddled together on the benches. They jump to their feet when Aruan and I enter the room.

Shooting an apprehensive glance at Aruan, Sandy rushes to me. "We were worried about you. Is everything all right?"

"I'm good. How's everyone doing here?" I frown. "Where's Karl?"

"Next door. He has his own room." Her gaze darts to Aruan, who's observing us with his arms crossed over his broad chest. "Can he understand us?"

"He doesn't speak English. I'll translate for him."

"You speak their language?" she asks, looking stung. "But how? You didn't mention it."

"It wasn't relevant at the time. Let's focus on the issue at hand, which is to make sure you're all okay."

The tense set of Sandy's shoulders relaxes a little. "You said his mother can get us out of here."

Having heard Aruan and his father arguing about that, I feel my stomach tighten with concern. What if the queen refuses to open a portal to Earth because the scrolls forbid it?

We'll have to talk to her about it, but for now, I want to make sure everyone is fine.

"One thing at a time," I say. "Have your needs been taken care of? Have you eaten?"

"They fed us well, don't worry. A guy looking a lot like your companion here came to check our injuries." She glances at Eucabeth, who stares into the distance with a dreamy look and glowing cheeks. "He cured Eucabeth." She continues in a disbelieving tone. "She can hear again." Lowering her voice, she stresses, "Her deafness is simply gone."

I smile. "That would've been Vitai."

"How is that even possible?" Sandy exclaims. "Irina's scars have disappeared, and for once, Maeva is calm."

"Vitai has healing powers."

"He was very kind to us. I like him. I can't say the same about the guy who brought the food. Now *that* one was scary. I swear he saw right into my mind. I had this weird notion he knew exactly what I was thinking, which was that he was a frightening son of a bitch, because he looked me straight in the eye and gave me a diabolical smile."

"That sounds like Kian."

"What is she saying?" Aruan asks.

I turn to him. "Sandy says Vitai healed them. Eucabeth was deaf, but now she can hear. Isn't that amazing?" I'm all but jumping up and down from the elation. "Apparently, Kian was here as well. He brought them food."

"Ask them if they need anything else," Aruan instructs.

After I've done so and told him that they're grateful for everything but eager to go home, Aruan tells me to explain to them that they have to be confined for safety reasons, and that we'll be back when we've spoken to the queen.

When I've conveyed the message, I ask Aruan in his language, "Is confining them really necessary?" Because that's just a nice way of saying he's locking them up. "The Phaelix kept them in prison cells. Don't you think they've been under lock and key for long enough?"

He addresses me in a stern tone. "You know why it's necessary." Turning on his heel, he orders, "Come. You can visit them again later."

Not wanting to evoke his ire by arguing, I say to Sandy, "I'll be back as soon as I can. You don't have to worry. I won't let anything happen to you."

"Wait." She grabs my arm, holding me back. "How long are they going to keep us here?"

"I really can't say, but I'll do my best to make sure you leave as quickly as possible."

A flame of hope kindles in my heart when I think about going home with the humans and seeing my parents. At the dark look that comes over Aruan's face, I suppress the thought. He can probably feel what I'm thinking.

"We can't just sit here and do nothing," Sandy says. "We'll go out of our minds."

"I'll ask Aruan if we can bring you something to keep you occupied."

"Let us help with the chores. At least that way, we'll feel useful." Sandy tilts her head toward the others, who're watching us from a safe distance. "Keeping busy will prevent us from going crazy."

"Time to go, Elsie," Aruan says, glaring at the spot where Sandy's fingers are locked around my wrist.

Blanching under his stare, she lets me go quickly.

Aruan heads toward the archway.

"Don't worry," I call over my shoulder. "I'll be back soon."

Sandy doesn't look convinced as I leave hurriedly with Aruan.

He seals the archway and makes his way with long strides down the hallway.

"What now?" I ask, running to keep up with him.

The stone walls light up as we pass, illuminating our way.

Aruan stops next to an archway on the opposite side of the living quarters. It gives a view of the ocean below. Taking my hand, he intertwines our fingers.

"Don't fret about those humans. I'll speak to my mother."

I hold his gaze, trying to get a read on him. Even as he tells me not to worry, I feel his concern through the bond that exists between us, albeit weakly. "What if she refuses to help? Your father said creating portals to Earth was forbidden."

He watches me quietly.

"Whoever brought us here broke the rules," I continue. "Do you have any idea who was responsible?"

"No." The set of his mouth hardens. "But I intend to find out."

"How?"

"I've already sent spies to the other kingdoms. If someone is creating forbidden portals, we'll sniff him out."

"You don't think the Phaelix are creating those portals."

"Whoever is creating them must be as powerful as my mother."

He doesn't elaborate, leaving me to arrive at my own conclusions.

"And the Phaelix don't have powers," I muse.

"Correct."

"You think it's an Alit," I say as the insight hits me.

He only continues to observe me with a muscle ticking in his jaw.

I frown. "If an Alit is involved, why would he or she provide slaves to the Phaelix?"

"That's what I'm going to uncover."

Wait a minute. "Is that why you're in no rush to send the humans home?" I prop a hand on my hip. "You'd better not think you can use them to somehow draw out the guilty party."

His smile is calculating. "I just want to question them. There's no harm in that."

"Every one of us ended up here via a portal with Phaelix. That's all we know." And then I understand. "Oh, my god. That's why Kian went to see them under the guise of delivering food. He read their minds, didn't he?"

"Maybe," Aruan says, an evil smile tugging at his lips.

"You're despicable. That's invasive."

"But necessary." He turns, pulling me with him. "You need to rest. You've been through a lot."

"If you think you can go back to sealing me into your quarters while you go off to do whatever it is you're going to do, you have another think coming." When he doesn't slow down or answer, I hang back. "Aruan."

At my frustrated tone, he stops.

Facing me squarely, he says, "Do you think I don't know what's going on in your head, Elsie? Our bond may not be complete, but don't let that fool you into thinking I can't read your intentions."

My mouth goes dry. "What do you mean?"

He fixes me with a silver gaze. "Swear on Betty's life

you won't run away again, and I won't have to lock you in."

My breath stutters. For a moment, I can't reply.

Disappointment moves across his face. "Back at the slave market, you vowed to stay where you belong if I brought the humans with us. When I said, 'in my bed,' I meant by my side. It didn't escape me that you didn't use those words when you made your oath."

His bitter disillusionment in me is a pain that blisters my heart.

"You didn't mean to stay *with me*, Elsie. Because you still believe this isn't where you belong."

I open my mouth to argue, but he doesn't give me a chance.

"I know you, mate." He studies me with that intense, brooding stare. "Did you really think you could trick me by sidetracking me from the real issue at stake with a seductive deal?"

"I didn't try to sidetrack you. I did what I had to do so you wouldn't abandon Karl and those women in the wild."

He drops his voice an octave. "I wouldn't have abandoned them."

I stare at him in disbelief. So I didn't need to bargain for their lives? "You tricked me." Anger surges through me. "You tricked me into making that promise."

His smile turns wry. "And you made that promise for them, not for me. You're not here because you chose your mate, Elsie. You're here because you wanted to save those Earthlings."

I clench my free hand into a fist. "How could you? You manipulated me."

"And you? Isn't the deal you offered me a form of manipulation too?"

I'm so angry I'm fuming. "I can't believe I was so blind I didn't see that one coming."

"If it makes you feel better, I had no intention of bringing them here. I would've kept them somewhere else until I figured out what to do with them."

I pull my hand from his. "You really make it difficult for me to like you."

His silver eyes gleam, making him look more dangerous than ever, but he maintains an icy veneer and a cold, cutting calm. "You make it difficult for me to trust you."

"I can't help how I feel. I have parents who don't know what's happened to me. Don't you get that?"

He works his jaw from side to side, his silence hurting me worse than his clever deceit. But deep inside, I also know he's right. I didn't promise him what he asked. I used that little clause, "where I belong," to justify my argument. Where I belong is a very subjective belief. Regardless of the promise I made to mate with him willingly, I have no intention of meekly giving in and staying here forever.

The unfriendly smile that curves his lips cuts me to the bone. "That's what I thought." He turns and continues on his way without bothering to check if I'm following. "I'm going to see Kian. If you're interested in knowing what he discovered from reading the humans' minds, you can follow me. If not, you'll wait in my quarters until I come back for you."

With that, he stalks away, leaving me sad and lonely for reasons I can't explain. Not having a choice, I push those feelings down and follow him.

CHAPTER 7
ELSIE

Kian doesn't have much to tell us about how Karl and the women ended up on Zerra or who created the portals except the facts I already pointed out.

I give Aruan a look that says I told him so.

Aruan paces in front of Kian's table, frustration etched on his face. "How is it possible that no one has heard of anyone with the same powerful ability as Mother? That kind of power isn't easy to keep a secret. On top of that, the person who tried to poison Elsie *and* the traitor who let the Phaelix into the palace are still hiding right under our noses."

Kian sits on a circular chair behind his table, observing us with a neutral expression. "If you let me read your mind, Elsie, I may be able to find some information. Something could've happened while you were unconscious."

"You can do that?" I come closer. "See what happened while I was unconscious?"

Aruan's, "No," echoes through the room. "You will *not* read her mind." His tense shoulders and fisted hands as he stops to glare at Kian say he's not going to budge.

In either case, I don't want Kian to sift through my most private thoughts. I was just curious about how the brain works, if the mind records information even while we're lights out.

Kian sighs. "Suit yourself, but then don't stand there and complain to me about the slow progress of our investigation."

"Sandy mentioned something," I say.

Both men turn their attention to me.

"She said an Alit came to visit the Phaelix at night, and that it sounded as if they were negotiating. She didn't catch a name or see his face. The topic of the slaves came up, and the man said the Alit don't mate with Earthlings."

"Interesting," Kian muses, steepling his fingers.

"And you didn't get that from reading Sandy's mind?" Aruan snaps at his brother.

Kian's tone remains level. "Reading everything would've taken all night. I focused on their arrival on Zerra."

Aruan resumes his pacing. "You need to read their minds thoroughly. Maybe one of them saw or heard something that'll shed light on the Alit's identity."

"Hey." I look between them. "What happened to

asking someone's permission before invading their thoughts?"

As expected, Kian ignores the morality question. "I can clear my official duties for the afternoon."

"Do it," Aruan says. "In the meantime, I'll speak to Mother."

Kian meets my eyes with an innocent shrug.

"Those humans had better be treated well," I say, giving Kian a narrow-eyed look. "Or you'll have me in your face, and believe me, you don't want that."

"Congratulations," Kian says with a smug smile.

I'm not taking the bait by asking for what. Of course, Aruan does.

He slams a fist on the stone slab of the desk. "Get your mind out of Elsie's head."

"I'm not in her head." Kian watches Aruan unblinkingly. "I don't have to be to know her power is back. Otherwise, she wouldn't have been so brave as to threaten me."

"Enough." Aruan's voice bounces off the walls. "We have ample problems as is. I don't need you to add to them."

Taking my arm, he leads me out of the room.

In the hallway, we bump into Vitai and Tarix.

Aruan motions at the basket of exotic fruit in Vitai's arms. "Where are you going with that?"

Vitai smiles sheepishly. "I was just bringing our guests a snack."

"It'll have to wait," Aruan says. "We need to talk to Mother."

"She's in private council with Father." Vitai shifts the weight of the basket. "They asked not to be disturbed."

Aruan exhales through his nose. "How long is it going to take?"

Vitai glances at me. "Who knows?"

"What about the humans?" Aruan scrutinizes Vitai. "Are their injuries sufficiently treated? Is there anything important I should know?"

While Vitai gives Aruan a rundown of the humans' physical conditions, Tarix pulls me aside.

"I'm so relieved that you're safe, Elsie. When the queen told us where she'd found you, we expected the worst."

"Thanks," I say half-heartedly because whatever happened to me, I brought onto myself. I don't deserve his concern.

Lowering his head, he asks in a voice that doesn't carry to Aruan and Vitai, "What was it like to be a prisoner of the Phaelix?"

I scrunch up my nose. "Like being a prisoner of anyone. It was awful."

"Did they say anything that could throw some light on their secret slave trading?"

"Like I already told Aruan, I didn't learn anything useful. At least their market has been destroyed." I don't feel pity as I add, "Along with the traders and buyers."

"Yes," he says in a far-off manner, frowning.

"Is everything all right? You look upset."

He appears to gather himself. "Of course. I'm just not keen on facing the queen with no new information to give her. I love her like my own mother, but she can be harsh if you don't deliver."

"We'll get to the bottom of it," I say, trying to sound confident when I'm not so sure myself.

He plasters a smile on his face. "I'm sure we will." His mood seems to improve a bit. "I overheard Suno asking you at the mating ceremony to tell him about Earth."

"I never got the chance."

"Maybe you'll indulge me? We can have wine and cake. I believe on Earth you call it 'having tea.'"

"I thought the subject was forbidden."

He winks. "I won't tell if you don't."

"Why are you and Suno so interested in Earth?"

"I can't speak for Suno, but I'm interested in everything. There's too much we keep hidden on Zerra, and no good ever comes of ignorance."

Does he disagree with the rules, which, in effect, could mean he's likely not a believer in the scrolls? Before I can question him about that, Aruan walks up to us.

"Speaking to my mother will have to wait." He drapes a possessive arm around my shoulders and says pointedly to Tarix, "Elsie has to rest." Addressing me, he continues, "I'll take you back to my quarters before I have to attend to some urgent matters."

"Which reminds me," Tarix says with an

uncomfortable laugh. "I have business to take care of for the queen."

He leaves with a hurried farewell, speed-walking down the hallway.

I tilt my face to Aruan. "That was rude. You literally chased him away."

"He had no business speaking to you like that."

"Like how?"

"Whispering in your ear. If he weren't my mother's favorite nephew, I would've snapped his neck for that."

"He didn't whisper in my ear. He just wanted to know if I came back from the Phaelix any wiser. He's worried about your mother's reaction if he doesn't have information for her."

"As he should be," Aruan says as he steers me back to his room.

Once we're inside, he seals the archway. "Do you need anything before I go?"

Not looking forward to being locked in here again, I hurry to say, "I was hoping I could visit the site with the scrolls again."

There's still so much about that strange technology I have to figure out.

His sharp "no" jolts me.

I blink. "Excuse me?"

He widens his stance and crosses his arms. "You're not going anywhere for a while."

I gape at him. "Why not?"

His tone is uncompromising. "You're going to oversee the Earthlings and allocate tasks to them to keep them busy. From now on, they're your responsibility. If any one of them steps out of line, I'll hold you accountable. When you've rested and recovered your strength, you'll spend every waking moment with them unless I require your presence."

"You can't be serious."

His smile is dry. "Do I ever joke?"

"But what about finding the perpetrator who's bringing humans here as slaves? I'll be of much more value to you if you let me help with the investigation. I can find the other Phaelix settlements much quicker from the sky."

"You mean on your dragon's back."

"Yes." I swallow. "I'm not going to fly off and leave the humans here alone."

"I don't think you will—leave them on their own, that is—but we don't need you to find the settlements. We know where they are."

"What about questioning the Phaelix?" I ask quickly. "If Kian gives me the ability to speak their language, I can help with that."

"We have that under control."

"You already have people going out there to question them?"

He doesn't reply.

"Aruan," I say with frustration. "I know you don't trust me, but this concerns me too. I'm just as invested in finding the person behind the slave trading as you are. The Phaelix brought me here, remember?"

"How can I forget?" He drops his arms to his sides

and steps right up to me. "The thought of those lizards with their claws on you still makes me want to torture them slowly while savoring their screams."

"Then what's the problem?" I ask, hoping to appeal to his reason.

"I'm not risking you in that way."

"I can take care of myself. I'll be vigilant. I promise. I learned from my mistake. I won't repeat that oversight."

"No," he says, not giving an inch. "You'll stay here and keep your friends on a tight leash. It'll be best to avoid contact with the royals and the inhabitants of the palace."

"But—"

He holds up a finger. "Consider it your punishment."

"*That's* my punishment?" I ball my hands at my sides. "That's unfair. You know I don't like being trapped between the walls."

There's no mercy in the smile that crinkles his silver eyes. "You're just going to have to get used to it."

"I—I…" I splutter, clenching my teeth.

"Hate me?" he says with a twisted expression.

The words were on the tip of my tongue, but I can't bring myself to say them again, not when I don't really mean them.

A calculated look comes over his features. I gasp as he backs me up to the wall and pins me against the stone bricks with his weight.

He wraps his fingers around my neck, holding me

in a dominant grasp, and lowers his head. His words feather over my lips, their meaning like arrows that find their target in my heart. "But you don't hate *this,* do you?"

Another gasp tears from my chest as he tilts his hips and presses his hardness against my stomach. The sound that escapes my lips is involuntary. It slips out before I can stop it, giving him his answer.

My belly heats as he brings his lips to mine. Everything I refuse to say hangs thickly in the air as he just hovers there, keeping that hairbreadth of distance between our mouths. Our breaths mingle with every labored exhale, our words caught in our chests. He remains like that, a hunter holding out a piece of bait, knowing the prey is going to eat right out of his hand.

And I'm the one who breaks first, who closes the distance and proves the truth he's taunting me with, the fact he's dangling in my face—that I can't resist him.

The minute I've taken that leap, he's no longer the patient hunter who's flaunting his power over me. He becomes wild. His instincts take over, like those of a predator who's smelled blood. His sole driving force becomes sinking his teeth into the meat that's right under his nose, all his for the taking.

It cuts me a little that the kill has always been a foregone conclusion. Yet I don't stop him when he chains my wrists in the iron grip of his huge hands and pins them above my head. I open my mouth for him, letting him a little deeper under my skin with every touch and every conquering caress.

He leans into me, his weight a secure anchor that wakes every nerve ending under my skin. The wall lights up around us, little sparks that buzz like fireflies in the background as he dominates my mouth and kisses me into submission.

My thoughts are all over the place, my head spinning with the delicious addictiveness of his touch. I revel in being caught in his cage, wanting him to not only ravish but completely ruin me. Even when he transfers both my wrists into one big hand and slides the other down my side to my hip, I don't try to break free. I stand quietly, chest fluttering and breaths heaving in the snare of his trap, willingly letting him devour me.

He bunches the fabric of my dress into his fist, pulling it up to my middle. Beneath, I'm naked and aching, ready for him.

His fingers find the truth; his lips growl an approval against my neck.

The nip of his teeth is going to leave a mark, but I'm beyond caring as he shoves a finger inside me.

I clench around him, willing him to take more. He peppers my jaw with kisses and bites while stretching me until I finally submit to the unbearable pleasure that tightens my core under the onslaught of his hand. At the same time, my inner muscles give for him, turning pliable and soft, as an invisible band squeezes around my pelvis.

"Aruan..."

I'm barely cognizant of speaking his name. Of moving. Of meeting the thrusts of the two fingers he plunges inside me. I let him keep me in the vise of his hands while he destroys me a little more with every wave of pleasure that exceeds the intensity of the previous one.

I moan when he deprives me of that destructive touch, mourning the delicious devastation it promised. Keeping my wrists constrained, he wraps one arm around my middle and lifts me. I lock my ankles behind his ass, keeping myself up with the support of the wall at my back as he lets my wrists go and works his pants open.

He angles my hips and keeps them in the position he wants with a bruising grip on the fleshy side of my ass cheek. I'm close to breaking when he finally enters me. He doesn't go slowly or carefully. He takes me greedily and messily, a beautiful disaster of total possession and brutal pleasure. His cock stretches me, his pummeling taking me to limits I shouldn't be able to handle, but it feels right. It feels as if I were born for this man and the carnal dance that walks a tightrope between pain and pleasure.

Keeping one hand on my ass, he slips the other between our bodies and brushes impatient fingers over my clit. I lean my head back and simply accept the sweet torture. A perverse part of me enjoys being this man's prey. I'm his to tear apart, to rip limb from limb.

The orgasm doesn't creep up on me with slow,

languid pleasure like earlier. This time, it detonates like fireworks in my belly. He stops feathering my clit to splay his fingers around my neck, applying proprietorial pressure as he keeps me in place while finishing inside me. He does so staring into my eyes, consuming me with his gaze and daring me to tell him no.

But I don't.

I don't tell him to stop.

I couldn't even if I wanted to. I need to finish this too much. I need this—him—like food, water, and air.

He lets me ride out the aftershocks slowly, making me take every drop. A long time passes before he's sated. And when he finally pulls out, his semi-hard cock already hardening for me again, victory glows in his eyes.

Because I let him.

I let him come inside me, the consequences left to run as terrifying and wild as our lust.

He kisses me tenderly before lowering me to my feet. My knees are wobbly and my mind disoriented. Our clothes disintegrate as if they never existed. He tells me how proud he is of me, what a good girl I've been, and that he's going to run me a bath and hold me in his arms for hours, his duties be damned. He whispers praise and sweet nothings in my ear as he cradles me to his heart, but all I hear is the powerful roar of his silent victory in the air… and the deafening defeat beating in my chest.

CHAPTER 8
ARUAN

The primal way I've marked Elsie fills me with possessive satisfaction, even as despondency sneaks in to foil the elation.

Because she's not happy.

Her discord slices through my ribs like a blade.

She didn't want me to fill her sweet pussy to the brim with my cum, yet I did it. Even now, as we stand facing each other naked, it drips down the insides of her thighs.

I step closer, plastering our bodies together. A primitive urge born from the basest of instincts compels me to gather the wasted seed and push it back in, my fingers slick in her tight, wet pussy.

Instantly, I feel the coldness inside her melt away, the dying embers of her arousal sparking back to life as I pump it all back, making her take every drop… and then my cock.

I wasn't planning on claiming her again so soon, not after taking her hard enough to leave her raw, but in this, my body has a mind of its own. I spread her out right there on the floor, cushioning her head with one hand while I fuck my cum into her sleek, hot pussy. If I could plug and seal that pretty hole until she conceives, I'd do it. Instead, I settle for fucking her like an animal, savage and without restraint. I'm propped up on one hand, carrying my weight with my arm as I stare at the ecstasy twisting her beautiful features. Biting her lip, she refuses to give me sounds, but her expression tells me everything.

She both loves and hates this.

Her body wants me, but her mind doesn't. As for her heart, I'm not sure she'll ever open that part of herself to me.

Because she didn't choose me. Nature made that choice for her. For us.

Leaning down, I kiss her to take the sting out of the bitter reality. And then I coax another orgasm from her spent body by removing my hand from the back of her head and wedging it between us to stroke her clit.

She surrenders her pleasure, drowning me in her tormented defeat as we come together. I'm buried to the hilt inside her, yet the ever-growing gorge between us runs a little deeper and stretches a bit wider. Trying to ignore it, I cup her hip and chase after her lips again, but instead of kissing me, she pushes on my shoulders.

I do what she wants—get off her—and let her sit up.

She flinches either with discomfort or regret. Or maybe with both.

I take her hand and pull her to her feet. "I'm calling Vitai."

"I'm not injured," she says with a bite in her tone.

I'm far from reassured. I'd like to have Vitai do a full-body healing session, but I don't want to force more on her than I already have. I wasn't going to take things so far, not again. With her, I simply can't help myself.

We have another bath. At the rate we're going, we'll end up with permanently wrinkled skin. She allows me to wash her and kiss her even though her mind is clearly somewhere else and her body is too wrung out to come alive under my hands again.

When I offer to dry her, she tells me she'd like to relax in the water for a bit longer, which is just another way of saying she needs distance from me. I open my mouth and close it again. This isn't the moment to talk about what happened, or rather, what *could* happen. I'm guessing that life-altering possibility has a lot to do with her withdrawal from me.

For the first time in my life, I'm at a loss for what to do. If I stay, my presence may upset her more than she already is. If I go, she may feel abandoned when she decides she needs me.

After a moment's deliberation, I add more healing salts to the water and leave her in peace. I don't go far —just to the bedroom, where I dress in the formal attire official business meetings require. My father is tasked with enforcing our laws and the necessary judgments and punishments that go with that responsibility. My mother is in charge of diplomatic relations. Kian oversees Lona's trade, and Vitai is tasked with health and sanitary regulations. Gaia is saddled with our charities. My duties include overseeing all of theirs and making sure the system runs smoothly. The other royals are allocated obligations within those areas and report back to my immediate family. When my father is inundated with disputes to settle, I lighten his burden by taking over some of the cases. It's a never-ending job that keeps me busy from sunrise to sunset, leaving little time for anything else.

But my father has taken on a great deal of the work himself lately, thereby giving me time to seal the bond with my mate. It's one of the only two occasions in a royal's life that he's granted that much spare time. The other is when his mate is pregnant. We take our responsibility in supporting and protecting our women seriously, especially when they're growing a baby inside them and are therefore more vulnerable.

There are a lot of assignments waiting for me, enough to keep me busy for many moon cycles to come, yet that's not what I'm focused on. My thoughts remain with the woman in the other room, a woman who belongs to me yet has a hard time accepting that fact.

When I've pulled on my boots, I hover for a moment, torn between going to her and giving her the space she demanded. The decision is made for me when the wall at the entrance lights up, announcing a visitor.

I know who it is by the distinct pulsing rhythm of the light even before I walk to the archway.

Behind me, the almost-silent footsteps of bare feet fall on the floor. Only my enhanced hearing allows me to discern the sound.

I look over my shoulder to find Elsie standing in the archway of the bedroom with a bath sheet wrapped around her naked body. She tries to hide her feelings from me by keeping her expression neutral, but her hurt reaches me through the vague connection of our incomplete bond.

She's upset—not as much with me as with herself.

"It wasn't your fault," I say gruffly. "You couldn't have stopped what happened even if you'd wanted to."

She studies me from underneath those long, russet lashes. "Could *you*?"

My jaw locks around the denial. I've always owned my actions. That's not going to change now. I don't regret coming inside her, and I won't blame it on the mating heat.

She sucks her bottom lip into her mouth, working it between her teeth for a while before pushing out a heavy question. "What if…?"

My reply is decisive. "Then we'll handle it."

She nods but not in an affirmative way. She looks

so frail and delicate standing there half-naked, drowning in a bath sheet, that a chilling fear eats into my gut. Now that it's a real possibility, the idea of Elsie in childbirth terrifies me. After what she's been through on Earth, coming so close to dying over and over again, I'm worried she may not be strong enough, that her body may relapse under the strain of growing a baby inside her.

I'll have to keep Vitai on standby for the full moon cycles of her gestation period. And I'll find out what happened to make her so sick in that other world, so I can make sure it never happens again.

I'll keep Elsie and any child she may conceive safe if it's the last thing I do.

In my peripheral vision, the pulsing of the light becomes insistent. Turning away from Elsie more to prevent her from reading my concern than to address the matter that demands my attention, I lift the seal I've put in place and let the archway appear.

My mother stands at the threshold, supported by my father on one side and Vitai on the other. Her guards form a close-knit half-circle at her back. She looks a little better, but she's still pale.

Seeing her with those thoughts still churning in my head brings back all the old anger and accusations. My mother lied to me. She told me my mate was dead, and I believed her. That fact alone has always made her the main suspect in the wrong that was committed when Elsie was banished to Earth. However, now that the Phaelix's slave trading has been blown wide open, I have to admit that my mother isn't the only one capable of sending someone to that other world. Although… the slave trading started a lot later than Elsie's disappearance, which logically still leaves my mother as the most probable guilty party.

"Mother. I was just about to come see you."

Her eyes flare as she focuses on something behind me, or I should say, on someone.

I know what she sees—Elsie covered in nothing but a bath sheet with *that* look on her face. It's a look only a well-fucked woman wears.

"You've mated," my mother whisper-exclaims.

Almost immediately, a frown pleats her brow. The tangible harmony that exists between mated couples is impossible to miss, yet the disagreeable atmosphere in the room is palpable. My mother's questioning eyes rest on my face. She's wondering why, if we've mated, that harmony is absent with Elsie and me. But she wipes her doubtful expression away quickly before schooling her features.

Holding my gaze with a tilt of her chin, she says, "I need to talk to you."

"By all means." I step aside. "Let's not do it in the hallway where the walls have ears." My smile is cool. "Come in."

"Alone," she says in a firm tone.

"What I have to say concerns Elsie too."

"Aruan," my father says. "What you want to say will have to wait. You will speak with your mother first." He stresses, "And you'll do it as she requests—alone."

Maybe it's better like this. Elsie's emotions are still too raw. It's best to give her more time to deal with everything before throwing the wrong that's been done to her in her face. Nothing can change what she's suffered. However, I'd be cursed if I don't make it right.

"As you wish," I say, my manner cold even as red-hot fury sizzles inside me.

My mother turns and heads down the hallway. "My quarters."

The look I give Elsie holds an unspoken message. We'll continue our conversation when I return.

The longer I stare at her vivid eyes, so alive with hurt and betrayal, the bigger the chance grows that I won't leave at all, so I tear myself away from her and follow in my family's footsteps.

Elsie's plea is spoken to my back. "Don't lock me in." Then she resorts to begging. "Please."

It's impossible to harden my heart against the outcry of my mate. I turn to face her. "You'll stay here."

She nods enthusiastically. "I won't leave your rooms until you get back."

She hasn't earned my trust, but I give it to her anyway. It's not because I feel guilty about taking her silence as her agreement to come inside her. It's a step in a new direction, showing her that I'm prepared to give her the benefit of the doubt. Or so I tell myself as I walk with long, angry strides to my mother's reception room.

It's so typical of the queen to face me standing instead of sitting, even in her weakened state. My father takes up a position at her right while Vitai stands a small distance to her left. She's dismissed the guards, which means the subject she wants to discuss is sensitive, too sensitive for the ears of the commoners, but she's summoned my cousins.

The presence of Suno and Tarix shows just how important the matter is. Suno is the legal arbitrator while my mother values Tarix's advice above that of everyone but my father.

My father isn't holding her elbow or supporting her arm, but he looks ready to catch her at the slightest sign of swaying or fainting.

My mother holds herself regally, an iron will shining in the silver gaze she fixes on me. "What happened? Why wasn't the mating successful?"

I clench my teeth. "I don't know."

She considers me for a moment before declaring, "She rejected you."

"Did she?" Vitai sounds surprised. "That's unheard of. No person on Zerra has ever rejected a mate."

"Our circumstances aren't exactly ideal," I say, a tad defensive.

"The bond won't be forged if she doesn't accept you," my mother says.

Irritation rises in me. "What does that even mean? I thought that fate was undeniable. I've claimed her. What else is there to do?"

"It won't work if she doesn't love you." My mother gives me a pitying look. "Establishing a physical bond is easy. Acceptance comes from the heart. You need both for the bond to be complete."

"This is the first I'm hearing of it." I scoff. "No other mated couple on Zerra has ever had this problem."

My mother sighs. "Normally, mated couples love each other. It comes naturally."

Vitai smirks. "It looks as if you have your work cut out for you, Aruan. You're going to have to win your mate over."

I slide my gaze his way. At my cutting look, the smile vanishes from his face.

"That's not why I asked you to come," my mother says.

"Naturally," I drawl. "What *did* you want to talk about?"

"I heard about something that happened even before Elsie tamed a dragon," she says. "The talk is that spiked pets and pixie dragons swarmed to her in frighteningly great numbers, right here in the palace. Does she know how to control her power?"

I cross the floor and stop in front of my mother. "Out of everything that's happened, *that's* what you're concerned about?"

"Elsie's power has enormous ramifications," my father says. "It could be dangerous."

The muscles around my eyes tighten. "Aren't all our powers dangerous in some way?"

Tarix steps forward. "We've had since our childhood to learn how to master them. Elsie discovered her power only recently."

I direct my ire at him. "And whose fault is that?"

Tarix cringes.

"Aruan," Suno says in a pacifying tone. "Your mother is simply concerned about everyone's welfare."

"If she can command animals," my mother says, "who's to say she won't eventually be capable of commanding more advanced species?"

Meaning us, the Alit. They're worried that Elsie would be able to control us. Interesting. I wonder if that's the case. If so, her power would be fearsome indeed, and just about every man and woman on Zerra would have a good reason for wanting her dead.

Just like they do with me.

"There's no evidence suggesting that," Vitai says. "Let's not get ahead of ourselves."

"The people are frightened." Tarix spreads his hands. "So are the royals."

"Are they now?" I face him with a mocking grin. "What do you want me to do about that?"

I won't lie. I'm enjoying the fear reflected in his eyes.

"Your mother needs to take Elsie under her wing," Suno says. He must see the anger on my face because he adds quickly, "To train her."

The anger boils over, escaping from the tight lid I've tried to keep on it. "Do you think for one minute I'd entrust my mate to the very person who banished her?"

"Aruan," my mother cries out as if I've insulted her.

I turn on her. "Isn't that true? Are you going to deny it again? To my face?"

She trembles as she stares at me, pursing her lips so tightly they turn colorless.

My father lays a hand on her shoulder.

The silence that follows is charged. She's denied it up to now, but I won't let her get away with it any longer.

"Do you know what happened to her, Mother? Do you know what she went through on Earth?"

And as she stares at me, I tell her everything, every little detail that Elsie shared with me, starting with her childhood ailments and their painful consequences and ending with how her heart almost gave out.

If it were possible for my mother's chalky cheeks to grow paler, they would. Even Suno and Tarix appear offended and moved for Elsie's sake. Only Vitai, whom I've already told Elsie's history, doesn't look surprised.

When I finally finish, I face my mother unblinkingly. "Are you still going to tell me you didn't do that to her?" My voice rises steadily. "That you didn't steal my mate from me?"

"It had to be done," my mother exclaims in a sudden frenzy. "There was no other way."

So it's true, what I've been suspecting. And despite those suspicions, I've never felt more betrayed in my life.

"Nia," my father says, his manner soothing.

My mother's proud posture sags. "I did it for you, Aruan. For all of us."

It takes everything I have to control the destructive

rage inside me. "Do not insult me, Mother. You did *not* do it for me."

Only Suno wears a shocked expression. Everyone else has already worked it out for themselves.

"She was going to be your downfall," my mother says. "Please, Aruan, try to understand. I did it because I loved you. Because I *love* you. I knew the prophecy would come true that day you set off the explosion." I wince at the mention, but my mother plows ahead. "That day, I knew you were too powerful, more powerful than any man who's been born. Everything in the prophecy pointed to you. Removing your mate was the only way to secure our people and our world." She comes closer, stretching out her arms with her palms facing up. "But I didn't kill her. I could never do that. I sent her away as much to save *her* life as yours because I knew she wasn't safe here. Don't you see? She was a target since the day it became clear that she was your destined mate."

"So you sent her through a portal to Earth," I say with all the bitterness I've been carrying inside me since the day I found out my family deceived me.

My mother hangs her head. If she means to embrace me, I won't offer her forgiveness so readily. When I step away from her outstretched arms, she looks up, and hurt washes into her eyes.

I take in her smooth skin and youthful features. The characteristics are familiar, but I see now that I never truly knew the person who calls herself my mother.

I never imagined she could be capable of such cruelty.

"Don't look at me like that," she says. "Don't you understand?"

"No." My voice is cold. Hard. "You sent Elsie away as a strong and healthy baby." I know it. I felt it. "What did you do to her?" The blade of her double betrayal twists into my gut. "Was banishing her not enough for you? Why did you have to make her suffer so much?"

Vitai looks on with an empathetic expression, but I'm in no state to figure out if it's meant for my mother or for me.

"Aruan, I—" My mother swallows. "It wasn't my intention. I swear that to you. All I can think is that, seeing that she wasn't fully developed yet, her body must've been put back together wrongly on the other side. It was the first and only time I sent a baby through a portal to Earth."

The sound of that makes me lose all reason. "She would've died." My voice grows in volume until the whole palace must be able to hear me. "If the Phaelix hadn't taken her, Elsie would've been dead."

Dead.

My vision goes hazy. Red bleeds into the edges. The injustice wakes a rage in me that knows no boundaries. My reason fails as a deep, dark void sucks me in. I'm aware of nothing but the power vibrating inside me, the darkness that's slowly creeping in and swallowing the light until the darkness becomes the light.

"Aruan!"

My mother's terrified scream reaches me through the power that's taken over my body and mind.

"Aruan." Someone shakes me. "Stop it!" My father.

"Aruan!"

I blink through the wave of haziness, slowly coming to my senses. The light is blinding. It streams through the windows, hurting my eyes and burning my skin.

The sun.

Through the arched windows, the flaming ball in the sky is a flaring mass of white light that steals the colors in the room. The beams bask everything in that pale, brilliant heat.

"Aruan." My father grips my arm hard. "Calm down."

It takes effort to do so. I will down the rage, getting a handle on it with difficulty.

Slowly, the sun shrinks to the size of a nut in the sky. The suffocating heat goes back to the humid hotness of a normal day. Colors return to the room. The landscape that's visible through the window is no longer a white portrait with stark lines of flashing black but simply the green grass of the rolling hill and the blue of a cloudless sky. Although, a few of the taller trees in the distance are black, as if they've been scorched by fire.

I register the people in the room. Suno is shivering, staring at me with round eyes. Tarix, who found shelter behind a sofa, is straightening on wobbly legs. A trickle of sweat runs down his temple, but he doesn't wipe it away. He clenches the back of the sofa in a white-knuckled grip, looking at me as if I'm a monster. Vitai leans against a wall, appearing equally stunned and impressed. My father has an arm around my mother's waist, holding her steady.

My mother finds her voice first. "If anything could prove my point, that was it."

"Nia," my father says in a tone I've never heard him use with her before.

I ball my hands into fists. "You harmed Elsie. You nearly killed her."

"She's here now," Vitai says. "That's what you have to focus on."

His words only aggravate me anew.

Vitai adds quickly, "And that she's perfectly healthy and not dying any longer."

"How is that possible?" my father asks Vitai. "Could Elsie's body have been restored to its original health when it was brought back through the portal to Zerra? Is that why her power reappeared?"

Vitai smoothes down his hair. "It's a plausible explanation. Aruan told me about Elsie's condition on Earth a while ago, and I've looked at it from all angles since, but I still haven't come up with a theory."

"It's the only explanation that makes sense," my mother says. "Going back through the portal somehow undid—"

"Is that why you tried to poison her?" I interject with a resentful smile. "Because fate ironically put a spike in your plan? So you thought you'd better finish her off for good this time?"

My mother gasps. "I would never! Besides, do you think I'd poison myself?"

The bitter disappointment makes me cruel. "You've proved yourself shrewd enough. I wouldn't put it past you."

"That's enough," my father snaps.

"I didn't try to poison anyone." My mother adopts a wounded look. "I swear that on the lives of my children."

I cross my arms. "Then who did it?"

My mother blows out a frustrated sigh. "I wish I knew."

Suno clears his throat. "We're losing sight of the matter at hand, which is determining the extent of Elsie's power and teaching her how to control it. As a person who possesses one of the strongest powers in the kingdom, the queen makes an ideal candidate to train your mate, but if you don't trust your mate with your mother, Gaia could be tasked with the duty."

"Gaia's power isn't as strong," Vitai says. "Elsie will make mush out of our sister—figuratively speaking, of course."

"It's true that Elsie has to be trained in using her power responsibly." My father looks at Suno. "What do you suggest?"

I sneer at that. "Have any of us had training?"

My father gives me a hard look. "You were taught how to apply your power ethically as a child."

He leaves the rest unsaid, namely that if Elsie can control more than animals, every person on Zerra is at risk. She could bring entire kingdoms to their knees if she wished.

People will fear her, and not just because she's my mate. They'll wish her away even more than they already do.

"I'm sorry, Aruan," my mother says. "I'm sorry for everything Elsie suffered. I hope you'll realize with time that I acted out of love for you because I couldn't bear losing a son to his own power. You may not think so now, but in my own way, I also acted out of love for Laliss."

"She prefers to be called Elsie," I bite out. "That's who she became."

Though the truth is a lot more complicated now and reality much more muddled. My mate is both women, Elsie and Laliss, and it's confusing for her to redefine herself in this new life.

"Fine. Elsie, then," my mother says. "A different name doesn't change who she is. I couldn't stand by and watch someone assassinate that baby. In time, maybe you'll be able to forgive me."

My mother is still talking, but I've stopped listening to her. Instead, I focus on a deep rumble in the distance. The sound rolls like thunder before cracking down like a whip, shaking the very mountain the palace is carved into.

"What the—" Tarix says, grabbing the back of the sofa for support.

Vitai rushes over to the window. "What's going on out there?"

"Aruan," my mother says. "You have to stay calm."

This storm isn't mine. For once, my power is under control.

Like a shadow that swallows the room whole, an ominous foreboding creeps up on me. I walk to the window and look outside.

The entire mountain above the village is alive, shuddering and groaning as if it's about to burst from its seams. I have a terrible feeling this is my doing, that I somehow set off the disaster when my power caused the sun to flare.

The top of the mountain starts sliding, a broad river of gray rocks the size of houses that rips trees out by their roots and drags them down its path, a path that leads straight to the village.

"Dear dragons," my mother says next to me, her voice pitched with distress.

I have no recollection of her crossing the floor or how my father arrived so quickly at my other side. All I know is that hundreds of people are about to be buried under a sea of rocks.

My mother grips my wrist, her nails digging into my skin. "Do something."

I focus my gaze on the mountain, using my mind to reassemble soil and stones, keeping the lot together before more damage is done.

The landscape stops shifting. The river of rocks filled with mangled trees and patches of grass that were plucked off the hills like tufts of hair from a scalp slows and then comes to a stop. People's screams replace the roar of the land as the villagers flee, running as fast as their legs can carry them.

Just as Vitai blows out a shaky breath, Gaia comes sprinting through the door with her hair flying behind her.

"Quick," she says. "There've been several landslides on the other side of the mountain, and half a moon cycle's villages are buried beneath rocks. We need all the help we can get."

CHAPTER 9
ELSIE

Destruction and chaos meet me as I step on Kian's heels through the portal he created. Deep grooves scar the side of the mountain where rocks have torn through the soil. The rockslide has swept away trees and everything else in its way. Severed roots, mangled branches, and crushed trunks stick out between the rocks that cover half a village at the foot of the mountain, not a rooftop in sight. On the untouched half, domed stone houses line circular streets. From the vantage point of the high outcrop on which we're standing, the layout looks like a snail shell coiling in circles from the center.

Disoriented, I look around me. People are screaming and running in all directions.

Shit.

How do we help them? A moment ago, it looked as if the sun was going to explode. I thought that was the end of all of us. Finished. Done. The life forms on

Zerra weren't going to be destroyed by an asteroid but by a supernova.

Miraculously, the sun returned to its original brightness, and things went back to normal. Until the mountain started shifting. Then, just as abruptly, it stopped.

I dressed hurriedly, grabbing the first gown and pair of shoes my hands fell on, and was just about to go check on our guests when Kian arrived.

Having sensed the distress in so many Alit minds, he came looking for Aruan. When I told him Aruan was with the queen, he said there was no time to waste. He sent a message straight to Gaia's mind, since he said it was open to his instead of closed like Aruan's, to alert Aruan and the rest of the family. Then he took my hand and brought me here through a portal he opened. He didn't mention a natural disaster or how we were supposed to make ourselves useful. I weigh a whopping ninety-two pounds. I won't be able to lift a single one of those rocks, and even if I could, it would take ages to remove everything.

I look at Kian for a clue. His expression is grim as he takes in the horrific scene.

My voice is shaky. "Where's Aruan? What's taking him so long?"

Surely, with his powerful ability, he can fix this in no time.

"He'll come as soon as he can," Kian says. "Gaia already delivered the message. There are several villages affected in addition to this one."

In the meantime, people here are trapped beneath the rocks. "What can I do to help?"

He closes his eyes without replying.

"What are you doing, Kian?" My anxiety climbs. "Now's not the time for meditation."

"Getting a headcount," he mumbles. "If you'd let me concentrate."

Portals open left, right, and center of us, letting guards through. They land on their feet running. The work has the queen's name written all over it, which must mean Kian is right. Gaia did indeed deliver the message.

More guards arrive, but there's no sign of Aruan. The only sentiments our bond reveals are urgency and diligence. What I wouldn't give for cell phones right now.

One of the guards stops in the clearing, puffs out his chest, and starts calling out orders. I jerk with surprise. The volume of his voice is so blaringly loud that my ears ring. Did the guy swallow a megaphone? He sounds like a thousand-megawatt speaker. Is that an Alit power, having a super-loud voice?

His words carry across the valley as he orders people to line up according to their talents, swiftly dividing them into groups of heavy lifters, runners, and caregivers.

Another guard is already hauling rocks twice his size from the pile while others are working in teams to move them. That guard is the man who flung the

Phaelix through the air without even touching them when they attacked the palace. I recognize his face.

In no time, the villagers have joined in. Everything is so well coordinated and happens so fast it makes me think this isn't the first time they're facing a crisis of such a scale.

A blur moves in my peripheral vision. I look toward it. The blur of motion dashing across the field turns out to be a man running so fast he appears like nothing but a series of hologram flashes.

What the…? Where's he going?

"To tell the other villages to bring food and blankets," Kian says. "We may have injured people who'll need care."

Did I ask that out loud? Or is Kian in my head?

The guard with the megaphone voice jogs to Kian. Like the other guards, he wears a white tunic and dark pants tucked into long boots.

He stops at the bottom of the outcrop and bows his head. "Your Highnesses."

His voice is like razorblades cutting into my brain. I resist the urge to cover my ears with my hands.

He raises his gaze to Kian, avoiding eye contact with me. When he speaks again, his voice is at a normal level. "How many people are trapped under the rocks?"

"Ten moon cycles." At the widening of the man's eyes, Kian adds, "It happened too fast. They didn't have time to sound the alarm."

The guard's expression is cautious. "Casualties?"

"Not yet," Kian says with a tight jaw. "The stone

structures are holding under the weight of the rocks. They still have air to breathe."

The big fat "but" he doesn't say hangs in the air between us.

"The rocks dragged the underlaying soil with them. We have to dig." Kian points at the foot of the mountain. "Get all the tools at your disposal and start the guards on the east side. The villagers can work from the west."

Adrenaline floods my body. The rush is like a kick-start to my brain. I scan the environment, taking in the absence of dinosaurs and insects. As animals often do, they must've sensed the danger and fled.

Instead of relying on my sight, I tap into that part of my power that revealed itself earlier when I sensed the animals in and around the palace. Back then, the feeling was faint, but now, it's pronounced.

A warm glow starts in the pit of my stomach. The heat expands until it fills every part of me. My skin begins to hum with a strange buzz. And then it all implodes from my brain outward, dunking me into a world of black.

I'm standing in the center of a dark sky, the whole planet a canvas of night dotted with stars. Each of those stars is a source of life—a dinosaur, reptile, or insect. I know exactly where and what they are, the whole of Zerra's animal life revealed to me in a blink.

The map embeds in my brain. I can't explain how or why it happens. I only know it's as natural and comforting as pulling on a favorite sweater. Cozy. Familiar.

As soon as the picture has formed, the daylight returns, and I'm back on the outcrop with Kian.

The rest happens automatically, like an inborn instinct awakening from a long slumber. I don't have to think about what to do. I simply act, focusing on a parade of pangolins that were hunting for termites on the border of the forest before the landslide hit. They took refuge in their deep burrows.

A mere thought makes them surface. Another sends them rushing to the site. They're powerful diggers, capable of excavating circular chambers large enough for an Alit to crawl inside and stand up. Together, they can do so in record time.

Kian shoots me a questioning look as the pangolins, normally solitary animals, arrive in hordes. With their cute armor of scales, they look almost exactly like the species on Earth, except that their scales don't cover their tails and legs. On Earth, they've been around for eighty million years, and now, sadly, they're endangered due to poaching.

Instead of waiting for the Alit to clear the rocks, they start digging from the border of the enormous pile, creating underground tunnels to the houses buried beneath the rubble.

Something like surprise and approval flashes in Kian's eyes as he glances at me. I don't get the same looks from the people who're digging as fast as they can.

Rather than being relieved to have help, they appear frightened of the pangolins. Or maybe the fearful looks they throw over their shoulders are aimed at me.

One of the guards is splitting rocks, chopping them into smaller pieces with his bare hands like an axe falling on wood. Another Alit power? Some of the people are lifting the pieces into carts while others, who must be as strong as oxen, are pulling the carts away.

I tap into my energy source again and bring a few quetzalcoatluses around. They're powerful enough to hook their claws into the broken tree trunks and carry them off before dumping them on the flat stretch of land next to the village to make the diggers' work easier.

My heart leaps when Betty appears in the sky. She sweeps down low, circling over me before joining the others. They fasten their claws around the rocks and fly them away at an astounding speed, working much faster than the men on the ground.

Even little Pip and a host of his friends show up for support. Aside from cheering on the quetzalcoatluses, the anurognathuses aren't much help, but it warms my heart that they've come unsummoned. Just as Pip saved me from drinking the poison all on his own.

Does that mean they feel the special bond we share? The connection between the animals and me is so much more than mind manipulation. They're like my family.

I hold my breath as the pangolins finish the first

tunnel, and the parents and children trapped in their house are brought through it to safety. Immediately, the pangolins move on to extend the tunnel to the next house.

A circle of lights appears on my right. Gaia rushes through the portal, holding Vitai's hand. A beat later, the queen steps through a portal with her husband. Aruan arrives on his own, answering my question about his ability to create a portal.

Finally.

Thank fuck.

A host of nobles and royals, still dressed in their smart tunics and gowns, follow through portals that the queen and Gaia open, but I only have eyes for Aruan.

In the light of the tragedy, I have an inexplicable need to be near him, to assure myself that he's safe. I haven't realized how nervous I was until he's standing in front of me, watching me with dark intensity that transforms his expression from disbelieving to thunderous.

"By dragons, Elsie." He charges toward me and clamps my shoulders between his big palms. "Why aren't you in my quarters?" He gives me a gentle shake. "What are you doing here in the midst of the danger?"

I blink up at him, surprised by the ferocity of his outburst. "Kian brought me."

Aruan lets me go and turns on Kian with clenched fists and flaring nostrils. "You masked her distress. You endangered my mate and prevented me from sensing it." He gets into Kian's face. "You put a shield on her mind to hide her from me." His voice rises steadily. "Worse, you mimicked her sentiments and deceived me into believing she was safely in my quarters."

"Elsie was needed here," Kian says with deceptive calm. "As you can see for yourself, she's doing a great job in helping." He gets in Aruan's face. "So, brother, I advise you to let her do what's necessary."

The king's voice booms through the space. "That's enough." He steps up and pushes them apart. "The two of you can fight it out when we've addressed the crisis. Elsie is here now. She'll do what she can. She has a responsibility to our people just like the rest of the royals."

Aruan works his jaw from side to side, but his father doesn't give him a chance to argue.

The king addresses Kian. "What's the status?"

Kian nods toward the rescue work. "We're making progress."

Just then, the second, third, and fourth families are freed through tunnels.

Everyone turns their heads toward them. Except Aruan. He's looking at me as if he's ready to storm over and rip me away in a second. I do my best to calm my erratic heartbeat and to show him through the bond that I'm all right.

After another beat, he tears his gaze away from me to look toward the village. The villagers and guards are stealing wary glances at the quetzalcoatluses and anurognathuses flying overhead. The queen looks equally uneasy.

"What about the other villages?" Kian asks.

"We checked," the queen says. "Everyone is safe."

Aruan may no longer be staring in my direction, but his attention lingers on me for another second, pulsing darkly between us, before he turns to the mountain. In a wink, the rocks and sand retract, falling to the wayside.

Holy macaroni.

The buried half of the village isn't only uncovered but clean, not a speck of sand remaining.

Vitai takes off to the side where the injured are gathering.

"I don't know if that's such a good idea," a man with white hair and a bushy mustache says with his face tilted toward the sky. "What if those dragons get hungry and decide to snack on a few Alit?"

"Don't worry," I say. "I can control them."

Aruan turns a cold glare on the man. "Are you implying Elsie is incompetent, Incus?"

The man cringes. "Not at all."

"Aruan," I say in a gentle tone, imploring him to calm down.

He doesn't have a choice as the rescue operation continues in all earnest. Luckily, none of the injuries are serious. Gaia explains that Lona is often plagued by landslides, which is why the houses are constructed from stone.

Everyone, including the royals, roll up their

sleeves and get their hands dirty. The queen gives orders for an area to be prepared where food and water can be served. While we're waiting for aid from the nearby villages, she brings staff with food from the palace. The king demands a large tent where Vitai can treat the injured, which Aruan fabricates with nothing but his mind. The villagers use their own powers, albeit clearly weaker than those of the royals, to lift heavy buckets of water and to light fires with their minds.

Seeing that everything is mostly back to normal, I let the animals return to their burrows, nests, and hunting. Aruan visits every house to repair any damage with his incredible power. I join Gaia in handing out bowls of hearty broth to the villagers while the queen ensures their stores and cellars are filled with fresh food and wine.

We work until late, helping with the chores and the children. When every single person has been taken care of, we're weary to the bone. It's late when Aruan takes my hand and transports me via a portal to his quarters. We step into his bedroom, facing each other with dirt-streaked faces and dusty clothes. The atmosphere is charged. With every second that he simply stands there, staring at me, the heaviness intensifies.

"I didn't know you could create portals," I say to break the awkward silence.

"Most of my immediate family can open a simple portal to a nearby location, but only Gaia and my mother can create them systematically and repeatedly, bending distance with their minds to create multiple portals over greater areas."

I nod at his patient explanation, racking my brain for something else to say.

He surprises me by declaring, "You did well today."

"You're not angry?"

"Angry?" He advances on me. "I'm furious, Elsie." Stopping short of me, he towers over my body. "Kian put you in danger, and you risked your life by following him."

I crane my neck to look at him. "You can't keep me locked up in your quarters forever and treat me as if I'm made of glass."

"Really?" His lips stretch with a calculated smile, the gesture narrowing his eyes. "Watch me."

"Come on, Aruan." I blow out a breath. "You said yourself my power is strong."

"The land was unstable," he bites out. "A rock could've fallen on your head."

"Does that mean you don't care about your siblings and your parents?"

He's vibrating with rage, barely holding himself back. "Of course I care."

"Yet you don't make a scene about them helping people in need."

He clenches his jaw. "You're my *mate*."

"Yes." I put a hand on his chest, right over the strong thuds of his heart. "So I think you can give me a little more credit."

Just like that, his anger fizzles out. It doesn't

disappear. It just gets buried beneath the weight of my admission. It's the first time I've acknowledged that I'm his mate. I've been kicking against it hard and long, but the bond between us doesn't lie. Now that I'm coming into my power, I'm forced to admit that I'm one of them, and my body has recognized this man as mine right from the start. And I'm not sure what to do with that yet, if staying here is what's best for me. Or for anyone.

"Elsie…"

The way he says my name is loaded.

I sweep my hand over the expanse of his chest, mapping the deep-cut muscles with my palm. "I'm just getting used to this new person I'm becoming myself." I add gently, "It will help if you give me the space to get to know her."

Emotions flash through his eyes. Taking my hand, he kisses my knuckles. "The thought of anything happening to you—"

"If I'm to live here, I have to learn how to take care of myself."

"You have me," he says stubbornly.

"Aruan." I sigh, pulling my hand away. "If you want me to be happy, you have to give me some room to breathe."

"Do you mean that?" He searches my eyes as if he's trying to spot the lie. "You'll try to be happy?"

I nod. What choice do I have? As long as I'm trapped here, there's no point in punishing both of us by remaining miserable.

As always, when the thought that I'm never going back to Earth manifests, I think about my parents. I remember the tough and the happy times, the camping trips and the puzzles we built when I was too sick to exert much energy. It's not the vacations abroad and the fancy hotels that I miss the most but the everyday moments, like Mom flipping pancakes at dawn because it's my favorite breakfast and Dad stopping at the bookstore on his way home from work to buy a book on archaeology that's just been released.

A lump lodges in my throat as hot tears build behind my eyes. How long before time erodes those memories and my parents' faces fade in my mind?

At the same time, the mere idea of leaving Aruan hurts.

"Elsie," Aruan says, sounding as if he's the one in pain.

He wraps me up in his strong arms, holding me to his chest. His embrace is comforting, but it doesn't take away the sadness.

"That's all I ask—that you try to be happy." He kisses the top of my head. "I'll do anything in my power to make this good for you, my sweet. If I'm angry, it's because I'm worried about you." He hesitates as if it's hard for him to admit, "But despite the danger you put yourself in today, I'm also proud."

I pull away to look at him, blinking away my tears. "Of me?"

"No." He smiles. "Of those pixie dragons who love to follow you around."

I swat his shoulder. "Don't make fun of me."

"I'd never," he says with mock offense.

Suddenly shy, I clear my throat. "You were pretty awesome yourself. What you did was amazing. You saved all those people."

A veil drops in front of his eyes, and all traces of emotions vanish from his face. "Keep your compliments. I don't deserve them."

"Are you kidding?" I gape at him. "You used your power for something good. Aren't you proud of yourself too?"

The mask he's donned cracks, and a sliver of self-loathing slips through. "Not if I'm the reason it happened."

"What do you mean? You didn't—" And then the meaning of his words sinks in. "The sun…" I swallow. "That's what caused the rockslides? That was you?"

He doesn't reply, which is an answer in itself.

I stare at him, unable to speak. I'm shaking, and it has nothing to do with being cold. I thought a nuclear explosion was the worst he could do with his power. But if he's able to affect the sun itself, then it's not just nuclear fission he's capable of but also nuclear fusion. With his *mind*, he's somehow able to change the burning power of a star that's millions of miles away.

How is such a thing possible?

No wonder people think he's the prince in the prophecy. I can't blame them.

His power is beyond belief, beyond comprehension.

It's absolutely terrifying.

And I *am* terrified… but at the same time, the vulnerability that stirs in our bond makes my chest clench with compassion. Aruan didn't ask for this. He's not doing these terrible things on purpose. I've gotten to know him well enough by now to be certain of that. Something must've set off his reaction.

Reaching out, I take his hand. "What happened?"

Finally, the mask drops. Anger contorts his features. "I know who sent you to Earth, and I think I know why you got so sick when you arrived there."

My heart starts pounding as I stare at him. "That's what made you so upset?"

Calculation crosses over his face. "Do *not* say that was because of you."

Despite my best effort to hide my perturbation, I can't help how breathless my reply sounds. "I wasn't going to say that."

He pins me with a look, cutting me open and seeing right through me. "But that's what you're thinking."

I'm thinking a lot of things, starting with, surprisingly, that I care. Aruan's pain is like white-hot coals smoldering in my stomach. All I want is to take it away. I don't even know when it happened. I only know I don't want him to suffer. And yes, I'm thinking that it's my fault. If not for me, he wouldn't lose control of his power like that.

The disasters he set off today because someone banished me send more shivers down my spine. If I stay, it's a risk. But if I leave, it will be just as perilous, if not more so.

My ribcage constricts, squeezing the air from my lungs as the impossible situation stares me in the face.

"It's not your fault, Elsie." A muscle ticks in his jaw. "I'll get a better handle on my control. It won't happen again."

That's not something he can guarantee, and I don't want him to make promises he may break, but we're getting sidetracked. "Was it your mother? Is that what she wanted to talk to you about?"

The set of his mouth hardens. "She wanted to talk about your power, which poses a risk if you don't use it responsibly, but I wanted answers."

"She admitted it," I say with a tremulous exhale.

He rubs his thumb over my knuckles. "She thinks your body was put back together wrongly when she sent you through the portal, seeing that you were only a baby."

"*That's* why I was dying?"

His eyebrows snap together, drawing deep lines over his forehead. "We believe so. Coming back to Zerra reversed the process."

I look down at my body. "Which explains why my old scars are gone and why my heart isn't failing any longer."

As incredible as it sounds, it does make sense.

My mind starts working a mile a minute, digesting what this means about these parallel worlds. If that's the case, it would explain how traveling through a portal is possible. The atoms making up our bodies are deconstructed on one side and reassembled on the other side of the time and space that've been bent.

This is incredible.

I'm so caught up in the mind-boggling discovery that I almost forget why we're having this conversation. The dark expression with which Aruan continues to stare at me gives me pause.

"I'm not dying, am I?" I ask quickly.

He lets go of my hand and cups my cheek. "No, Elsie. You're not dying. If anything, you're getting stronger. What you did with your power today was proof alone."

"Then why are you still upset?"

"I'm angry about the time that's been stolen from us. I'm furious with my mother for taking you from me. My own family betrayed me."

I search his eyes. "Why did she do it? Was it because of the prophecy?"

"Yes," he says with gritted teeth. "And for that, I'll never forgive her. I vowed the guilty party would pay, and I never break an oath."

"What are you going to do?" I pull away. "She's your mother, Aruan."

He drops his arms to his sides. "She claimed to have banished you out of love for me and to save your life, but what she did was cruel and inexcusable."

Empathy compels me to say, "I'm not happy about the situation I find myself in either, but I'm sure she loves you. Parents sometimes make the wrong decisions when they try to protect us, doing things they think are in our best interest even though we disagree."

He studies me with a perceptive gaze. "You're speaking from experience."

I shrug. "My parents didn't want me to study. They thought I was just wasting the little time I had left. They didn't understand why it was important to me."

"Then why do you still want to see them?"

"Because I love them, and that will never change."

He considers my statement for a moment. "You're not angry with them."

"They sometimes annoy me like all parents irritate their kids at times, but they do what they do because they care about me."

He narrows his gaze. "Are you saying my mother shouldn't be held accountable for her actions?"

"I'm saying that there are always two sides to a story and that you shouldn't judge her too harshly for acting in what she believed was your best interest."

His eyes flare. "You're defending her."

Again, there's a painful tug in my chest when I think about my own parents and how much I miss them, knowing that I may never see them again. "I'm just saying things aren't always black and white."

The silver of his irises darkens to the color of molten steel. "Intelligent and strong, as well as kind and fair. You'll make a great queen."

I laugh uncomfortably. "You'll give me a big head."

The heat in his eyes morphs into an intention I recognize only too well.

"Aruan—"

His name has barely left my lips before my mud-stained shoes and dress vanish, and I stand in front of him naked, wearing only the necklace he gave me.

"That's better," he growls with satisfaction, already reaching for me before I have time to gasp.

His own clothes evaporate before he yanks me against him in a crushing embrace.

My body agrees. It wants this. But my mind is still lucid enough to recognize our work is far from over.

I strain in his grasp. "I need to check on the humans."

He presses a kiss on my neck. "They can wait."

"No." I use all my strength to push him away while I still have some self-control left. "It's late. They'll be worried, not knowing what's going on."

He spears his hands through my hair. "A little worry has never killed anyone."

"It wouldn't be fair to them."

His voice drips with dark seduction. "You know what wouldn't be fair?" Taking my hand, he cups it over his hard-on. "Leaving me like this." His warm breath fans over my lips. "You did this. Now, fix it."

Damn.

He feels good.

And just like that, all my noble intentions vanish and my resistance crumbles. When I lean against him, a wicked smile curves his lips. He lifts me up, waiting until I've hooked my legs around his hips before he carries me to the bed.

I lock my arms around his neck, staring into those mercury-colored eyes. "I want to take Karl and the women outside. They need fresh air."

He's all flexing muscles and virility, his large body engulfing mine. "You can take them to an inner courtyard."

"The Sky Bridge."

His powerful steps jostle me in his arms. "Ten minutes."

I'll take that. "And I want to see the scrolls again."

"Next week."

My smile is challenging. "Tomorrow."

His eyes turn into slits. "Are you using sex for bargaining with me again, mate?"

I fake innocence. "You know what? Actually, I'm exhausted. Maybe we should wait—"

"Fine," he growls impatiently. "Tomorrow."

I'm about to gloat about that victory and rub it in his face, but everything I wanted to say is forgotten when he splays his fingers over the back of my head before closing them in a fist in my hair. With a gentle but decisive tug, he tilts my face back, exposing my mouth for his taking.

Whatever I was thinking turns to ashes in the wake of the flames that blaze between us.

Before my back hits the bed, he's already kissing me like there is *no* tomorrow.

CHAPTER 10
ELSIE

Guilt sets in when bright sunlight wakes me. I'm snuggling in Aruan's bed with my back against his chest. He has one arm thrown over my waist, anchoring me to him, and I'm using the bicep of his other arm as a pillow. His breathing is even, but he's awake. I sense it.

When I turn in his arms, he's staring at me with such an intense gaze that goosebumps break out over my skin. The butterflies in my stomach are both from apprehension and something entirely different, something that feels a lot like... I can't describe it. Contentment? Excitement? Nerves?

Wait a minute.

Am I freaking falling in love?

The idea is so disconcerting that I jackknife into a sitting position.

What the fuck am I doing? I haven't even decided if I'm staying or going. I have no business developing feelings for my mate. Because what we share is only physical. For now. I can still leave without either of us getting hurt.

But if I allow feelings to enter the equation, it won't be so easy to simply hoof it out of here as soon as I find a portal to Earth. Feelings will complicate everything. Besides, Aruan's interest in me is of a proprietary sexual nature. It doesn't go further than that, and it will be stupid to make myself more vulnerable than I already am.

Becoming aware that he's diverted his gaze from my face to my naked breasts, I tug the sheet up to my chin. It takes effort to push my startling train of thought down and not to let him know where my mind has been wandering. To my surprise, I find that I can block him from probing our bond.

He raises a brow, letting me know he's onto me.

It takes a lot more effort to keep my voice normal. "How long have you been awake?"

His lips quirk. "Long enough."

I have an inexplicable urge to run my fingers through his dark hair. Which frightens the fuck out of me. Instead, I get up, taking the sheet with me and selfishly exposing him to the fresh air. Although, he doesn't seem bothered. Neither does he try to hide his hard-on when he stretches out on his back and crosses his arms behind his head.

I quickly avert my eyes and go next door to do my morning grooming.

As always, I'm ashamed of myself for how easily I

forget about everything and everyone when Aruan touches me. He came inside me—again—and even though I know better, I simply can't gather the willpower to stop him or to care. Not in the moment. Not with the heat that seems to fry my brain and leave it totally useless. Regret only comes when my body is sated and reason returns. But that just lasts until the next time he lays his hands on me.

That I allow him to take things so far is a huge red flag in itself, a big, blaring sign that I need to get away from here. From him. But at what price? Will his reaction at finding me gone actually set off a supernova, destroying this entire solar system? Or… not a supernova. This star is probably not massive enough for that. If Zerra is indeed a parallel Earth and this sun is identical to ours, then Zerra's eventual death will come by way of this sun becoming a red giant.

If I recall correctly, the explanation behind it is something like the sun runs out of hydrogen that fuels its fusion reactions, and then its core condenses to dump a whole bunch of heat into its outer layers, causing it to expand and swallow the planets in its vicinity. Then I think it's supposed to become a white dwarf. Or is it a red dwarf?

I wish I had Google to check.

Either way, none of that matters if Aruan can cause the sun to flare like that—if his power is that strong and lethal.

And if it is indeed somehow tied to *me.*

Sighing, I wash my face and brush my teeth. I can't

dwell on Aruan and this whole surreal situation any longer without going insane, so I focus on the simple task of my morning routine. Someone has set out clothes for me on the bench, or maybe Aruan fabricated the garments with the sheer power of his mind. I'm surprised to find black fitted pants and a white shirt in my size instead of another glamorous gown. A pair of soft socks finish the ensemble.

When I return to the room, Aruan is dressed in a tunic and dark pants tucked into his boots. His hair is brushed back and tied at his nape, leaving his stunning features exposed. For a moment, I falter. My pulse quickens. He looks impossibly handsome. And damn, he smells good.

Get a grip, Elsie.

He stands at the foot-end of the bed, dangling a pair of brown boots in one hand.

They're definitely not his size. His palm alone is bigger than the sole.

Rushing over, I snatch the boots from him. I'm so ridiculously happy to have practical shoes again that I have to fight an impulse to hug them to my chest.

"Thank you." I can't help the silly grin that splits my face. "Did you make them?"

He nods. "You seem to like them better than the shoes the females prefer to wear in the palace."

I sweep a hand over the soft, suede-like material. "I love them."

He nods again, looking pleased with himself.

"I appreciate the clothes too." He did make an effort

for me, and it will be rude not to thank him. I'm not making a pass at him or anything like that.

A smile plucks at his lips as he drags a gaze over me.

I look down at myself. "What?"

When I meet his gaze again, amusement sparks in his eyes.

"The men's clothes and hairstyle suit you."

My heart skips a beat at how that smile transforms his face with attractive laugh lines crinkling the corners of his eyes.

Focus.

I touch my spiky hair. "I kept it short because of the chemo."

He frowns.

"It's a cancer treatment that made my hair fall out." At the dark look that comes over his face, I add, "But I happen to like my hair short."

His easy smile doesn't mask the strain in his voice. "Me too." His tone is still a bit clipped when he points at the bed and says, "Sit."

I obey without arguing, not because I'm giving in easily but to give me time to gather myself.

What the hell is wrong with me this morning?

My breath catches when he goes down on one knee and takes my left foot in his large hand. Our eyes meet as he brushes his palm up my calf. My heart beats so loudly I'm sure he can hear it. His touch is light, but he's lingering longer than necessary.

Holding my gaze, he gently frees one of the boots from the death grip in which I'm clutching them. I haven't noticed how I've tightened my hold on the boots or how I've clamped my knees together until he cups one knee and parts my legs.

A gasp forms in my throat. Only sheer willpower prevents the sound from making it to my lips. I stop breathing, watching him watching me as he carefully pulls the boot over my foot and ties the laces.

By the time he's fastened the second boot, my pulse is all over the place. Pulling on boots shouldn't be so sensual, but the way he kneels in front of me while doing something so simple yet so thoughtful sets my heart racing. I could've easily pulled on the boots myself, but how he's taking care of me warms my belly. And other parts of me too.

Yet this isn't about sex. This is about something else, and it scares me. Just as much as falling for him scares me. Maybe more. We may be destined mates, whatever that means, but being physically compatible doesn't make him the right man for me. He's overbearing and overprotective. He'll smother me without even trying. Not to mention, melt anyone for looking the wrong way at me and cause the sun to explode if I'm in danger of getting hurt.

Yeah, my mind refuses to wrap itself around that last one.

Regardless, I don't see how this can work.

I hop off the bed, standing over him where he's still kneeling on the floor with the hand he had curled around my calf now empty and poised in the air.

My voice comes out squeaky. "I'd better get going.

Sandy and the others must be going out of their minds."

He straightens unhurriedly with a knowing smile on his lips. "We'll eat first."

Taking my hand, he leads me to the adjoining room. He seats me at the table and then disappears, returning a short while later with servants carrying trays loaded with food.

While the servants set dishes and jars on the table, he watches me quietly. Being the focus of so much undivided attention has me squirming in my seat.

"You promised to let me visit the sacred site today," I say to break the intense spell.

"I remember," he drawls.

"What's your schedule like?"

He arches a thick, black brow.

"When will you have time?" I clarify, knowing he must be busy with his official duties.

The servants retreat.

He serves generous helpings of the food I like on my plate. "I have an engagement this morning. I can make time in the afternoon."

"Great." Not wanting to sit there with my hands folded while he does all the serving, I take the jug of juice and fill two glasses. "That will give me the morning to spend with the humans."

At the approval that burns in his gaze when I offer him a glass, heat creeps into my cheeks. He's making it clear that he appreciates the gesture of me serving him like he's serving me. Why does his appraisal make me so self-conscious? And why does it make me feel good?

Ducking my head, I pretend to be absorbed with the task of eating. Though I have to admit that after yesterday's activities and another night of mind-blowing sex, I'm starving. Somewhere between giving me multiple orgasms and soaking in the pool, Aruan woke me up to feed me a snack in bed, but it wasn't enough to replenish the energy I spent.

The juice is spicy but surprisingly refreshing. I help myself to seconds and eat another one of those delicious *thoska* cakes, minus the snake egg topping.

Aruan's appetite is astounding. He polishes off the food on almost every platter and finishes the enormous jug of juice.

When breakfast is over, he comes around the table and offers me a hand. I place my fingers in his and let him help me to my feet. The touch sends a jolt through my body, my awareness of him always like a live wire ready to catch fire with a single spark. However, this morning, the all-consuming heat isn't the same. Beneath the scorching flames, something fragile is smoldering, something that warms me in a different, deeper way.

I pause for a moment, trying to get a read on what's changing. The bond between us is still vague, so it can't be that.

"The waterfall that gives access to the Sky Bridge is sealed for security reasons," he says, pulling me from my thoughts. "If you're going to take the humans to the outlook point, you'll have to ask Gaia or one of my cousins to open the archways and the waterfall. I'll let them know I authorized it, and I'll leave the archway to my quarters open for you."

He's making sure I take a chaperone. He's not taking the risk that I may use the opportunity to run away. "You forgot your brothers. Can't they open the waterfall too?"

His jaw hardens. "Ask Vitai if you can't find Gaia."

So he hasn't forgiven Kian yet for taking me to the village yesterday. I have a feeling Kian did that on purpose, that he was trying to make a point. But what point?

Aruan goes to the trunk and removes a jacket. I walk to the archway, hovering a few paces away. Will I be able to part the wall one day? Otherwise, as with the waterfall, I'll always be reliant on someone to do it for me. I suppose as long as there's a window, I could always get out with the help of a pterosaur.

Curious, I focus my attention on the exit. Just like yesterday at the village, when I felt my power flowing through my body, fire zaps through my veins. I concentrate harder, willing the wall to open… and then a small crack appears.

"Aruan," I exclaim, bouncing on the balls of my feet. "Look!"

He walks over, peering thoughtfully at the fissure. "Your power seems to be growing stronger."

"This is so cool." I clap my hands. "Do you think I'll be able to do the evaporation trick too?"

He studies me with a strange light in his eyes. "I think you'll be able to do whatever you set your mind to."

Too excited to analyze the shift in his mood, I concentrate on the wall again. In my mind's eye, I imagine the stone separating into grains of sand, and then the grains of sand breaking apart into individual molecules.

The gap slowly but surely grows bigger.

Aruan's voice seems to come from somewhere far-off. "That's enough, Elsie."

The hole in the wall expands a little more.

Almost there.

A hand falls on my shoulder. "Elsie."

Voila.

The exit is open.

When I come to my senses, I'm shaking, and perspiration beads on my forehead.

I gape at the wall, saying more to myself than to Aruan, "I did it."

He doesn't sound pleased. "You'll wear yourself out. Coming into your power can be dangerous if you don't know how to control it. You have to move slowly."

I turn to face him, his words barely registering in my mind. "I did it!"

He sighs. "Yes, you did."

I tilt my head. "You don't seem surprised."

"I never doubted that you would."

"You have an awful lot of faith in me."

He cups my shoulders between his broad palms.

"You have a strong power, Elsie. You have to be mindful of how you use it."

I'm still high on my achievement. "Do you think I'll have the same power back on Earth?"

His gaze darkens, and his grip tightens. "It doesn't matter. You're not going anywhere."

I almost waver under his broody stare. "I was just wondering how it works."

Clenching his jaw, he says, "Going there is forbidden, so I guess you'll never know."

I stare at his handsome features, now hard and relentless when he was being so accommodating and considerate a few moments ago.

"It will be the same," I say, throwing the statement out there for no other reason than testing my theory by whatever reaction it will evoke from him. "I became sick because I was a baby when your mother sent me to Earth, but adults don't change when they go to Earth through a portal, do they?"

The truth shows in the cold, stony gleam of his eyes. "The subject is forbidden, or did you forget?" He bites off every word. "We won't talk about this again. Did I make myself clear?"

All the fuzzy warmth that accumulated in my chest turns into ice. That fragile thing that almost bloomed to life dies a premature death when I shut down my emotions and say in a voice devoid of feeling, "Perfectly."

I turn on my heel and walk through the archway,

not bothering to close it behind me, or rather, not bothering to try.

"Elsie!"

Aruan's voice chases me down the hallway, but I don't stop to listen to whatever he wants to say. I march to the Earthlings' quarters, half relieved and half disappointed that he doesn't follow.

CHAPTER II
ARUAN

I've lost count of how many times I've wanted to go after Elsie but let her get away instead. Some of those times, I knew she needed space, and I did my best to respect it. Granting her that space took immense self-control. Just like now, as I watch her march all three stones of her meager weight down the hallway, walking so fast the wall lights have a hard time keeping up. They go off in flashes, mapping out her angry steps as she stomps farther away from me until she turns a corner, and I lose sight of her.

I clench and unclench my fingers. And count to several moon cycles. The atmosphere between us was changing this morning. Finally, she was softening up to me. Then the possessive beast inside me reared his head, and I opened my big mouth and said things I wish I hadn't. Trust me to spoil a perfectly good moment. I want to chase her down with everything I've got, but I have someplace to be, and I'm already late as it is.

Trying my best to put Elsie out of my mind—and failing spectacularly—I portal myself to the clearing in the jungle behind the palace. Kian is already there, pacing in the circle of gum trees and flexing his muscles. Warming up, no doubt.

A sardonic smile finds its way to my lips. "Practicing your rusted skills?"

He stops and pins me with a narrow-eyed look. "You're late."

"Impatient." I click my tongue. "It's not like you, brother." Peeling my lips into a wider grin, I walk to the center of the clearing. "Did you miss me?"

"Was it difficult to get out of bed?" he taunts me with a laugh. "Was it nice and warm with your mate in it?"

The mention of Elsie in such a disrespectful manner sets me off like a strike of lightning. I charge at him like a rabid dragon, pulling back my arm and aiming for his dirty mouth, but Kian is fast. He can't read my mind because I've blocked it. Nevertheless, he sees me coming.

He sidesteps to the left and slips behind me, catching me off-guard with the fist he smashes on my side. I barely grunt, although I feel it. I turn around and swing another punch at him, but he's skirted around me again. I definitely feel the fist he jams into my lower back.

I leap out of reach and prowl in a wide circle, getting the coward in my vision. A parasite vine that creeps around a tree decides it's a good moment to try and strangle me. It knots its tentacles around my neck, its multiple suckers already drawing blood through my skin.

Kian chuckles as I wrestle with the parasite. I could've easily melted the carnivore, but no powers or weapons are allowed in the clearing. Just our bare hands.

My brother is unscrupulous enough to take advantage of the situation by pounding his fists into my stomach. I tear the tentacles straight off the trunk of the creeper, but the faster I dismantle them, the faster they grow back.

The next blow falls on my chin. My head snaps back from the impact. Another one hits me straight on the mouth. A metallic taste coats my tongue. Enraged with the pesky creeper, I rip it off my neck so hard the whole vine comes off the tree. I chuck it aside and wipe the blood from my split upper lip while Kian laughs at me.

Coward. Kian has always fought like a sand snake. He likes to come up from behind and bite you in the heel or to lurk in the grass until you're incapacitated before he strikes. But I'm done playing.

I hook a fist under his chin, sending him flying. The air leaves his lungs with a thud as his back hits the ground. An opportunistic trumpet worm sees his chance and lunges for Kian from the undergrowth on the border of the clearing, fangs bared and saliva dripping.

Kian swipes at the worm irritably, backhanding it on the sensitive membranes behind its feelers hard enough to make it reel. I catch it behind its head and squeeze, preventing it from snapping its jaws at us. Kian pushes to his feet, grabs the tail-end, and flings the worm into the jungle. Then he turns his attention back to the fight, bouncing like a dancer.

He may be light and fast on his feet, but I can read him too. I've been sparring with my brothers in amiable and not-so-amiable fights for many moon cycles. When he pounces, aiming another jab at my jaw, I duck and whack him on the ribs.

He grabs his side and doubles over, leaving his face wide open. I plant a fist on his cheek, sending him stumbling backward. Before he's caught his balance, I knock the wind out of him.

"Enough?" I ask, raising a challenging brow.

Usually, we fight until one of us surrenders, but neither of us wants to make that call because saying it means admitting defeat. More often than not, we go at each other until someone can no longer get up from the ground, and that someone is never me.

Kian spits out blood. "In your wet dreams."

I grin. "I was hoping you'd say that."

I go for him again, letting him get a few jabs in to make the fight a bit fairer. Just as he really gets going, raining vicious punches on my abdomen, I hook another left under his chin. The force of the blow makes his teeth clack together.

A ground crawler, who's smelled blood, quickly inches closer, its stinger already poised for attack. It's small enough for Kian to flick it away. The crawler, a leechlike species that's not easily deterred, dives for the few drops of blood that have already drained into the soil. It swiftly vacuums up the sand. The crawler has the ability to filter blood from anything and to secrete the undigested waste material. It can even swallow stones. We let the small vulture be. Let it suck up whatever it wants as long as it doesn't interfere with our fight.

Kian circles me. I can tell from his labored breaths that his cracked ribs are bothering him, but he doesn't show pain. For what he did, he deserves a lot worse.

"You endangered my mate," I snarl, storming him again.

I ram headfirst into his stomach but not before he thwacks me on the nape.

"It was necessary," he throws back at me.

I take up a defensive position. "You don't get to make that call."

"The people need to learn to trust her. She has to make a place for herself in Lona, and she can't do that if you keep her locked away."

"That's dragon shit." I sneer. "Don't pretend to care about how Elsie is settling in. Caring about others isn't your style. You never do anything for anyone unless it serves your own purposes."

He picks up a handful of sand and throws it in my face. For a moment, I'm blinded, but I hear the sand crunching under his boots as he sneaks to the side. The arm he pulls back is nothing but a wisp that displaces the air, yet I feel the movement. My enhanced senses pick up his subtle inhale as he fills his lungs with air before striking.

I'm ready, catching his fist in my palm and restraining him in the vise of my hold as I hit him hard enough on the side of his head to see stars.

While he comes to his senses, I wipe the dust from my eyes. Kian is breathing hard, staring at me with unconcealed animosity—a rare display of emotion for my brother.

I walk right up to him, putting us chest to chest. "If anything had happened to Elsie, this fight wouldn't end with you crying defeat. It would end with you dead."

He holds my gaze without blinking. "There are more ways to lose someone than in death."

The statement is like scratching at a festering thorn under my skin. I've been fretting over losing Elsie since the moment she came back into my life.

"She's mine," I growl in his face. "No one and nothing will take her away from me again."

His swollen lips lift in one corner. "Are you sure about that, brother?"

I grab him by the collar of his tunic. "What the dragon is that supposed to mean? I'll kill anyone who tries."

He watches me with a steady gaze. "Even Elsie herself?"

His meaning hits me between the eyes. "She won't leave." Because I won't let her.

His expression turns pitying. "You can lock a pixie dragon in a cage and pretend you can tame it as much as you like, but the moment you open that cage, you know what's going to happen."

Fury rises like lava inside me. For good measure, I punch him again. He doesn't even try to deflect the blow. He takes it stoically, all the while staring me down.

"You did not take Elsie to the village to do her or me a favor." I let him go and ball my hands at my sides to prevent myself from strangling him. "You did that just because you could, because you like to provoke me."

"You and your big ego." His smile turns condescending. "Everything isn't always about you, Aruan."

"Then why did you do it?"

"Her loyalty had to be tested," he replies evenly.

The anger that surfaces isn't like molten lava this time. It's cold and lethal. "What did you say to me?" He dared to test Elsie as if she's a simpleton, some experiment, and not with the respect owed to *my mate*?

"We needed to know how she'd react in a crisis, if she'd make the right choices."

"Right choices?" My laugh is scornful. "You mean if she'd run away or help you."

"We needed to know the extent of her power."

I pull my eyes into slits. "You endangered Elsie to submit her to a *test*? You went against my will and explicit orders." I raise my voice loud enough to make the small winged dragons scatter from the trees. "You masked her mind and prevented me from feeling her through our bond. For that alone, I can kill you."

I dive at him, not holding back any longer. We go down, fists flying through the air as we roll on the ground. He pummels me in the ribs, not tamping down his strength either.

I find purchase in the fabric of his tunic, kneeling over him and holding him down as I slam my knuckles into his face. "If you come near Elsie again—"

He bends his leg and knees me in the groin. "Maybe you should let her decide who she wants around her."

Son of a dragon. I hit him again, hard enough to register the pain in my knuckles. "You deceived me. You masked my own mate from me."

"That was me," someone says at my back.

I pause with my fist in the air. Turning my face a fraction, I take in my father who stands at the edge of the clearing. He's wearing his crown, which means he was attending official and very important business. He only wears it for ceremonial events in the palace.

He walks to us with easy strides, his face giving nothing away—I'd even go as far as to say he appears bored—but I sense his coiled anger. In many ways, our father is like Kian. He only shows people what he wants them to see. He's not easy to read, but I've learned to pay attention to the energy rolling off him rather than visual clues.

I let go of Kian. "What did you say?"

"That was me." My father stops next to us. "I shielded Elsie's mind and mirrored her emotions."

My father possesses the most deceitful of all powers in the five kingdoms. He has the ability to not only copy but also store in his mind anyone's sentiments at any given time. His specialty is the unique connection that exists between mates, allowing them to sense one another through their bond.

That ever-growing pool of personal information in his mind is an infinite source he can tap into whenever he wants. He can camouflage several minds at the same time, making it impossible for mates to feel their bonds. He can go one step further and project a memory he recorded to fool anyone about the whereabouts or feelings of their mates.

The most famous use of his power was when he kidnapped my mother from the Red Kingdom. He married her before her father could catch wind of her disappearance. As far as my grandfather was concerned, my mother was still safely locked in her tower, far removed from the vicious prince of Lona, who, very unfortunately, turned out to be her mate.

"Why?" I push to my feet. "Why would you let me believe Elsie was safely in my quarters when she could've been in danger?"

"Kian is right." My father gives my brother a hand to help him up. "We needed to know where we stood with Elsie and how far her power extends."

I grit my teeth. "Did you get your answers?"

"Yes." My father smiles. "She behaved very commendably during the crisis. She could've fled, but she used her power for a greater good."

"You mean she didn't abuse it," I snap.

"We doubt she's able to command more intelligent species. If she were, it would've manifested by now."

"You had no right to do that."

"I'm the king. If the safety of Lona is at stake, I can do anything I want. If you two have eaten enough dirt, we have guests waiting. You'd better clean up before meeting them." He looks me up and down. "We don't want to make a bad first impression."

The sideways glance Kian shoots me says he knows who these surprise visitors are. Why do I get the feeling I'm the only one in the dark?

"Who?" I ask as my father opens a portal and strolls to the circle of lights.

"Elsie's uncle and aunt, the king and queen of Marikanea."

"What? You want her to meet her family?" I want to add, "*Now?*" Our relationship is much too unstable. Too much has been happening. I'm not sure Elsie is ready for this. "Why?"

He turns around. "It's time for Elsie to see where she comes from."

He can't mean what I think he does.

And then he proves me wrong by saying, "It's time she visits her birthplace. She leaves with them. Tonight."

CHAPTER 12

ELSIE

With my feelings still bruised from Aruan's callous words, I arrive at the quarters where Karl and the women are housed. I go to the women's side first.

This time, I manage to dissolve the archway without breaking into a sweat. I'm surprised to find Vitai there, having breakfast with our guests. Karl has joined them too. They're seated on cushions around a flat rock on which a spread of dishes is set out. From the way everyone is laughing at what Vitai has just said, he's doing a good job of entertaining them.

They look up when I enter.

"Elsie," Sandy, who sits next to Vitai, exclaims. "I thought Vitai just opened the wall for another server. He hasn't stopped feeding us. You have no idea how glad I am that it's you." She jabs Vitai with an elbow. "You could've told me Elsie was here before you let her in."

Oops. I was so excited to test my new powers that I didn't think before I opened the archway.

Vitai frowns at me, but I simply shrug without correcting Sandy or explaining that I opened the wall.

"Sorry I took so long." I give her an apologetic smile. "We had an emergency."

Sandy pushes to her feet. She's wearing a blue dress that compliments her eyes and complexion, and with her hair hanging in waves around her shoulders, she looks gorgeous, a far cry from the dirty woman with the dull hair and sunken eyes I met at the Phaelix settlement. It warms my heart to see her appearing so healthy and radiant.

"Are you okay, hun?" She eyes me with worry. "Vitai told us about the rockslides. And was that a sun flare that happened just before?"

"Yes, but everyone is fine." Not wanting to linger on the subject in case they're wondering about the cause of the disaster, I address Vitai. "I didn't know you speak English."

"I asked Kian to help me so that we"—he motions around the table—"could understand each other. He got the skill from Sandy's mind and gave it to me."

Why would he go to so much effort? He didn't have to.

I study him more closely. "It's kind of you to keep them company."

His smile is neutral, giving nothing away.

Sandy takes my hand and pulls me to the table. "Have you eaten?"

"Yes, thanks." The memory of the agreeable breakfast I shared with Aruan only acts as a magnifying glass on the unpleasant way we parted. "Do you need anything?"

Alexa sits back on her heels. "Everyone has been very kind. Clothes were sent, and food is delivered regularly. Vitai has been very accommodating too. He's been telling us interesting stories about his fishing adventures."

Irina grins. "Like the time a finned dragon took his bait and dragged him with his fishing rod and all into the water." She turns to Vitai. "But you didn't finish the story. What happened after you fell into the lake?"

Vitai chuckles. "I was lucky I made it out alive. Those finned dragons aren't fussy eaters. If I didn't have the presence of mind to grab my basket of bait when she took off with me, she probably would've taken a bite out of me. Instead, she went after the bait and swallowed everything whole, including the basket."

Eucabeth stares at him with a doting expression, hanging on his every word. When he meets her gaze, a blush tints her cheeks pink.

When she catches me looking at her, she averts her eyes and stands. "Would you like a seat, Elsie? You can have mine."

Her voice is gentle and melodic. It suits her. I'm so happy and grateful Vitai healed her. A lump lodges in my throat just from hearing her speak.

I swallow my untimely emotionality down. "I actually came to invite you for a walk."

At that, everyone's eyes light up. They're on their feet in an instant.

"We can't go far," I warn, but they're already dashing for their shoes that are lined up next to the archway, not paying me any heed.

Vitai, left on his own at the table, unfolds his tall body and stands unhurriedly, stretching to his full impressive height.

Not wanting to be rude, I ask, "Would you like to join us?" I did interrupt their breakfast, and he's been nice to my uninvited guests.

Eucabeth gives him a soft smile, her doe-like, ochre-brown eyes sparkling.

Is her reaction what I think it is? I hope she's not falling for Vitai. He must have a destined mate. Eucabeth knows as well as anyone here the Alit don't mate with humans. She was present when Sandy mentioned the conversation she overheard between the Alit and the Phaelix. I'll have to remind Eucabeth of this. I'd hate for her to get hurt, especially after everything she's suffered.

"Please, do," Sandy says to Vitai. She adds with a wink, "You can protect us if there's danger."

The corner of Vitai's mouth lifts. "Who am I to deny a lady's request?"

We exit the quarters with Sandy and me leading the way and Vitai at the back of the line. The group gawks at the window archways that give views of the ocean. Up here, in the higher part of the palace, the long mossy creepers that grow from the summit hang like strings of beads over the windows. The roar of the water spouting from the top is louder, but it's not as deafening as where the flow accumulates in the waterfall that crashes on the broad rock ledge in front of the Great Hall.

The humans chat excitedly as I lead them down the spiral staircase and through the hallways with their illuminating stone walls. We stop in the Great Hall to admire the statues and the view of the cultivated hills with the wild jungle beyond. Vitai amuses them by reciting all the names of the kings and queens eternalized in stone.

"These statues are so detailed they almost look real." Irina trails her fingers over the intricate folds of a queen's gown. "Who made them?"

"A family of village artists," Vitai says. "With their power, which is passed down through generations, they can chisel in stone anything they lay their eyes on."

"Interesno," Irina says under her breath, studying the stern stone faces.

Vitai is generous in divulging information about the Alit and their powers. I'm not sure the king or Aruan will appreciate that. They seemed inclined to share as little as possible with the group from Earth. Maybe Vitai thinks it doesn't matter if the humans learn more about his culture and people. Perhaps he figures they've already seen a lot of Zerra anyway.

I walk to the waterfall and stop a few paces away, unsure if I can do it. But it turns out to be surprisingly easy. I don't even have to focus hard for the water to part, revealing the bridge against a peachy, misty morning sky.

Wow. That's so cool.

"Well done, Elsie," Vitai says next to me. "Your power is strong."

I glance over my shoulder. The humans are still engrossed in the statues and the views. They haven't seen me parting the water, and the noise of the waterfall is drowning out my conversation with Vitai. For all they know, it was Vitai who opened the waterfall. I haven't told them I'm an Alit. I don't want them to think I'm not on their side, not when I want them to return to Earth as much as they want to leave this world.

I look at Vitai, who's fallen quiet. He's studying me with crossed arms and a deep line running between his eyebrows.

"Any Alit can do that," I say.

He raises a brow. "Not any Alit. Seeing that we have guests who shouldn't leave, Aruan put a seal on the waterfall. It takes a great power to break such a strong barrier."

"Is that why you came with us?" I scrutinize him. "To open the waterfall?"

He doesn't answer, but I don't miss the guilt that flickers in his eyes before he wipes it away. "Aruan would've opened it for you."

"But he's not here, is he?"

He turns his face toward the horizon. "You would've found someone in the palace to help you."

Is it me, or is he hiding something? "Is there something you're not telling me?"

"It's not my place to tell you anything." He cuts a sideways glance my way. "That's Aruan's privilege as your—"

"Mate." I roll my eyes. "Yes, I know."

Vitai doesn't reply.

"Come on," I call to the group. "We only have ten minutes on the bridge. Let's not waste it."

The women stare with apprehension at the sheer drop. A swing bridge with wooden boards and ropes on the sides spans between the palace and the cliff on the other side. A circular platform in the center serves as a lookout point.

Karl goes after Sandy and me, and the rest follow. They cling to the dewy ropes that serve as rails as we make our way to the platform.

Vitai hangs back until the last person has walked onto the bridge, which happens to be Eucabeth, and then he falls in step behind her.

I stop on the platform, gripping the thick ropes in both hands. Mist hangs over the land. The trees are so tall their tops pierce the white fog that envelopes the sea and hills like a soft cloud. Above it, streaks of orange and pink are painted across the sky. A few stars are still visible in the purple band that separates night from day.

I fill my lungs with the fresh morning air, inhaling

the scent of forest moss and salty ocean. Like before, the oxygen infuses me with energy. I've never felt healthier or stronger.

Sandy leans on the rail next to me. Her gaze is trained on the distance as she asks in a low, serious voice, "Any news about sending us home?"

"I was going to speak to the queen, but then the rockslides happened." Heat climbs up my neck as I give her only half the truth. "We came back very late. I'll try today." I turn around, facing the hills, and rest my elbows on the rope. "Don't worry. I'll get you out of here." One way or another.

She observes me with an earnest expression. "What about you?"

I blow out a sigh. "It's still complicated." I don't want to tell her that Aruan is literally keeping me captive here. For some reason, I don't want her to have a bad impression of him.

"I've gathered."

She opens her mouth to say more, but a scream cuts her short.

We both give a start. I spin around just in time to see one of the boards fall down from the bridge. It hits the rocks below with a thud that echoes through the space. Eucabeth stands on the board in front of the gap, her left foot poised in mid-air.

Shit.

She must've stepped on the board that collapsed.

Vitai freezes two paces behind her. His tone is clipped. "Don't move."

The board under her right foot creaks. She raises huge, fearful eyes to us, tears glimmering with a plea in their expressive depths.

I rush to the edge of the platform that gives access to the bridge. Irina and Maeva are in front of Eucabeth. They close the remaining distance with two big steps and leap to the safety of the platform, causing the bridge to sway dangerously.

Eucabeth screams again as she loses her balance and stumbles. Everyone screams at the same time before a deathly quiet falls over the group. We hold our breaths while Eucabeth rights herself with a white-knuckled grip on the rail. She lands with both feet on the unstable board, putting her full weight onto it.

We all stand frozen in horror.

"Just keep still." Vitai comes up behind her and focuses his gaze on the floor of the bridge from over her head. "I'm not going to let you fall."

The board beneath her feet stops creaking and looks more solid.

I charge forward on autopilot, but someone grabs me by the back of my shirt. Karl.

"The bridge is unstable," he says in a strained voice, yanking me to the middle of the platform.

I haven't tested my power enough yet to know if I can fix a board with my mind. I've just learned how to open walls and part water. Before I can put my new skills to the test, Vitai cups Eucabeth's hips and steers her forward carefully.

One of the boards on which Vitai steps gives way. It

falls for three, four seconds. A crunch follows as the wood breaks into pieces on the rocks.

"Vitai," Eucabeth cries out.

"Don't worry." His voice is soothing. "You're fine."

Two more steps, and they're on the platform.

Just as I'm about to let out a relieved sigh, the ropes make a funny noise. They groan with strain, stretching… stretching. The bridge starts to sway in the breeze that picks up.

A chorus of gasps rises from the platform.

A sharp snap sounds. The bridge tips sharply to the right. A few boards fall to the bottom.

More screams pierce the air. The women cling to the ropes, their faces pulled into masks of horror. We're trapped on the platform.

The platform jolts.

"The ropes." Sandy's face is as white as chalk. "They're fraying."

Instinctively, I focus my mind on them as Maeva starts crying.

Shivering from head to toe, Alexa says, "We're going to die."

"We're not," Vitai says with a tight jaw.

The ropes knit together again, and the remaining boards grow in size, covering some of the gaps.

It's Vitai's doing, not mine. I clearly need more practice.

Either way, now that they're wider, the boards look thinner and flimsier, and I don't know if they'll hold under our weight.

Desperate, I scan the horizon, but the mist obscures the sky.

Betty, I need you, girl.

I close my eyes and tap into that dark world of stars. It's quicker this time, the map already there. An istiodactylus is the closest. The other dinosaurs are still skittish after the rockslides and haven't returned from their hideouts yet. The istiodactylus is profiting from the bigger carnivores' absence, fishing in the lake.

I bring him around.

A moment later, he appears through the mist. He thrusts his long, orange-tipped, yellow beak forward as he dives down. With an impressive span of at least fifteen feet, his wings quickly eat up the distance.

The women duck and yell, making the platform sway.

"He won't hurt you," I say, doing my best to keep everyone calm. "Trust me."

Betty follows short on the istiodactylus's tail, her majestic body gliding through the air as she aims straight for the platform.

God, I love you, girl.

The istiodactylus follows my mental command and positions himself under the bridge while Betty hovers next to it. She flaps her large wings to stay in place, nearly knocking a few of us off our feet.

"Down, girl!" I point below the bridge. "You can do it."

Immediately obeying the command, she descends and lines up in front of the istiodactylus, whom I decide to call Ducky. Together, they're long enough to cover the length of the bridge and provide support for our weight in case the boards don't hold.

Vitai nods at me, clearly understanding my intention. "Let's go."

"No," Maeva squeals, her expression terrified as she looks down. "We'll fall!"

"We won't." I take her hand. "Vitai stabilized the bridge, and the dinosaurs will carry our weight. Just follow my lead."

"Don't you mean dragons?" Vitai asks.

Now's not the time to explain.

Eucabeth retreats to the center of the platform. "No." She trembles. "I can't."

"Yes, you can." Vitai's tone is both stern and encouraging. "I'll carry you."

I go first, pulling Maeva behind me. Sandy is next. Irina, Karl, and Alexa follow. Vitai is last, carrying Eucabeth in his arms.

The large wings of the pterosaurs stir up a breeze. I'm walking as if on eggshells. The boards tip left and right like seesaws on the uneven expanse of Ducky's back, but he manages to keep more or less motionless in the air.

A few of the thin boards crack. Some break when I step on them, and I'm not the heaviest of people. I glance past Ducky at the abyss below, my stomach climbing into my throat as I slowly cross the bridge.

By the time I reach Betty, my palms are clammy, and a trickle of sweat runs down my back. The people behind me cry out every time another board splits in two beneath their feet, but we're making progress.

I can feel Ducky's stress. Staying in place puts enormous strain on him. Reaching out to him with my mind, I calm and encourage him with a mental pep talk.

I'm almost on the other side when a portal appears on the ledge. I feel Aruan's presence before he steps through the circle of lights. I don't have to look at the dark, frantic expression on his face to know what he feels. Anxiety and terror reach me through our bond. Then I notice the purple bruise darkening his jaw and the black circle around his left eye. His upper lip is cut and swollen.

A new kind of fear slams into my chest.

What happened to him?

His calm reassurance reaches me through our bond, letting me know he's all right. I'm far from put at ease, but I don't have time to linger on why he looks as if he's been in a fight because Maeva trips on one of the boards and goes down face first, sprawling out behind me. Still clinging to my hand, she nearly pulls me down with her.

Aruan's voice reaches me both from the ledge and through our bond. "Elsie!"

I hurry to say, "I'm fine." I help Maeva to her feet. "We're fine."

I don't want Aruan to storm to me, which is exactly what he wants to do. I can feel his intention. However, I have a bigger problem than dealing with my mate's anguish right now. It's vital that we cross over quickly because Betty is getting tired.

"Come on," I say over my shoulder. "We have to hurry."

We make it across in a few more strides.

The moment my feet hit solid ground, Aruan is in front of me. I let Maeva go and move aside to make space for the others. They stumble onto the ledge, falling down on their knees, crying. When Vitai clears the bridge with Eucabeth in his arms, I release Betty and Ducky.

Ducky heads toward the waterfall and perches on the ledge to rest. Betty lands a safe distance from him. I sigh with relief, my heart still beating a mile a minute. I don't even want to think about what would've happened if Vitai hadn't fixed the ropes. In my mind's eye, I see them give and the bridge swing through the air before crashing against the rockface, splintered wood flying everywhere. But we're here, safely, thanks to Betty and my new friend.

Aruan locks his hands around my waist and stares into my eyes. Everything we're not saying but thinking passes between us. He's both relieved and furious. Alarmingly so.

I blow out a shaky breath when he pulls me closer and wraps me up in his arms, soaking up the warmth and the feeling of safety until he kisses the top of my head and whispers in my hair, "We'll talk about this in my quarters."

I push away, picking up on something else that worries me—a thought that's not my own.

Someone tampered with the bridge.

I go cold, searching Aruan's eyes for confirmation. Yes, that's what he thinks, what he *knows*. The bridge didn't collapse from wear and tear. Why would it? The Alit would never be so negligent as to let the sole access to their palace deteriorate.

This was no accident. Someone cut the ropes and loosened the boards. Why? Because one of us is a target, and it's not Vitai or the people from Earth.

It's me.

First the poison and now this. I almost got seven people and myself killed.

"No." Aruan's voice is unrelenting. "You're not responsible for someone else's actions."

Maybe. Either way, now is not the time to argue. I put my hand on his cheek. "What happened to you?"

He cups my hand, pressing my palm against his face. "Nothing."

"That's not nothing." I pull my hand free and trace the cut on his lip. "Someone hit you."

"It was nothing I couldn't handle."

Quoting his earlier words, I say, "We'll talk about this in your quarters."

He doesn't protest when I walk to the two pterosaurs, though the surfacing of his power comes through our bond. He's being cautious, ready to melt them just in case.

"Good girl." I pet Betty when she lowers her head to

nuzzle my hand. "You did great." Going over to Ducky, I give him a scratch under his chin, which makes him close his eyes in bliss. It's insanely cute. "You too, buddy. Thanks for your help."

I become aware of Karl and the women staring at me. They're quivering on the ledge, looking at me strangely.

Right.

I sometimes forget how frightening the sight of a dinosaur is.

I say goodbye to Betty and Ducky, giving each a last caress. When I return to the others, they pretend to be studying the remnants of the boards that lie scattered far below.

Betty and Ducky stretch their necks. Their piercing cries reverberate through the valley. The mist has evaporated. A brilliant sun shines over the black sea. The pyramid mountain with its foaming waterfall and moss-covered cliffs stands out against the backdrop of the green jungle. With the rainbow colors of the pterosaurs perched on the ledge, it makes a striking picture. Maybe it's just the thrill of having escaped with our lives, but I don't think I've seen a more beautiful scene.

What happened must've attracted the other royals and Aruan's parents because they come rushing through portals into the Great Hall.

Not appreciating such a big audience, Betty and Ducky launch into the air. They spread their wings, turn west, and take off over the sea.

The queen is the first one who reaches us. "My son!" She rushes with outspread arms to Vitai, forcing him to lower Eucabeth to her feet. "Incus just told me what happened. He saw it all through the archway of his chamber."

She embraces Vitai, hugging him to her chest, and therefore not seeing the fierce look in his eyes as he holds Eucabeth's gaze over his mother's shoulder.

The king walks through the parted waterfall, resembling a dark devil as he takes in the damage.

Kian appears next, suspiciously sporting a few bruises and a swollen upper lip himself.

The queen wraps an arm around Vitai's shoulders and leads him to the Great Hall. "I think we can all do with a strong drink."

Tarix, who's appeared out of nowhere, follows like a lapdog on the queen's heels. "And this in the midst of an important visit. Whatever will the Marikanears think of us?"

The king addresses Kian. "Escort our guests back to their quarters." He cuts a gaze to Aruan and me. "Elsie and Aruan have someplace to be."

As the queen ushers everyone inside, Sandy holds me back with a hand on my arm.

"Why didn't you tell us, Elsie?" She appears wounded. No, disappointed. "Is it because you're in cahoots with them? Is that the deal? You pretend to help us to keep us pacified while we're your prisoners?"

"No," I exclaim. "Of course not! It's not what you think. I'm just as much a prisoner here."

She nods a couple of times. "Are you locked in?"

I hesitate. "Not exactly."

She nods again before turning around.

"Sandy, I—"

She looks over her shoulder. "You deceived us, Elsie. We thought you were one of us."

She walks away without another word, leaving me on the ledge with Aruan, who's taken in the exchange with a tight jaw and flaring nostrils.

In one long step, he puts our bodies flush together. "My quarters." The way he adds, "Now," makes me shiver.

I want nothing more than to be alone with him right now.

For once, we agree.

CHAPTER 13
ARUAN

I'm bristling, scarcely holding myself together when Elsie and I enter my quarters. Even before I've finished closing the archway, I'm framing her hips between my hands. My mouth is on hers in a desperate, searing kiss, a necessary confirmation that she's here with me. Safe.

By dragons, she tastes sweet. Her small body is warm beneath my palms. She's gorgeous, hard-headed, too brave for her own good, and everything I want. She's everything I ever dreamed of having, the girl I saw growing into a woman in my mind's eye, a beautiful woman who's strong yet vulnerable. There's not a part of her I don't like or admire, nothing I won't do for her.

Except let her go.

Her arms come around my neck as I tangle our tongues in a deeper kiss and cup the round globes of her perfect ass. She goes on tiptoes, pressing her breasts flat against my chest, and it's all I can do not to shred her clothes and sink my cock up to the hilt inside her.

I pull the shirttails from her pants as I walk her to the bed. I can easily dissolve our garments, but I want to undress her slowly. I want to savor it this time. I need to. I need this like I've never needed anything.

When her heels hit the edge of my bed, she lays a palm on my chest and tears her mouth from mine.

Her voice is breathless. "Aruan."

I reach for the button on the waistband of her pants. "What is it, my sweet?"

Her gaze plays over my face. "Your bruises are gone."

I kiss her neck while popping the button from its hole. "I just healed them."

She bends backward to look at me with big eyes. "You can heal living matter?"

I plant another kiss behind her ear and nuzzle her temple, my lips sweeping her skin as I rasp out a reply. "Not nearly as well as Vitai. With my skill level, I can mend a few cuts and minor injuries, and I do it best on myself."

"You didn't tell me."

I put just enough distance between us to push her pants over her hips. "There's a lot about me you don't know." Holding her gaze, I crouch down to free her feet. "There's more to me than natural disasters. Sometimes, I use my power for good."

"I don't doubt that," she says with a sad little smile.

As I straighten, I trail my fingers up the backs of her legs. Her breath catches when I reach the junction of her thighs. The fingers I splay over her lower back anchor her to me securely. It's a dominant touch, a possessive hold—another thing I need. Keeping her in that tight grasp, I make sure she can't escape as I trace her slit with a finger.

Dragons.

She's soaking wet.

A groan tears from my chest. I press her closer, trapping my rock-hard cock between our bodies. I watch her face as I part her carefully before slipping a digit inside. Her eyes are stunningly expressive, showing me how much she likes this. She grips my biceps and throws back her head when I start to pump. She's impossibly tight, but after a moment, her inner muscles give enough for me to add another finger.

The whisper I brush over her ear sounds close to a growl. "I could've lost you, Elsie."

I almost did. Again. And the thought makes me rabid.

Her nails bite through the fabric of my sleeves. "I didn't know what was going to happen this morning."

I pull my fingers from her body, inviting a protesting moan. "I'm not blaming you." I take her wrists and lift her arms. "I blame myself."

Ire sparks in her eyes. "Unless you can tell the future, you couldn't have predicted it either."

"No." I pull the shirt over her head and drop it on the floor. "But I shouldn't have let you go without me."

I bend down and kiss a nipple. Searching her gaze, I circle the tip with my tongue. "Which is why it won't happen again. From now on, I'm keeping you at my side, night and day."

"I—"

She sinks her teeth into her bottom lip when I suck her nipple deep into my mouth.

I bite down gently before arching a brow. "Was that a protest?"

She shakes her head. Her chest rises and falls with her panting. I can hear the fast pace of her heartbeat and smell the sweet scent of her arousal. I can see the vein that throbs in her neck and the black of her pupils that's almost swallowed the turquoise of her irises. I can feel her wetness when I cup her pussy. But I don't need my senses to know what she wants. The bond reveals that to me, as it's meant to do. As it should. And yet, it's still not complete.

I pull my hand away and set her free. She looks so disappointed I have to suppress a smile. I strip naked, taking my time and letting her watch. She likes this too —what she sees. Good. Because she's stuck with me. For many moon cycles to come. For eternity.

When I advance on her, she wets her lips with the tip of her tongue in an action that seems nervous.

My command is clipped, my self-control already close to breaking. "Show me what a good girl you are for me, and get on the bed."

Perhaps sensing that now isn't the time to test me, she climbs onto the soft bedding and faces me with her knees pulled up to her chest. "Maybe we should talk first."

"Turn around," I say in a tone brusque from pent-up desire.

"What?" she stammers.

"You heard me." I kneel on the bed, forcing her to scoot back to make space for me. "On your hands and knees."

"Are you going to…?" She swallows without finishing her question.

"Take you from behind. What did you think I was going to do?"

Her cheeks turn crimson.

My smile is wicked. "Were you hoping I'd spank your ass?" I trace my bottom lip with a thumb. "If that's what you're into…"

Her lips part as she stares at me for a speechless moment. When she finally finds her voice again, it's to stutter, "I'm not."

And I'm done waiting. I show her just how impatient I am by gripping her hips and positioning her like I want her.

Locking her elbows, she braces herself on her arms. "Aruan, I—"

I don't know if she was about to beg me to go slow or to kill this need eating us alive hard and fast, but her words are cut short when I enter her with a single thrust, pushing halfway inside. She makes a choking sound, crumpling the bedding in her fists. I keep her up with one arm around her middle and grit my teeth hard to prevent myself from losing control. This is new for both of us. Hurting her is the last thing I want.

Keeping still, I give her time to adjust while caressing her slender back. I can't resist drawing a finger over the elegant line of her spine, memorizing her shape with my sight and touch. I inhale her floral scent, burning that into my memory too.

When her muscles soften around my cock, I slide in another inch, and another, until she's taken everything. She's panting as hard as I am, both of us fighting our own battles—me not to get swept away by the unbearable pleasure and risk tearing her in a moment of wild lust and she struggling to take me inside her small body.

She's even wetter than earlier, easing my way when I pull out and push back in, but her tight pussy milks my cock mercilessly. I have to grip the base and squeeze hard not to come. Slipping my free hand between her thighs, I play with her clit the way she likes. I have to bring her closer to the edge so I can take care of her pleasure before I'm unable to hold back.

It doesn't take long before she comes, nearly setting off my own climax. Cupping the soft curve of her hip in one hand and a pert breast in the other, I take her with a few shallow pumps until she gets the rhythm.

Soon, she's following my lead, pushing back with every thrust, urging me to take her harder and deeper until I'm pummeling her ass with my groin. Her moans only spur me on. I tweak her nipple, enjoying the hardness of the little bud between my fingers. She gasps and hollows her back, but she doesn't try to stop me. If anything, she grows wetter around me. I move faster still, pleasure gathering at the base of my spine.

The threat on her life has set off every protective response inside me. Elsie is mine, and I must keep her safe. The terrifying thought of losing her pushes me to wrestle a confirmation from her.

"You're mine, Elsie." I burrow the fingers of both hands in the silky skin of her waist to keep her in place and hammer my hips faster against her groin. "Say it."

"Yours," she cries out as her pussy spasms around me, triggering my own release.

I come so violently that streaks of light flash like shooting stars behind my eyes. My release goes on and on, the pleasure lasting for a long time. Thick jets of cum fill up her pussy until her body can't hold any more, and it starts leaking out.

Unwilling to sever our connection, I sit down on my heels and bring her with me. My cock has gone semi-soft, but like an unsatiable beast, I'm already growing hard inside her again. Only she can have this effect on me.

Her knees are pressed together between mine. I spread them, letting her straddle me with her back against my chest, and then I take her again, spearing into her with sharp upward punches of my hips. I play with a nipple and rub her clit with the heel of my palm while making her ride me until she comes again. My cum is still warm in her pussy, the excess dripping down her inner thighs, when I push her onto her stomach and spread her legs. Securing her to the bed with a palm on her lower back, I give her another orgasm with my hand.

I only stop when she begs me, telling me she can't take more.

Lying down next to her, I pull her head onto my chest. We're quiet for a while, catching our breaths. I'm both sated and unsettled, content and wary.

Elsie broaches the subject responsible for my turbulent thoughts first. Intertwining her fingers on my chest, she rests her chin on her hands and looks me straight in the eyes. "Who do you think tampered with the bridge?"

I clench my jaw. "It must've been somebody inside the palace."

"Someone could've done it from the side of the cliff."

"The stairs are guarded. We would've known if someone who doesn't belong in the palace climbed up to the bridge."

She ponders that for a moment before asking, "Who knew I was planning on taking the humans onto the bridge?"

I brush a hand over her hair, enjoying the silky feel of the short strands under my fingers. "I told Gaia and Vitai you'd need someone to open the waterfall. My parents were present, as well as my cousins."

"Do you think your mother…?" she starts uncertainly.

"The truth is that anyone could've eavesdropped."

A frown pleats her brow. "What are we going to do, Aruan?"

I like the sound of that—of "we." Since the day I found Elsie on Zerra, there've always been two people instead of one in this new equation of my life. And lying here with her in my arms, I know exactly what I'm going to do. I'm going to take her away from the danger until I can find the person or persons responsible for the attempts on her life. I'm going to take her to Marikanea. At first, when my father brought it up, I thought it was too soon. I was going to say no. But now I think it may be the best decision. I'll take Elsie there myself to make sure no one harms her.

"We're going on a trip," I say.

She eyes me curiously. "Where to?"

"Marikanea."

"Gaia mentioned that kingdom to me." Her turquoise gaze brightens. "To meet my biological family?"

My smile is wry. "Actually, they're already here."

She shoots upright, sitting on her knees. "Here?"

"I just found out myself. My father told me the news."

Narrowing her eyes, she scrutinizes me. "Would that have been while you and Kian were giving each other black eyes?"

A smile plucks at my lips. "Black eyes? I've been told mine are the color of a gray sky."

She draws a circle with her finger around her eye. "Bruises."

"Why?" I tease. "Were you worried about me?"

She crosses her arms. "Why did you fight him? Was it because he took me to the village?"

Reaching out, I untangle her arms. I like to look at her pretty breasts. "He endangered your life and disrespected my wishes by taking you there."

"I'm a big girl, Aruan. I know how to take care of myself."

I push up on one elbow. "That's my job, even more so when there's an assassin on the loose." My tone is cold and hard, making it clear how serious I am about this. "In the future, think twice before you let Kian convince you to make wrong decisions. He's lucky my father showed up when he did. Next time, my brother won't walk away. The only way he'll leave that clearing is if he's dragged out by his feet. I can assure you that Vitai will have his work cut out for him if that happens."

She scoffs. "For grown-up men, you're behaving an awful lot like children."

I shrug. "That's how we settle arguments in Lona."

"With your fists? You could simply lash at each other with your powers, throw sticks or something at one another with your minds."

That makes me chuckle. "Our powers aren't allowed in the clearing. That'd be cheating."

"What's the point of giving someone a beating if Vitai is going to heal him anyway?"

"The point, my sweet, is showing that I'm stronger

and that I won't hesitate to kill anyone, family or not, if their willful actions cause you harm."

"That's harsh."

"That's our law." I sit up and get off the bed before offering her a hand. Now that the brutal pleasure of our physical bonding has faded, the violence runs hot in my veins again. "Come. We smell like we've been fucking. We'd better have a bath before we question the palace inhabitants, unless you don't care if they know what we did."

She rolls her eyes, climbs from the bed, and takes my hand. "You're crude, you know that?"

My smile is forced this time, my mind already on the next steps.

First, I'm going to interrogate a few people and get Kian to read some minds. Then I'm going to have a word with the human woman, Sandy, for the way she spoke to Elsie. And then I'll take Elsie away, making sure she stays out of Lona for a while.

I won't rest until I find the piece of swamp slime who sabotaged the bridge, the traitor who's trying to kill my mate.

CHAPTER 14
ELSIE

The visitors from Marikanea—my biological family—have retreated to rest. Aruan tells me they were eager to meet me, but in light of what happened, the king convinced them to let me find my bearings first. I believe it's just an excuse to win time to investigate the sabotage. Kian is already reading the minds of the palace residents, and Aruan is questioning everyone in case someone saw something.

So far, we're none the wiser.

The plan was to leave for Marikanea after dinner tonight, as per my family's request. Apparently, they don't want to leave the kingdom unattended for too long. Seeing that the queen is organizing a banquet in their honor, she managed to twist their arms into leaving tomorrow morning.

True to his promise, Aruan keeps me at his side. He even takes me with him when he conducts the questioning in the banquet hall. I've been on edge throughout the morning. I suppose multiple attempts on your life will have that effect.

To my surprise, Aruan also keeps his promise to take me to the sacred site in the afternoon. I didn't think he'd cut his interrogations short. Maybe he thinks the outing will take my mind off this morning's events. He knows how curious I am about the scrolls.

I'm dressed for the occasion in a clean pair of pants and a shirt with my favorite boots. As usual, when he's not taking care of official business, Aruan wears a tunic and dark pants. We're strolling hand-in-hand over the hill, enjoying the sunshine and the quiet—and each other's company, to be honest—when voices reach us.

Laughter comes from the tall shrubs that line the path. Three boys jump out of the thick vegetation with makeshift stick dragons that they fly through the air. At the sight of us, they drop their toys with exclamations of fright and sprint down the path in the direction of the village.

I turn to Aruan. "They can't seriously be *that* terrified of us."

The line of Aruan's jaw hardens, but he doesn't reply.

"Or…" A nasty suspicion settles in the pit of my stomach. "Are they just afraid of me because I can control the dragons?"

"Come." He pulls me along. "They're just kids."

"They probably listen to scary stories their parents tell about us at night around the dinner table." The thought leaves me sad. "How can you blame them for being frightened?"

"It'll take time."

Yeah. That doesn't sound convincing. Which brings me back to the same question. Is my presence a blessing or a curse? What if the killer eventually succeeds in offing me? How will Aruan react to that? Will it be the end of Zerra? And even if Aruan's dangerous reactions weren't a factor, what about my parents? They don't deserve to be abandoned and left in the dark. My heart clenches painfully at the thought of them.

Aruan stops and turns me to him with his hands on my shoulders. "Do you miss them that much?"

Of course he knows what I'm thinking. Not trusting my voice to speak, I swallow and nod.

"I understand," he says, catching me off-guard.

I didn't expect him to sympathize, and strangely, it helps a little when he acknowledges my feelings without trying to invalidate them.

He stares into my eyes as if he can see into my soul. "If you give us a chance, you can be happy here."

He sounds so certain of himself. Can I? Will the sword of the prophecy always hang over my head? There's so much I don't understand yet. Where do our powers come from, and why are they all different?

He speaks again, interrupting my train of thought. "If you let me, I can make you very happy, Elsie. Let me show you how good it can be for mates when their bond is complete."

How am I supposed to do that? I'm not even sure about my future here.

"When you hold back," he continues, "you prevent me from not only being a proper mate but also from protecting you."

"Aren't you already protecting me?"

He tightens his grip on my shoulders. "The bond allows mates to be in touch with each other's thoughts and emotions, as well as their locations, at any given time. It brings mates great peace and joy. You know as well as I do what we share is vague at best. When you're away from me, I can't even tell where you are. That's why Gaia had to open several portals to find you when you first arrived on Zerra. That's why my mother had to find you when the Phaelix put you up for auction at the slave market. I can't protect you if I don't know where to find you."

Why is he always blaming me for the incomplete bond? I raise my chin. "Who says I'm the problem?"

A sardonic smile thins his lips. He drops his arms at his sides and takes a step back, creating distance between us. "I'm not the one holding back, my sweet."

"Are we back to slinging accusations and blame around?"

"It's not about blame. It's about fixing what's broken between us. It's about letting me protect you as I should."

"As you're not letting me out of your sight, it shouldn't be a problem," I shoot back.

He narrows his eyes. "You can let me in and be

happy or keep on shutting me out and remain unfulfilled. It's not going to change the fact that this is where you're staying." He delivers the verdict almost like a threat. "Indefinitely." Grasping my chin between a forefinger and thumb and tilting my face to meet his gaze, he adds in an oddly gentle way, "The choice is yours." He sets me free only to offer me his arm, asking as if nothing is wrong, "Shall we?"

I accept the offer without a fight, putting my hand on the crook of his arm. We continue in silence while I contemplate my options, which, as he said, are limited. By the time we reach the site, I still have no idea what the right thing to do is. All I've achieved is giving myself a headache.

The same man from before guards the entrance. Aruan dissolves the big rock and leads me through the tunnel to the cist at the back, where the strange silicone-like pyramids project flashing images on the walls while the men in white tunics chant. None of them acknowledge our presence. We stand at the back, watching for a while.

I can't make out much of the images. They're moving too fast and with a staccato rhythm. Here and there, I recognize human forms. And… flying cars? I peer closer. Maybe. Skyscrapers? Yep, I catch a flash of a tall building here and there.

Was there an advanced civilization here on Zerra at one point, after all?

The existence of these "scrolls" certainly seems to imply that.

What happened to that civilization? If it existed, why don't I see signs of ruins everywhere?

I motion at the kneeling men and keep my voice to a whisper. "Aside from the infamous prophecy, what do they believe these pictures say?"

Aruan crosses his wrists behind his back. "All kinds of things. Some that make sense, such as us having mates. Others are rather nonsensical."

"For instance?"

"Some priests believe that at one point, the Alit were like the humans on Earth, without powers. Then they took tiny smart particles into themselves, made them part of their brains, and gained the ability to manipulate matter the way we do."

The way Aruan says it makes it clear he thinks it's all bullshit, but my heart is beating faster.

Tiny smart particles? Like nano-computers? Maybe quantum nano-computers with advanced artificial intelligence?

I suck in a breath.

Could the humans of that long-ago Zerran civilization have merged with AI using brain implants, thus becoming the superhuman Alit?

It's a wild theory, but it would explain so much.

"Can the priests slow the images down?" I ask in excitement. "So we can better see what the recordings show?"

The red, green, and blue light plays over his face as he studies the wall. "The priests don't control the projections. They run on a loop. The best they can do is watch them repeatedly and try to form a bigger picture in order to decipher them." He points at a corner where an image of a smiling couple is already disintegrating before it's been fully shown. "That part refers to mates."

I blink at the bright light, trying my best to make out something, but the picture is gone as fast as it appeared. "What do they think it says?"

His voice is gruff. "That every Alit has only one mate, and that mating is for life."

I glance at him quickly, catching the piercing look in his eyes as he scrutinizes me. Unable to hold his intense gaze, I turn back to the images.

If the Alit *are* part AI, could this whole mates business be a byproduct of their programming? Ensuring that pairs are perfectly matched to avoid the unhappiness stemming from breakups makes a lot of sense. Maybe some kind of code in the AI part of the Alit seeks a complimentary code in the mate.

I've already concluded that Zerra must be a parallel Earth. Only here, an asteroid didn't end the existence of the dinosaurs. Maybe the human race developed in coexistence with the animals which, on Earth, are long since extinct. They could've created powerful supercomputers and artificial intelligence, just like humans are starting to do, and merged with the latter to become a new, stronger race with seeming superpowers.

I'm so lost in the incredible possibility that I jump when Aruan touches my shoulder.

"You look pale." He frowns. "Are you all right?"

My voice comes out scratchy. "Yes." I clear my throat. "It's just a lot to take in."

He strokes my arm before taking my hand. "Shall we go? We have to get ready for the banquet."

I look up at him as he leads me back into the sunshine. "Aruan?"

He smiles at me. "Elsie?"

"Does Vitai have a mate?"

"Every Alit has a mate."

"Does he know who she is?"

He steers me around a puddle of mud. "He hasn't sensed her yet."

"When does an Alit sense his mate?"

"It happens at different stages of maturity, but for most, it's during young adulthood. Why?" He stops and gives me a dark look. "You're not interested in Vitai, are you?"

"Of course not." I bite my lip, considering how honest to be. I don't want to betray Eucabeth's feelings, especially as I haven't spoken to her and am basing my assumption purely on observations. "I was just wondering."

"As long as you don't get any ideas." He tugs me closer, pulling me into a possessive hug against his side. "I don't want to have to kill my youngest brother."

And he's not even joking.

CHAPTER 15
ARUAN

The reason I'm in a rush to get back to the palace isn't only because we have to get ready for the banquet. I've interrogated everyone who was near the Great Hall this morning, but I still have a warning to deliver.

Once Elsie and I arrive, I lead her to the guests' quarters. She shoots me a questioning look when I stop in front of the entrance. The wall is already dissolving before she can question me.

The group, minus the male—Karl—is having the refreshments I ordered to be delivered. For good measure, I instructed the cook to mix a little calming potion into the honey wine. Everyone was shaken after this morning's outing that nearly ended in disaster.

At the sight of me, they climb to their feet warily.

Elsie tugs on my hand, strain etched on her face. She's wondering what we're doing here.

"I need to question Sandy." I keep my tone soothing.

"She may have noticed something. Why don't you check on the others to make sure they're all right?"

The explanation reassures her enough for the tense set of her shoulders to ease marginally. She nods before going over to the table where the women are gathered.

I catch Sandy's gaze and tilt my head toward the archway. "A word, please."

Her throat bobs as she swallows. She wrings her hands together but does as she's told.

When we're out of earshot in the hallway, I get straight to the point. "You'll never speak to Elsie again like you did this morning. One wrong word out of your mouth, and it'll be the last word you say." I lean closer. "Am I clear?"

She nods vigorously, her eyes as big as full moons.

Or better yet… "If you can only use your words as poison or a weapon, I forbid you to speak to my mate."

"I didn't mean any disrespect." She cowers under my glare but plows ahead. "I just felt deceived and betrayed."

My anger ignites. I rein it in with fisted hands and gritted teeth. "If not for Elsie, you'd probably be dead by now."

"I know," she says quickly. "But she could've told us. There were many opportunities to come clean, yet she kept quiet."

My smile is sardonic. "And being an Alit makes her so unlikeable?"

"No," she exclaims, trembling. "I just thought—" She cuts herself short, staring at me with wide eyes.

"You just thought what?"

"That we were invested in the same thing," she admits, shaking even more.

"If by 'the same thing,' you mean going back to Earth, I can assure you that's all Elsie has been begging for."

"But..." She frowns. "Why would she have to beg?" Her cheeks turn even paler than what they already are. "Are we your slaves?"

I chuckle. "We condemn slave trading, which is why we're wiping out the operation. Elsie was a victim, just like you."

"I don't understand. I got the impression the slave traders didn't abduct Alit. I thought they only stole humans from Earth."

"Elsie grew up on Earth." I don't want to tell this woman my mate's whole history. It's too personal. However, I want her to understand because I sensed Elsie's hurt when Sandy accused her of having ulterior motives for bringing them to Lona. "She only found out she's an Alit herself recently."

Sandy's mouth pulls into an O.

"Next time, don't be so quick to judge." My tone is cold. "Wait until you know the facts."

"I'm sorry," she sputters.

I turn around, indicating the matter is closed for discussion, and head back toward the rooms.

"Wait." Sandy runs to catch up with me. "What about sending us home?"

I stop. "Believe me, we want you gone from here just as badly as you want to leave."

When Sandy and I step back into the quarters, Elsie is talking to Eucabeth. Elsie is frowning as she speaks while the latter is listening with averted eyes and flushed cheeks. They hug briefly, and then Eucabeth hurries away, pretending to be busy with folding clothes and packing them into trunks.

"Ready?" I ask Elsie.

She follows me outside wordlessly.

"What was that about?" I ask when I've sealed the archway. "The conversation between you and Eucabeth seemed serious."

"Nothing," she says, sounding distracted.

"I know when you lie to me, mate."

She opens her mouth, but a portal appears in front of us, and Gaia steps out of it.

"There you are," my sister says. "Mother is looking for you." Only, instead of facing me, she's facing Elsie. "I thought I might find you here."

"She wants to see Elsie?" I ask.

Gaia smiles. "Both of you, actually."

Turning on her heel, she bounces down the steps. "You'd better not make her wait. There's a lot to do before the banquet."

Concern shifts through Elsie's eyes. I can't say I'm not worried too. Being summoned by my mother usually means nothing good.

I wrap my fingers around Elsie's hand, offering her

a measure of comfort as we walk to the queen's quarters.

My mother is seated on her thronelike chair in her reception room, flanked by Tarix and my father. The backrest of the chair is a dragon sculpted from yellow stone, its wings expanding from the sides. Its paws serve as the feet of the chair, and its tail is coiled around the bottom. My mother sits with a stiff back on the padded seat, her hands folded in her lap.

"Elsie," she says in a jovial tone, waving her closer. "How are you feeling?"

"I'm fine, thanks," Elsie mumbles.

My mother adjusts the silver ring on her finger, turning the heavy opal stone that has twisted sideways back up. "You had a great scare this morning."

Elsie glances at me. "We all had a scare."

I smile at Elsie, reaching through our bond to soothe her even as I keep one eye on my family. I have no idea why my mother has requested our presence, and I don't like surprises.

My mother addresses Elsie. "You've been very courageous, not only this morning but also during the rockslides."

Elsie frowns, no doubt surprised by my mother's compliment. "Um, thank you?"

"Thanks to you, many families in the village were saved." Emotions flicker in my mother's eyes. Her chest rises with a deep breath as she clearly struggles to compose herself. It takes a moment before she can speak again. "And this morning, you saved the humans' and my youngest son's lives."

Elsie shifts her weight. "Vitai repaired the bridge."

"But it wasn't strong enough to support your weight. Vitai told me. If you hadn't summoned your dragons…" The queen falls quiet, leaving the rest unsaid.

My father lays a hand on her shoulder. "I assume we share the same suspicion."

"That someone sabotaged the bridge," I bite out.

My father looks at Elsie when he says, "I want you to know we'll do everything in our power to find the guilty party. This crime will not be left unpunished."

My mother straightens her skirt. "I'd like to show my gratitude by rewarding you for saving my son's life."

"Oh." Flustered, Elsie says, "That's not necessary."

"But of course it is."

My mother flicks her fingers, at which Tarix hurries to open several trunks at the foot of her chair. One contains white opals, another black ones, and yet another, the rarest of red opal stones. Each lid that's lifted reveals priceless treasures, including moon flower seeds, handcrafted rings and bracelets, flacons of perfume, fabrics spun with silver and embroidered with gemstones, rare elixirs, and a dragon tooth necklace.

"Choose anything you like, Elsie." The queen waves a hand over the trunks. "Whatever your heart desires is yours."

Elsie peers at the wealth spread out at her feet, wetting her lips with the tip of her tongue in that nervous habit of hers.

"What's the matter?" My mother appears taken aback. "Is there nothing you like?"

My father narrows his eyes at Elsie, a non-verbal warning not to throw my mother's kindness and generosity back in her face.

"I, um…" Elsie shoves her hands in the pockets of her pants, causing my father's frown to deepen. He's not a big fan of Elsie's chosen attire. "No, everything is beautiful, and that's very kind of you."

The queen lifts an eyebrow, waiting for Elsie to continue.

Elsie squints at my mother through one eye. "Anything I want?"

My mother tilts her head. "That's what I said."

"In that case…" Elsie inhales deeply before blurting out, "I'd like you to send the humans home." She hurries to clarify, "To Earth." As if there were any confusion about where "home" for them is.

My mother is silent for a moment, her expression unreadable and her eyes veiled. My father watches Elsie quietly, but something like respect flashes in his eyes.

My mother leans forward. "That's what you want?"

Elsie bobs her head up and down. "Yes."

My mother and father exchange a look. The nod he gives her is almost inconspicuous, but I notice.

Turning back to Elsie, my mother says, "Very well,

then. My husband and I have been in council with our advisors and the representatives of the guardians of the scrolls. They've agreed this is indeed a rare situation and, seeing that these humans have been stolen and aren't deliberately disregarding the rules, an exception can be made."

"Great." Elsie wipes her hands over her thighs. "That's settled then. When can I tell them?"

My parents still make her nervous. And she has reason to be wary. My mother banished her as a baby, nearly causing her death. As her mate, my father must've been aware of my mother's actions. There's no way she could've hidden something like that from him. Which makes both of them culpable, at least of *that* crime. As for the person who's trying to kill Elsie, for all she knows, it's the very people facing her. No wonder she doesn't trust them. I'm not sure I do.

My voice booms through the room. "The gesture is very noble, but Elsie deserves something for herself, don't you think?"

My father smiles, looking mildly intrigued. "What do you have in mind?"

I look at my mate, seeing a beautiful, young, valiant woman, and so much more. I see a selfless and generous woman, a warrior and a worthy mate. But I also see her conflict and confusion. I see the pain she carries deep inside because of my mother's actions. And I see a way that may buy redemption.

I face my mother squarely. "As you can imagine, the transition to Zerra hasn't been easy for Elsie."

My father's smile slips. My mother stares stone-faced at me. Yeah. They don't appreciate being reminded of their wrongdoing.

Too bad. I continue without wavering, "What Elsie deserves is to see the parents who raised her so she can reassure them and herself."

"But—" my mother starts.

I don't give her a chance to finish. "This is your opportunity to redeem yourself, Mother."

Elsie jerks her face my way, staring at me with surprise and shock painted over her features. My father's expression hardens. My mother is left speechless.

The statement I pose at my mother holds a challenge. "Creating a portal for Elsie to visit her parents is the least you can do, don't you agree?"

Tarix, who's been quiet up to now, steps forward. "I don't think that's a good—"

I pin him with a look. "I didn't ask your opinion."

He cringes.

Facing my mother again, I continue in a calm but lethal tone, "And I'm not asking."

My mother purses her lips. She looks at my father. They hold each other's gazes for a moment, a silent message passing between them.

"Of course, I'll go with Elsie," I say, "to ensure her safety."

Another moment of silence passes during which Elsie moves closer to me. Something touches my fingers, light like a feather on a breeze. I look down.

The back of her hand is brushing mine. When I meet her gaze, the softest of smiles transforms her features as she ever-so-gently slips her hand into mine. My heartbeat speeds up in my chest. I wrap my fingers around hers, enjoying the warmth of her small hand in mine while securing her to me and greedily taking what she's offering.

"Very well," my mother says after another beat. "If that's what Elsie wants."

I'm hardly listening. My pulse is deafening in my ears. Because this is the first time Elsie has come to me like this—on her own, without lust driving her actions. And a whole league of dragons can claw me to pieces if this isn't the sweetest moment of my entire life.

CHAPTER 16
ELSIE

What Aruan has done for me leaves me with a warm, fuzzy feeling. I still can't believe I'm going to see my parents. It's as if I'm floating on air when we walk back to his quarters. I'm still battling to process the incredible turn of events.

Once inside his room, I throw my arms around his neck and breathe, "Thank you," against his chest.

The words are inadequate to express how grateful I am, but with my mind foggy with delirious happiness, I'm incapable of stringing together a sentence.

He kisses the top of my head. "My mother owed you, and you deserve nothing less."

I wish I could show him how much I appreciate his consideration.

Tilting back my head, I stare at his perfect features. "Why did you change your mind?"

"I didn't." His tone is solemn, and his serious gaze carries a warning. "It's just a visit, Elsie."

"I know."

I bite my lip. Is it, though? If I'm there, will I want to come back? And does it even matter? Because Aruan won't let me. That's why he's coming with me.

Still, the concession he made, getting his mother to agree to an act that's considered forbidden, has somehow tipped the scale in the dynamic of our relationship. He's shown me that he's capable of being kind to me even when it doesn't serve his own agenda. There's nothing he can gain from taking me home. He's doing that for no other reason than making me happy. And if my happiness is important to him, he must care about me, even if it's just a little. Which only makes me fall for him more, and that scares the hell out of me.

He frames my face between his large hands, his sensual lips curving into a soft smile. "What is it?"

"I'm just…" I swallow away the tightness of my throat. "Happy." Yet I can sense his tension at the prospect of going to a place where he doesn't want me to return.

"Good." He gives me a peck on the lips before setting me free. "We'd better get ready. We don't want to be late." He tilts his head toward a pale pink gown that's laid out on the bed. "My mother had a dress delivered."

I walk over and trail a hand over the soft fabric embroidered with silver thread. "Who makes these beautiful gowns?"

"We have several excellent seamstresses in the village as well as my mother's personal dressmaker in the palace."

"The dress is beautiful." I trace the tiny silver flowers on the bodice. "That was very thoughtful of her."

He goes toward the cleansing room, pulling his tunic over his head in the walk. "It's her way of making amends, or at least trying to."

I suck my lip between my teeth, admiring the well-defined planes of his broad chest.

He tosses the tunic in the wicker hamper in the corner. "It's also part of her duties as queen."

I raise a brow. "To make sure the royals' dress code is up to standard?"

"To be a good hostess until you've had time to select and employ your own dressmaker."

That sounds over the top. "Does Gaia have one?"

"Every royal female has one."

That's a lot of staff. "Where do they all stay?"

"Some of them live in the staff quarters in the palace." He brushes his hair back from his face, making his upper arm muscles bulge. "Others live in the village."

I tear my gaze away from his impressive biceps. "Well, your mother has excellent taste. She's always immaculately groomed. Come to think of it, she doesn't look a day older than Gaia. She must have a great skincare routine."

He chuckles. "My mother is nearly three times my age."

"What?" I gape at him. I remember what Gaia said, that Aruan was five years old when I was born—which means he's twenty-seven. "That makes her just over eighty!"

"I take it that's old in human years," he says over his shoulder, amused, as he continues on his way.

"It's obviously not on Zerra." I follow him into the cleansing room. "How long does the average Alit live?"

He sits down on the bench to pull off his boots. "At least ten times my mother's age."

"Holy cow." I stop in front of him. "Will I live that long as well?"

"Yes, my sweet. We'll grow old together."

I'm struggling to wrap my mind around the stupefying fact. "That's almost a thousand years. People on Earth don't live much longer than a tenth of that."

I can't even begin to imagine how it must be to live that long.

His gaze darkens when I undress and get into the pool that's already filling with warm water, which must be Aruan's doing, as I'm not testing my new powers. I can't deny that his reaction to my body pleases me. It's good to know I affect him as much as he affects me.

"Don't look at me like that," he says in a gruff tone. "Not unless you want me inside you."

I roll my eyes, ignoring the way his words heat my belly. "You'll make me think you only have one thing on your mind."

"With you?" He raises a thick, dark eyebrow. "How could I think about anything else?" Openly staring at my breasts and then lower, he adds in a low, dark voice, "I could never get enough of your body."

I flush hotter, then remind myself that he wants me because we're mates, which is a result of our programming. The mating system is ingenious from a biological point of view. It not only ensures procreation but also prevents the messiness that comes with breakups and divorces. Yet I still wish he liked me for me and not because some ancient programming in our DNA predestined us to be together.

His gentle question pulls me back to the present. "What are you thinking about that puts such a deep frown on your pretty face?"

"What you told me about the priests' theory." I sit down on the bench and stretch out my legs, enjoying the soothing warmth of the water. "About the tiny smart particles and all that."

"Oh?" He rakes a gaze over my body as he sheds his pants. "Do tell."

The sight of him naked always does things to me, things that make it hard to concentrate. I know where our bath is going to end if I don't get my mind out of the gutter, so I force myself to focus on his handsome face.

"I think those priests are right. On Earth, we're currently developing what could eventually become similar technology—some combination of artificial intelligence and nano-implants. So if that's what happened here, then you and I—and every Alit—are products of a highly advanced ancient technology, the end result of a merger between humans and AI."

He climbs down the steps into the water and sits down next to me. "I'm not sure I understand what you're talking about."

"It's…" How do I explain AI and computers to a person who's essentially from a medieval society? "You know what? Never mind. The key thing is, that could explain the mating phenomenon. You and I are literally *programmed* to be drawn to one another."

"That's what being mates means," he drawls, locking his hands around my waist and pulling me onto his lap so that I'm straddling him. "We're fated to be together."

"Not fated, *programmed*. Like two pieces of software."

He nuzzles my temple. "Uh-huh."

"Do you realize what that means?" I lean back on his lap. "If it's been done before, here on Zerra, there's a very probable chance that humans on Earth will also succeed in developing into a species like the Alit."

"Perhaps," he says, his lips quirking.

I pout. "You're not taking me seriously."

"Oh, I am." He strokes his palms down my thighs, grips my knees, and spreads them wide. "I just have other things on my mind right now."

My reprimand is half-hearted at best. "Aruan."

He goes from playful to serious in a second. "I want you, Elsie."

My core tightens. I wrap my arms around his neck,

knowing I'll need to hold on. "Nothing has stopped you from taking what you want before."

He encircles my waist and yanks me hard against him. "There's something else you need to know about an Alit's age, specifically about a female Alit's maturity." He smooths one hand up my side to cup my breast. "It takes only a few moon cycles for an adult woman to become fertile once she's mated."

My stomach contracts at the mention of the risk we're taking every time we have unprotected sex.

Reading my mind as always, he says, "If it's that important to you, we can wait."

The declaration takes me by surprise. "Really?"

"Yes, really."

"I thought you didn't want to." I search his eyes. "Wait, I mean."

His gaze plays over my face, his expression honest and open. "I already told you. I want you to be happy."

"Having children is important to you." I can sense it through our bond. I can feel how badly he wants that.

He gives me a crooked smile. "It's not going to happen overnight, so I may as well wait until you're ready."

"Why?" The word is a mere whisper. "What's changed your mind?"

"You're making an effort for me. I want to make one for you too."

Wow. This is huge. Aruan is willing to compromise. For me.

"It's not that I don't want kids. It's just…" I hesitate.

"Things are a little crazy right now." Waving a hand through the space, I continue, "This is a lot to take in, and there are so many pitfalls to navigate."

He brushes a thumb over my nipple, sending ripples over my skin. "Pitfalls?"

"Obstacles to overcome and problems to solve."

The light in his silver eyes is earnest. "I understand." He draws lazy circles around my breast with a finger. "We won't talk about it again until you tell me you're ready. In the future, I'll keep potions handy that'll prevent you from conceiving."

Is this the same man who's keeping me captive here?

His voice heats. "In the meantime…" He slowly lowers his mouth to mine, making his intention clear. "I'll pull out."

~

Three orgasms later, my knees are still a bit wobbly when Aruan and I leave his quarters in what must be Lona's finest attire. He wraps a hand around mine, offering me an encouraging smile, and I lap up the silent support he offers.

Instead of heading toward the banquet hall, he turns in the opposite direction.

I glance at him. "Where are we going?"

"To meet your family before the banquet."

"Why?"

He squeezes my fingers. "I think it will be less

stressful for you to meet them without the masses looking on."

"This was your idea?" His attentiveness makes more warmth spread through my chest. "How considerate of you." I do my best to smile with confidence, but I can't hide my nervousness from him. "Thank you."

"It's my job to take care of you, and that means keeping you healthy and alive in every way that matters."

I aim for humor. The situation is already serious enough as it is. "What's *my* job?"

"To rule as my queen."

The statement knocks my world off kilter. I expected him to say something with a sexual nuance, such as that my place is in his bed, but no. He's perfectly serious.

Before I can think of a suitable reply, we're in front of his mother's quarters.

"Ready?" he asks, rubbing a thumb over my knuckles.

Unable to speak, I nod.

He dissolves the wall, revealing a small group gathered in the reception room. The king and queen are present, but it's the man and woman standing with their backs to me who draw my gaze.

The wall seals behind us, enclosing us in the privacy of the queen's quarters. At the silent announcement of our arrival, the strangers turn around. We face each other quietly, the moment too charged for words.

A curtain of straight hair cascades over the

woman's shoulders to her waist. We share the same color hair and eyes. Her face is oval, like mine, and her skin is just as pale, but she's much taller, literally a giant towering over me. Her sky-blue dress hugs her curves, accentuating her perfect body and tall, slender legs. The fabric of her dress glitters, tiny sparks firing off in the light that pulses in the walls. Her shoes are the same color as her dress, the toes pointy and the heels wedged.

We hold one another's eyes for a few heavy heartbeats before I shift my gaze to the man. A broad forehead, high cheekbones, and square jaw give his face a hard, angular look. His blond hair is cropped close to his skull, matching a short-trimmed beard. He's wearing a tunic of a slightly darker hue than the woman's dress with a midnight-blue sash over white pants and tan boots.

What's most striking about him are the vivid blue of his eyes, not another speck of color visible in the solid circles of his irises, and the blue and green lines painted horizontally over his cheeks.

The woman steps forward, exclaiming in a voice as light and crisp as a windchime, "Laliss." Her eyes turn brighter with unshed tears. "I can't believe it." She stops a couple of paces away from me, spreading out her arms. "May I?"

Aruan's fingers tighten around mine. I'm not sure how to react. To be honest, I'm not even sure how I feel. Numb would nail it. The moment seems unreal.

When she remains in place with her outstretched

arms and tears running over her pale cheeks, I nod awkwardly, at which she immediately wraps me up in a hug, forcing Aruan to let me go.

She presses me tightly against her chest while I just stand there, not sure what to do. Her hair smells like exotic flowers, a soft but intoxicating perfume that reaches my nostrils.

After a second, she releases me from her firm grip to hold me at arm's length. "Let me look at you." Her gaze dances over my face before moving in a slow path from my head to my toes. "You look just like your mother." She turns to the man. "Doesn't she, Kal?"

The man jerks up his chin, which I suppose counts as a nod.

After smoothing her hands over my shoulders in a final caress, she sets me free. "I'm your aunt, Evolet, your mother's sister, and this is my mate, Kaleam." She waves at the man. "But everyone calls him Kal."

My voice scrapes in my throat. "Elsie."

Evolet smiles. "They told me that's what you call yourself now."

"Drink, anyone?" the queen asks.

She walks to the table where a carafe of golden liquid—my guess is honey wine—and goblets are set out, the wide skirt of her shimmery red dress swishing around her slipper-clad feet.

Evolet stiffens. The tension in the air climbs a few notches.

"No, thank you," Kal says in a curt manner. "The

sooner we get this dinner over with, the sooner we can spend time alone with my mate's niece."

Unaffected, the queen pours the wine into the goblets. "We have reason to celebrate. Elsie and Aruan's mating has brought together two powerful kingdoms."

"Or driven them to war," Kal says through clenched teeth.

Aruan and his father both take a menacing step toward Kal, but the queen holds up a hand. "I think there are some things we need to say to clear the air."

"Is that why you're wearing your war paint, Kal?" the king asks with a mocking grin.

"It's ceremonial paint," Kal says. "Which you would've known if you were familiar with our customs."

"Which you're not." Evolet shoots daggers with her eyes at the king. "Because your mate severed the sacred bond that should've existed between our families when she banished my niece."

The king crosses his arms. "Is that why you came? To declare war in my face?"

Aruan steps in front of me, blocking me with his body. His voice drips with pure malice. "Or did you think you could take my mate home with you?" His power rises to the surface, a faint vibration that won't stay faint for much longer if the meeting continues like this. "Away from me?"

Things are quickly getting out of hand. The atmosphere is volatile enough to blow up in our faces.

"Guys." I walk around Aruan, placing myself in the middle of the small group of angry people. "Aren't we missing the point here? Isn't this supposed to be a happy occasion? After wondering all my life who my biological parents were, I'm finally meeting the only family who can tell me anything about them. I'd prefer it if we could do that without you killing each other."

The king inhales deeply and straightens his tunic. "Elsie is right. I didn't invite you here for a fight."

I look at the king in surprise. "You invited them? I thought it was Aruan." After learning that Aruan's mother sent me to Earth, I never expected her or her mate to invite my biological family for a visit.

Aruan places a hand on my shoulder, offering me comfort with his touch and through our bond.

"I invited them because you're an Alit," the king says, looking me straight in the eyes. "And every Alit should know where she has her roots."

I turn my face toward the queen, expecting her to be upset by such an action from her mate, but she appears serene.

"We've been honest with you," the queen says, addressing my aunt, "because that was the right thing to do."

Kal sneers. "Now you're concerned about what's right."

The king takes another step toward Kal. "Be careful how you speak to my mate."

"We're done here," Aruan bites out, taking my hand.

I hang back. "Wait."

Aruan only stops when his mother speaks again.

"Aruan, wait," she says. "Evolet and Kal are forgetting an important point."

"And that is?" Kal asks, his upper lip curling.

The queen picks up two goblets. "If I hadn't sent Elsie away when I did, she would've died in the volcanic eruption with her parents. My action saved her life."

Evolet and Kal stare at each other. They're quiet for a moment. The way they look at each other is intense. I bet they're communicating through their bond.

For the first time, I envy that. I'm suddenly and inexplicably jealous of something they share that Aruan and I don't have. I wonder how it feels when the bond is complete?

After another second, Evolet sighs. "As much as I hate to admit it, you're right, Nia. The day we lost my sister, her mate, and so many of our family and people was a dark day in the history of Marikanea. And as much as I condemn what you've done, I'm also grateful that Elsie survived."

The queen hands Evolet a goblet. "I say we leave the past where it belongs and embrace the future." She adds with meaning, "Elsie and Aruan are going to need all the support they can get if they're to become the best rulers they can be. Lona needs them, and Marikanea will always have our support and alliance."

Kal accepts the goblet the queen offers him, albeit

with a tight jaw. "If that's what my mate desires, so be it."

The queen smiles from ear to ear. "I'm glad that's settled." She hands out the rest of the goblets and raises hers. "To Elsie and Aruan. May they live a long and happy life and be blessed with children." She holds her son's eyes as she takes a sip of her wine. "May their bond be strong."

I stifle an embarrassed sound that turns into an uncomfortable cough. There's no doubt about what his mother means. She must know our bond isn't complete, and for some reason, that bothers me. It feels too private.

A mumbled chorus of, "To Elsie and Aruan," follows.

Aruan shoots me a look that says we have our work cut out for us as he brings his goblet to his lips. Reinstating peace between our families may take time.

"I have so many questions for you," Evolet says to me. "I can't wait to show you your home."

The look in Aruan's eyes is downright dangerous. "This is her home."

"Yes, of course." Evolet smiles. "When I said 'home,' I meant the place where Elsie was born."

"I can't wait to see Marikanea," I say quickly, trying to diffuse a potentially explosive argument, which I'm a hundred-percent sure will either end in an uninvited reaction set off by Aruan's power or in bloodshed. Basically, it boils down to the same thing.

"How will we travel there?" I ask to change the subject.

"I can create portals between kingdoms," Evolet says.

The queen takes another sip of her drink. "Of course, I'll also be happy to assist."

I look down, making sure the stone in my necklace remains red before I drink the wine.

"A poison stone," Evolet muses, tracing the silver setting with a finger. "That's very prudent."

Not wanting to go down that road either, I force a laugh. "Rather safe than sorry, right?"

Evolet smooths a hand over my short hair. "When rumors reached us that Aruan's mate had returned from the dead, I didn't want to believe it. First of all, the name was different—Elsie instead of Laliss. Secondly, they said you were a small woman, and us Marikanears are known to be taller than average. Your mother certainly was." She gives a sad smile, pausing as if she's lost in her memories before giving herself a visible shake. "Then, great tales of how this small woman had controlled dragons reached us, and I knew it had to be true."

"Rumors travel that far?" I ask, not that I know exactly how far away Marikanea is, as maps are nonexistent on Zerra.

Kal replies. "Alit travel extensively for trade. Portals make it easy."

"How did you know the rumors were true?" I ask Evolet. "Could my mother command animals?"

Evolet makes big eyes and leans closer. "Your mother could make plants grow."

"Really?"

"Her power was just as great as yours. One touch from her, and a seedling could turn into a tree overnight."

Riveted, I ask, "And my father?"

"Your father could create rain," Kal says. "All he needed was a humid sky. Together, they made a formidable pair."

Evolet's eyes glimmer with reverence. "Creating life."

"Wow," I say a little wistfully. "Like sun and water."

Evolet grips my shoulder and gives a quick squeeze. "Precisely."

I glance at Aruan. If my biological parents were sun and water, what are we? Destruction and chaos? The end of the world as they know it? Or could we be something beautiful, something nurturing and life-giving?

I give a start when Aruan takes my hand and lifts it to his lips. The dark look in his eyes says he knows what I'm thinking.

I hope not.

But then he confirms my first notion when he kisses my fingers and says, "Sometimes, my sweet, destruction can be beautiful."

I fear he's right.

I fear he's already destroyed me, and now it's too late to salvage my heart.

"Don't worry," he says, pressing a whisper on my ear. "I'll make it good."

Jerking my face up, I stare into his silver eyes and find the meaning there.

By "it," he means my surrender.

CHAPTER 17

ELSIE

Aruan and I get ready to leave for Marikanea with the queen's assurance that she'll wait until our return before sending the humans home. I'd like to say goodbye and, if I'm lucky, make peace with Sandy before they go. I'd hate for us to part on bad terms, especially after everything we've been through together. Having shared the same horrible fate makes me feel close to all of them.

I wrangle a promise from Gaia and Kian to take Karl and the women for walks and to keep them busy. Since Eucabeth confirmed my suspicion that she's developed a crush on Vitai, I prefer not to ask him. There's no point in making the situation tougher on Eucabeth than it already is. If her blossoming feelings are left to run their course, she'll be devastated when Vitai senses his mate. She went as far as to suggest staying behind on Zerra while her friends return home, and the king and queen will never allow that.

The king pulls Aruan and me aside and ensures us he'll continue the search for the person—or persons—who sabotaged the bridge. He makes it sound as if we're going away for a month when Aruan agreed to a week.

My aunt and uncle leave straight after breakfast, going ahead of us. One minute, we're saying goodbye to Aruan's family in front of the portal his mother has pulled up in her reception room, and the next, we walk out onto a white shore that glitters like snow under a pale sun.

Aruan kisses the back of my hand. "All right?"

"Yes." Just excited and nervous.

Gaia advised me to wear a nice dress, but I figured my pants, shirt, and boots were more practical for exploring. I hope I'm not going to stick out like a sore thumb. Aruan is dressed in his habitual tunic and boots, his hair tied at his nape. He's scanning the surroundings with vigilance.

I look around me. Turquoise water laps at the shore. The sea is calm and flat, not black and turbulent with crushing waves like back in Lona. The water is so clear I spot pink, blue, and orange corals on the shallow reefs. Hybodus are gliding over the sand bed. I recognize the prehistoric sharks by the strange horns on the tops of their heads. How cool. They have two sets of teeth, one for gripping slippery prey and another for crushing shells. They float by soundlessly, on the hunt for prey.

A kalligrammatid flutters by and disappears in the

vegetation. Bright green ferns taller than I am sway gently from side to side despite the fact that there's no air movement, not even a breeze. Their leaves rustle as they unfurl and curl up again.

See-through, tube-shaped plants grow on the fringe of the beach. Black veins knit through their walls, contracting and expanding with a lazy rhythm. Behind them, thin, black, stick-like trees the height of a three-story building sprout into the air. At the top, their offshoots are connected, forming a circle of hugging branches without leaves. Maybe it's one big body and not several trees. Pink clusters of delicate little bell flowers hang like chandeliers from the pin-like branches. Beyond the border of the trees, cycads with red fruit resembling pineapples grow wild, each fruit sporting a white candy floss beard.

We must be on a high plateau because the air feels thinner and less humid. It smells sweet, like lilies. The sky is light blue with a pinkish hue, and although it's clear, the cries of pterosaurs are audible in the distance. I can sense their presence all around us, the dinosaur population here much denser than in Lona.

I turn to Aruan. "Have you been here before?"

"Many times." He stares off in the direction of a shimmery white cliff that frames the water. "I've been coming to this place ever since they told me you were dead. But I just got to know the surroundings and the animal and plant life here. I could never bring myself to go inside the palace."

The forlorn, desolate feeling that reaches me

through the bond is harrowing. The cold emptiness is like a parasite sucking the life out of every other emotion that's left.

The bleak, grim hollowness jars me, unsettling me in a way I didn't think was possible.

Is this what it feels like to lose a mate? All this time, Aruan suffered these painful emotions, and I was blissfully unaware of any of it. I lived my life on Earth, not knowing I had a mate in a different world, a mate who was slowly dying inside because a part of him—me—was gone.

I never really understood before. Now that I do, I don't know if I can leave him. I don't want him to go through something like that ever again.

I never want to hurt him.

Slipping my hand into his, I stare up at him. "Is this how I'll feel if you're gone?"

He meets my gaze, his silver eyes brimming with emotions, yet his lips curve into a smile. "That's the fate of all men and women who lose a mate."

That sad smile breaks my heart. "I'm sorry, Aruan. I'm sorry you had to go through that. I had no idea."

He tightens his grip on my hand. "You don't have to apologize. It wasn't your fault."

But rejecting him will be. Not being able to give him a completed bond *is* my fault. He said so himself… on various occasions. And I have no idea how to fix that. Maybe sending me to Earth harmed more than my body. Maybe it damaged our bond for good. Now Aruan is forced to exist like this, having found his mate who came back from the dead, only to live with a bond that will never be whole.

The thought floors me. A stone sinks in my stomach. I can never be the mate to Aruan he deserves. I've wondered whether he would've been better off if the Phaelix had never decided to kidnap me, but now I know better. His existence would've been nothing but loneliness and pain. And I don't know what's more perilous for Zerra: my presence or my absence. I suspect that an unfeeling Aruan is a hundredfold more dangerous than a feeling one, even when he's angry. If he had no emotions left, no remorse or affection for anyone or anything, there'd be nothing to prevent him from unleashing the full force of his lethal power.

Despite the pleasant warm weather, a shiver rakes down my spine.

"Come." He tugs me toward the cliffside of the beach. "Your aunt will be waiting."

I ponder everything our bond has revealed to me as we trudge across the fine, snowy beach that sucks at our feet like quicksand. My gaze is trained on the distance, my attention focused inwardly, so I don't spot the big hole opening in front of us until Aruan hoists me into his arms and carries me out of harm's way.

I glance back at the hole of swirling sand, my heart galloping in my chest.

He lowers me to my feet carefully. "You have to watch where you go. Don't step on the darker patches of sand."

"Jeez." I dust down the legs of my pants. "That was close."

"Not with me by your side." He takes my hand back in his. "I'll never let anything happen to you."

I let the reassurance of that promise settle me as he leads me underneath the thin trees. Jingling as clear as a bell rings through the air. In a second, the whole bunch of flowers above our heads are chiming, creating the most beautiful, haunting music.

I gape at the flowers, having a sudden urge to reach out and touch them. "What's that?"

"An alarm system."

Stopping, I turn in a circle with my head tilted back. "A what?"

"It alerts your family that they have visitors."

When I raise my free hand toward a cascade of flowers, Aruan grips my wrist.

"They're dangerous," he says.

"What?" I utter a laugh. "These pretty little delicate flowers?"

"They're disguised to deceive." He picks an unassuming yellow flower from a scrawny bush at our feet and, holding it by the long stem, lifts it to the tiny flowers that drip like a purple waterfall from the high branches of the trees.

Immediately, the air smells sweeter. The chiming turns louder. The flowers directly above us emit the high-pitched sound of an idiophone that vibrates through the air. The moment Aruan touches them with the yellow flower, they close around it. Their pitch amplifies as the petals of the yellow flower turn brown before disintegrating as if being burned by a flame. Their music increases until nothing but the stem is left, and then they turn quiet.

"That's creepy," I say, equal parts horrified and fascinated.

"They feed on small winged water dragons and moths, but they're capable of devouring something as big as a flying dragon." He continues onto a pebbled path that runs through the undergrowth. "They lure them with their music and scent."

Small tufts of the cycad beards drift into the air as we pass to float around us like fluffy white balls.

I point at one that passes in front of my face. "What are those?"

"They're a different kind of alarm system. They float ahead of us to let the dragons know there's prey on the loose."

"What do they get out of it?" There must be a reason the plants would be so "generous."

"Those cloudy pieces will land on the carcass the dragon leaves after his meal and absorb the blood. Once they've soaked up their quota, they become heavy and dense enough to roll back to the plants that released them. They ferment on the ground, and the roots of their hosts can reabsorb them."

The mental image of the blood-soaked cottonwool-ish balls makes my skin crawl. "That sounds like something from *The Little Shop of Horrors*."

He smiles. "What kind of shop is that? It sounds like a place of torture."

"It is, in a way, but it's just a story."

At the end of the cycad field, we reach a flat slab of stone that drops away at our feet. A vast pasture spreads out in front of us with stegosaurus and brontosaurus grazing in the yellow-green grass.

I suck in a breath. The sight is a dream come true.

"You like the view," Aruan says.

When I look at him, I catch him studying me. "I've always loved dragons. Since I was a little girl, I had pictures and toys of them in my room. I read every book about them I could get my hands on."

The light in his eyes is both soft and sad. "Maybe a part of you remembered where you came from. Even though your power wasn't developed, it was always there."

"I suppose that makes sense." I stare back at the picture in front of me, unable to believe that it's real. "On Earth, we call them dinosaurs. Only there, they're extinct. They lived millions of years ago before an asteroid caused major climate changes that caused them to disappear altogether."

"You're passionate about this subject."

"It's that obvious, huh?"

"You'll have to tell me everything about your dinosaurs."

"Why?" I search his eyes. "I thought you didn't want to talk about Earth, seeing that it's a forbidden subject."

"Everything that's important to you is important to me."

I'm stunned into silence, contemplating the meaning behind his declaration. Could he actually care about me for who I am and not just because I'm his mate?

The breeze picks up, blowing wisps of his hair that came loose around his face.

Glancing at the horizon, he says, "We'll have time to come back here." He pulls me behind him toward the white cliff. "The eastern wind is rising."

I recognize a few of the creepy-crawlies from Lona. A long line of the same spidery ants I saw in the jungle cross our path. The giant tube worms are everywhere, but I'm not worried, knowing I can control them. Anyway, Aruan will melt them if they snap their fanged maws in our direction. A colony of those prawn-like insects are hard at work in the trees, cutting larvae from their cocoons.

As we round the foot of the cliff, a gap appears like a dark distorted mouth in the rockface, giving the impression of a grimacing mask. We go inside. Light comes from the other end, so it must be some kind of tunnel running through the mountain.

Hissing reaches my ears. I access the map in my mind, but there's no animal life around us. I'm about to ask Aruan what's making that noise when my gaze falls on movement in the shadows. When my eyes adjust to the dark, I almost jump out of my skin.

A creature that looks like a giant snake slithers from

behind a rock. Beady little eyes shine like black marble from a triangular head. It pushes up onto two front paws, observing us slyly. I nearly fall onto my back when the human-sized snake opens its mouth and speaks with hissing and clicking sounds.

I cling to Aruan's hand as he listens attentively. When the creature falls quiet, I whisper, "What the hell is that?"

"They're one of the intelligent species on Zerra. We call them Slitheax. They're stealthy assassins."

The Slitheax says something, its red forked tongue peeking out as it spits and hisses more foreign words.

I suppress an urge to jump behind Aruan's back as it slides through the sand toward us. "What did he say? Or is it a she?"

"They're hermaphrodites. It was asking what our business is here. Your aunt employs them as guardians for the palace. That way, the Alit and Slitheax live together in peace."

A whole army of Slitheax crawl out from behind the rocks, hissing and clicking their tongues as they surround us.

I swallow. "What did you tell them?"

"They know who I am." Aruan pulls me closer with an arm around my shoulders. "They're curious about you."

Unable to stop myself, I yelp when they narrow their circle around us.

"Just keep still." Aruan's tone is reassuring. "They only want to get to know you."

It's difficult to stay still when "getting to know me" means licking my face with their sandpapery tongues.

"It's their way of smelling you," Aruan says with a grin I can't see, as I'm currently being blinded by tens of licking tongues and snake-ish saliva, but that I can hear clearly.

They're only happy when my entire face is covered in glob, and sticky slime is dripping from my chin.

Wiping a hand over my eyes to clear the muck that glues my eyelashes together, I swallow down the need to throw up and ask with sarcasm, "Do they know me now?"

Laughter is thick in Aruan's voice. "They've certainly made your acquaintance."

"Great," I grumble, wiping my sleeve over my face. Long dregs of slime stick to the fabric. "Eww."

The Slitheax who addressed Aruan first says something in its lisping language, and then they retreat to let us through. They push up onto their front paws, watching us with their long tongues flicking from their mouths. In the light spilling from the exit on the other side of the tunnel, I can make out the vibrant orange scales on the undersides of their otherwise black bodies.

Outside, I shake the hand I cleaned my eyes with, trying to dislodge the slime, but it only stretches like melted cheese before bouncing back to my splayed fingers.

"Come here," Aruan says, chuckling as he guides me to a pond in a hollow of the rock slab.

He crouches down in front of me, pulling me with him onto my haunches. He scoops up a handful of water and gently rinses my face. I don't miss the quirk of his lips as he tries hard to suppress his laughter.

I narrow my eyes. "You think this is funny, don't you?"

He flashes me a grin. "Don't worry. The price is worth the gain. They never forget a scent. Once they've smelled you, they'll never mistake you for an enemy. You'll always have a guaranteed passage through their terrain."

"Did Kian give you the ability to understand them?"

He nods.

"So there are Slitheax in Lona too?"

"No." He pauses. "On one of my visits, I crossed one that was injured. A dragon had chewed off his tail before he managed to get away."

I shiver at the mental image. "What happened?"

"I took him back to Lona in the hope that Vitai could heal him, but he'd lost too much blood. His injuries were extensive, and he didn't survive the shock."

That's sad. "So Kian transmitted his language to you."

"We needed to communicate if I were to find his family. They deserved to know what had happened to him." The look in his eyes intensifies as he says, "There's nothing worse than not knowing."

Oh, Aruan. I place a hand on his arm. "Is that what you went through when I disappeared?"

He continues to rinse my face, his lips pressed in a hard line. Just when I think he's not going to answer, he says, "When my mother told me you were dead, I didn't want to believe it. I kept on feeling your existence the way the mind tricks one into feeling a severed limb that's no longer there. And then it was just gone. Dead." His silver eyes grow hard and cold. "I had no choice any longer. I had to accept what the severed connection told me."

"I'm so sorry," I say, squeezing his arm. If I could, I would've taken that pain away from him.

"But you're here now." He brushes the hair back from my forehead. "And that's more than I could've ever hoped for."

"I'm staying," I say on the spur of the moment, willing to give my soul to make right all the wrongs that have been done to him.

I can't explain my impulsive need. I only know I can't bear his suffering. Not from the past or the present. Even if it means giving up everyone and everything I love, I'll do it. For him. Because it's in my make-up. It's part of my DNA.

Despite the heaviness of the moment, the possessiveness I've become so familiar with passes over his features. "I know, my sweet."

We fall quiet as he takes care of me, each of us wrapped up in our own thoughts, but thanks to the bond, none of those thoughts are completely private. He knows I'm mourning everyone I've lost to find him, and I know he knows that a part of me will always long for the people I left behind and that my heart isn't one hundred percent here.

He cups my face when it's clean and wipes the water from my cheeks with his thumbs. "Better?"

Trying to lighten the mood, I say, "I won't say no to a bath."

He straightens and offers me a hand. "It'll have to be a shower. They don't have pools in Marikanea."

"Why not?"

"In Lona, the Water Palace is fed from an underground source. Here, they have to rely on rainwater that accumulates in large containers."

We leave the tunnel behind and round another cliff. A gasp catches in my throat. The scene in front of us is like something from a fairytale. The rock formations are carved into a myriad of canyons. Towers and turrets shaped by nature create a giant sandcastle. Great pans of water in dams with clay walls shine like mirrors in between. The pointed stone cones that rise like giant termite heaps from the ground are reflected in the flat surfaces of the water. A few windows are visible here and there.

"If Lona is known for its palace that reaches the sky," Aruan says, "Marikanea is known for its palace that touches the belly of Zerra. The royal family constructed their new palace here when the volcano eruption destroyed the old one and half of their city."

We walk to the edge of the cliff. A deep canyon runs like a moat around the palace, making access on foot impossible. The cliff is too steep to climb down, and there are no bridges.

Aruan holds out a hand. "Shall we?"

I sense his intention to create a portal for us.

A cryodrakon is hunting for lizards between the rocks. It would've been nice to see the palace from his back. I bet the aerial perspective makes an impressive picture. I'm a lightweight, much lighter than I should be thanks to all my childhood diseases. But a pterosaur won't be able to carry the weight of a normal full-grown Alit, let alone Aruan's. So I take his hand and hold on for the sensations that come with going through a portal.

We walk out onto a large, flat surface between two dams. My aunt waits outside, her white dress billowing in the wind that has suddenly picked up.

She embraces me before offering Aruan her wrist. He presses his wrist against hers in the customary greeting. By now, the wind is so strong that it's pelting my face with sand.

"Quickly." Evolet grabs my hand. "It's the eastern wind. We'd better get inside."

"What's the eastern wind?" I ask as she drags me toward a cavernous entrance.

"It's strong enough to blow an Alit away." She rushes us inside. "And when it does, those unfortunate men and women are never found."

The entrance seals behind us, which I presume is Evolet's doing.

"We're safe now." She blows out a sigh. "I'm glad you got here in time."

"I know the wind patterns," Aruan says. "I timed our arrival."

Evolet pats his shoulder. "Did you show Elsie around?"

"Yes, but I'm sure she'd like to explore the surroundings at her leisure later."

"Is that why we landed on the beach and not in the palace?" I pose the question to Aruan. "Or did you just want to see me covered in snake slime?"

Evolet laughs. "You met the Slitheax. Good. Once they know you're one of us, they won't be tempted to crush your bones in a death hug before swallowing you alive."

I repress another shiver at the memory of their tongues on my face.

"They're actually a very peaceful species," my aunt continues. "They only kill to feed."

Okay. That doesn't make me feel better.

"Everyone is eager to meet you." Evolet leads the way, taking us into a maze of underground tunnels that are lit with the same pulsing light stones as in Lona. "But I'll let you freshen up first."

She shows us to spacious quarters with stone furniture and murals of dinosaurs, some rising from the water and others flying over the land.

She motions at the bed, which is elevated and not sunken as in the Water Palace. "I took the liberty of setting out some clothes for you."

I look at the long, white dress and matching shoes. "You didn't have to."

"Of course I had to." She waves a hand. "You can't exactly travel with a trunk through a portal, can you?"

Oh. I didn't think about that. There's a tunic and pants for Aruan too. Something lacy sticking out from under the dress catches my eye. Curious, I go over and pull it out. It's a type of thong. And something that resembles a strapless bra.

Aware of Aruan's stare, I tuck the flimsy garments back into place. "You have underwear in Marikanea?"

Evolet shoots me a puzzled look. "Every kingdom on Zerra has underwear."

My mouth drops open as I turn an accusing gaze on Aruan, who only shrugs with a wicked smile.

Evolet, quick to catch on, says, "Oh, I see."

I don't take my eyes off of Aruan. "It seems I still have a lot to learn about Zerra."

"Well." Evolet clears her throat. "Take your time to clean up." She wrinkles her nose. "You have a distinct odor of Slitheax. I'll wait for you outside."

I prop my hands on my hips when she's gone and the archway is sealed. "You deliberately made me walk around naked under my clothes."

"What can I say?" Aruan crosses his arms. "I like you naked under your clothes."

I saunter over. "Now that I know, I'm going to get a trunk full of underwear."

"That could be one way of taking revenge."

"Oh, absolutely." I stop toe to toe with him. "Have you ever seen a woman in underwear, Aruan?"

His gaze darkens, predatory intention sparking in his eyes. "There's only one woman I'm interested in seeing, and that's you." He closes the hairbreadth of distance between us, putting our bodies flush together. "Preferably without clothes."

My growing arousal makes me brave. "There's a reason underwear is considered sexy."

He rolls the word off his tongue. "Sexy?"

"Sometimes, hinting at something that's just out of reach is a more powerful magnet than outright flaunting it."

"Do you think if you hide your perfect body, I'll want it more?"

"Maybe," I tease.

He grips my chin and tilts back my head. "Then you don't know me very well, mate."

"Is that so?"

"I always want you. Nothing can make me desire you more."

"Right answer," I whisper, going on tiptoes and locking my arms around his neck.

His mouth is on mine before I have time to breathe. I give in to the kiss, just for a moment, and then I pull away, inviting a growl that tears from his chest.

"My aunt is right outside."

He aims for my lips again, whispering a promise over them. "I'll be quick."

"I smell like snake spit."

"I don't give a dragon."

"Aruan," I exclaim when he grabs my shirt and rips it down the middle.

With one swoop, he lifts me into his arms. "I'll fix your clothes."

"That's not what I meant." I wrap my legs around his waist. "I do mind."

"What? This?" He flicks his tongue over my nipple before sucking it into his mouth.

I throw my head back as pleasure coils through my core.

"See?" Wickedly, he nips my contracted nipple before moving to the other one. "There are advantages to not wearing underwear."

"Wait." He's distracting me, making me forget what I wanted to say. "I do need a shower."

Carrying me to an archway, he says, "And my mate will always get what she wants."

Our clothes disintegrate on our bodies only to be reassembled on the bed, perfectly clean.

I shift my hips, enjoying his hard length that's pressed between my legs. "You're any housewife's dream."

"Housewife?"

"There will never be laundry or dishes to do."

"Laundry? Dishes?" His voice is gruff. "Is this your 'sexy' talk?"

He walks into a cubicle and pulls a leather cord that

hangs on the wall. In an instant, warm water cascades over us.

Blinking drops from my eyes, I stare at the holes in the ceiling through which the water is pouring. "How do they heat the water?"

"That's what you're thinking about?" He pushes me against the wall, holding me up with his hands on my ass cheeks. "Now?"

I shrug. "I'm curious."

"Insatiable." He chuckles. "They warm it in cauldrons over a fire."

"In every room?"

"They produce pellets from dried grass and pulp from hard wood trees that burn for a long time."

"Like coals," I muse.

Using the wall to support my back, he slips one hand between our bodies and enters me with two fingers. My inner walls flutter from the stretch, my belly tightening with pleasure.

"We don't have much time," he says, "so I want you to keep your eyes on me, and don't you dare look away."

I try to focus on his face as he presses a thumb on my clit, but the pressure is enough to bring me to a quick release.

"Aruan."

"That's right, my sweet. Show me how you come apart for me."

The words push me over. I clench around his fingers, coming hard and fast but still needing him.

I bite my lip to stifle my sounds. Keeping his fingers inside me, he kisses me as if this is our last day together. It's wild and uninhibited, two people drowning in lust and not coming up for air. The aftershocks of my orgasm pulse through my lower body, ripples of ecstasy like the flapping of butterfly wings.

I trail my hands over the smooth planes of his chest, tracing the hardness of his muscles and the deep grooves. When he finally lets me breathe, my lips are swollen, and my skin is chafed from his stubble.

Leaning my head against the wall, I grip his shoulders. "I need more than your hand."

"If you want my cock, just say so."

"You want a verbal confirmation? I want your cock inside me, Aruan. Now."

The silver of his eyes darkens. "Then take it."

He wants me to admit what I want, to show him I need him, so I do it. When he pulls out his fingers, I grip his cock and guide the head to my entrance. The moment I part my folds with the tip, he doesn't constrain himself any longer. He takes back control, spearing into me with a single thrust. The punch of his hips moves my body up the wall, but I couldn't care if he breaks me in two as long as he doesn't stop.

I thread my fingers through his wet hair, holding on as he pounds pleasure into me. The sensations are overwhelming, and exactly what I asked for. What I want. What I need. Like he demanded, I keep my eyes open, showing him everything he does to me.

The pleasure builds slowly this time. I already know it's going to hit me like a wrecking ball before he ups the pace. I hold on for what it's worth, knowing he's going to destroy me. Again and again.

He wraps an arm around my middle, bracing me for the final blow, and splays the fingers of his other hand over my chin and cheeks. Holding me in place, he kisses me until I taste blood on my tongue—his blood, I realize, where my teeth have cut his lip. I tilt my hips, chasing the friction I need. And then I'm there.

He thrusts deep one last time, setting off my climax as well as his own. Like he promised, he pulls out. Every line on his face draws taut with pleasure. He lets my face go to grab the root of his cock, painting my breasts and stomach with hot ribbons of cum.

I breathe hard in the aftermath, unwilling to let him go, already feeling empty without him inside me. He breaks away first. With a last peck on my lips, he lowers me to my feet.

Rubbing a thumb over the stubble burn on my chin, he asks, "All right?"

I only manage a nod.

The water is already running lukewarm. He makes quick work of washing us both with a bar of soap that smells like cinnamon milk and leaves silky bubbles on my skin. Once he's rinsed us, he pulls the cord again. The holes in the ceiling close up, some kind of panel moving over them.

Instead of using the bath sheets left on a bench, he

uses his evaporation trick to dry us. We dress in the clothes Evolet supplied, and exit the quarters. Thankfully, my aunt isn't there. She must've gotten tired of waiting. Instead, a young boy of about ten is sitting cross-legged on the floor.

He jumps up when we enter the hallway. "I'm here to take you to the celebration."

I look at Aruan. "Celebration?"

"I'm sure your aunt would like to celebrate your return."

I'm nervous again as we follow the boy through a maze of tunnels. On the way, I notice ventilation holes that let fresh air in from outside. We stop in a huge hall painted with the same type of murals as in our quarters. The walls between them are lined with black polished stones that serve as mirrors. Our images are reflected back to us from around the room, creating the same effect as a hall of mirrors.

The wall on the far end dissolves. The boy waves us inside.

I pause at the threshold. Another hall, twice the size of the mirrored one, is filled to the brim with people. They're all wearing white, staring at us with welcoming smiles and friendly expressions.

Something gives in my chest. I breathe a little easier. At the same time, nostalgia overwhelms me, the feeling sweetly painful. I always felt a bit like an alien in Cleveland, as if I were different, but I always thought it was just because I was constantly dying. That definitely differentiates you from the living. Yet here, it's as if a puzzle piece that's been lost for ages has finally been found again, and this is the moment when that piece slides into place.

For the first time since I ended up on Zerra, I feel like I'm home.

CHAPTER 18

ARUAN

Bringing Elsie to Marikanea has an added value, a benefit I didn't bargain on.

For me, it's just a way of keeping her from danger while my father, brothers, and cousins search for the enemy plotting against Elsie.

For her, it's a homecoming, the final realization she needs to admit she belongs here. I should've thought about this simple yet clever strategy earlier. Visiting Marikanea so that an inborn part of her could recognize the place where her roots are ingrained would've helped in motivating her to stay on Zerra, and in essence, with me.

The only reason she's excited about leaving Marikanea is the prospect of seeing her adoptive parents. Otherwise, I'm not sure she would've left willingly. I probably would've had to throw her over my shoulder and carry her away. And if I know her, it would've been with kicking and screaming.

Unknowingly, Evolet fuels Elsie's eagerness to return to Lona by reminding her of her Earth parents when she tells us how Elsie disappeared as a baby. She explains how her late sister came into her daughter's room to feed her baby, only to find the crib empty. They'd searched high and low and finally offered rewards for information about the infant's whereabouts, but no one knew what had happened to the baby.

Some Alit said a Slitheax or a dragon stole her through the open window. Others argued the eastern wind had barreled through the window and carried her away. They speculated that she might've been dropped in the sea or crushed on the cliffs when the wind eventually stilled.

But none of them could've guessed the culprit was the queen of Lona, the mother of Elsie's own mate. Now that I know the truth, it makes perfect sense. My mother could've easily portaled herself here, sent Elsie through another portal to Earth, and been back in Lona before anyone was the wiser.

After promising Evolet and Kal that we'll be back for another visit soon, Elsie takes leave of her newfound family, which includes an abundance of cousins, second cousins, and distant relatives. I can't remember half of their names.

I portal us straight back to my room. Betty flies past the window, welcoming Elsie. The pixie dragon, whom she baptized Pip, seems to have taken up permanent residence in my quarters. Since Elsie is overjoyed to see the sly little creature, I don't protest. Every extra incentive that makes her happy to stay here—with me—helps.

While a squadron of my most trusted guards escorts Elsie on a visit to the Earthlings, I go in search of Kian. I don't like not having Elsie close to me, but there's a good reason I don't want her to be present for our conversation.

Kian is leaving my father's quarters, where he's been in council with the king and Suno, when I run into him in the hallway.

"Here," he says, pulling me into an empty room before sealing the archway.

"What have you found?" I ask, searching the bond to assure myself that Elsie is safe.

For the moment, she's happy, or as happy as she can be under the circumstances, so I trust my guards to protect her with their lives while I interrogate my brother.

"Nothing." He watches me with a steady gaze. "Which is a big revelation in itself."

Beyond frustrated and not a little impatient, I ask in a measured tone, "How the dragon can nothing be big?"

"I read the mind of every person in the palace, yet no one was near the bridge the morning Elsie took the Earthlings out there."

I walk to the window and grip the ledge hard as I study the bridge that runs to the other side of the cliff. "It had to have been someone in the palace. The bridge was fine the night before. Mother walked out on it for a stroll with our aunts, and we had no visitors." Turning to face Kian, I express the ugly thought that's been lodged inside my head since the incident. "Unless Mother..." I don't even dare to say the rest.

He crosses his arms, not denying or confirming the possibility.

"Did you read her mind?" I ask.

"You know she blocks me from reading everything, although she can't expel me as thoroughly as you can."

"So you think...?" I leave the rest hanging.

"I don't think it was her."

"Why not? She's done it before."

Kian widens his stance. "She's too invested in the new alliance she's forged with Evolet. I doubt she'd jeopardize that."

"Then what is this big revelation of yours?"

He drops his arms to his sides, comes closer, and says in a lowered voice, "The big revelation is, brother, that whoever it was is strong enough to prevent me from reading those memories in his mind."

"Or her."

"Right." He continues in a voice that doesn't carry far enough to be overheard by any eavesdroppers on the other side of the wall, "Whoever it was, what matters is that he—or she—is *very* strong."

The way he emphasizes the word gives me pause. "What are you saying?"

"You block me from reading anything in your mind. Father mirrors certain memories, trying to trick me. Mother can filter out some events, but they leave a blank that lets me know some of her recollections are purposefully missing. But there's another scenario I hadn't considered before. What if someone can change his memories to reflect what he wants me to see?"

"Twisting the truth? An Alit can lie with his words but not with his mind. You told me so yourself."

"Unless that Alit has a very strong mind power."

I reflect on that for a moment. "No one with such a selective mind power exists."

His lips curve into a humorless smile. "Not that we know of."

"You think the guilty party is hiding among us, right under our noses."

"There's no other explanation."

"That's your big revelation?"

"Think about it, Aruan. You interrogated everyone. I read their minds. Not having found anything is an answer in itself."

"Tarix? You always say you're battling to read his mind."

"He's vague, but not *that* vague. However, at this stage, I think you'd be wise to consider everyone a suspect."

"That doesn't help much," I say grimly. "Which means we're back to square one."

"Maybe we've been asking the wrong questions and using the wrong methods. Instead of looking for the guilty party by reading minds, we should use logic. Who knew that Elsie would be on the bridge that morning, and who wants to see her gone?"

I stab my fingers into my hair. "Anyone could've found out she'd be going there. You know how the walls have ears." My smile is hard. "As for wanting her gone, that makes up the entire population of Lona."

"You're exaggerating."

"You didn't see how the village kids reacted to her. They're frightened out of their wits every time she happens to cross their path."

He studies me. "Why?"

"You know why. It's because of the prophecy. Even our own mother acted in the name of that cursed prediction."

"Only the supporters of the scrolls believe in the prophecy."

"There are many in the palace," I say dryly. "Mother and her advisor, for starters. Father and most of the royals."

"But not Suno, not our siblings, and not *all* the royals."

"Great." I pace the floor. "That eliminates a handful of people at most."

He follows my agitated movement with his gaze. "That's why we have to set a trap."

I stop dead. "No." My reply is harsh. "I will not use my mate as bait. It's much too dangerous."

He watches me with that habitual eerie expressionlessness in his eyes. "Do you have a better plan?"

I grit my teeth because I don't. As much as I hate to admit it, we're at a dead end. Whoever is trying to kill

Elsie, for whatever reason, isn't going to give up. The multiple attempts on her life are proof of that. He'll continue until he succeeds.

My power surfaces at the thought, anger pushing up inside me until cracks run through the walls and every window in the room explodes.

Kian stands motionless in the midst of the chaos, not showing any reaction to my loss of control. Anyone else would've condemned me or told me how this little demonstration plays into the hands of the believers. His lack of emotion serves to calm me, helping me to force the uninvited violence down.

Neither of us says anything as I mend the cracks and fix the windows. If only it were that easy to fix the problems I'm facing. I haven't even started on the slave-trading operation yet. Elsie remains my priority. I won't rest until I find the enemy trying to hurt her.

"How do you want to move forward?" Kian asks.

Knowing I can trust my brother, I put him in charge of the investigation while I kept Elsie in Marikanea. I'd hoped he would've sniffed out the perpetrator by now, but if he's right and someone is clever enough to twist the truth in their memories, we have to change tactics.

"I want every person in the palace watched," I bite out. "I want to know everything about everyone, down to what they eat for breakfast, lunch, and dinner."

"You want me to put spies on the royals?"

I give him a hard look, leaving no doubt about my meaning. "*Everyone.*"

"That's plenty of Alit. We'll need a lot of spies."

My chuckle is wry. "I'm not increasing the risk by bringing more people into the palace, and I don't trust anyone except for the guards I vetted myself. Present company excluded, of course."

"So who will handle this?"

I grip his shoulder. "You, me, and a few guards."

He lets out a long breath. "You should consider pulling Vitai and Gaia in. There's too much ground to cover for just the two of us."

I pull my lips back into a dark grin. "Who needs sleep?" I didn't enhance my senses to hear and see through walls for nothing.

A portal appears in the center of the floor. Jaw ticking, I release Kian.

My mother steps through the portal with Tarix short on her heels. "Aruan." She nods in greeting, wisely not trying to hug me.

I'm not sure how long it's going to take before I can forgive her for what she did. Maybe an eternity.

"They told me you were home." Her smile is stiff. Uncertain. "How was your visit?"

"Good," I say, not giving her more. "Is there something you wanted?"

She folds her hands in front of her, her posture the epitome of serenity and innocence. "It's time. I'm sending the humans home." She faces Kian. "Your father and our advisors agreed it's best if they don't remember Zerra."

"You want me to erase those memories," Kian says.

Not deeming it necessary to confirm the statement, she addresses me. "It's time for Elsie too."

Time for Elsie to pay her adoptive parents a visit.

Without another word, she turns around and leaves through the portal she left open.

Tarix glances at a few small pieces of glass that remained forgotten on the floor when I repaired the windows I'd broken. His gaze flits between the shards and my face as he hurries after my mother.

When I look at Kian, he's assessing me.

"What?" I snap.

"How much are you going to tell her parents?"

"You mean the people who raised her."

"Yes." He continues with the same monotonous intonation, "Her parents."

"Just what they need to know."

"That their daughter is a powerful Alit mated to a prince and now living on Zerra?"

I raise a brow. "And?"

"That's more or less everything they were never supposed to know."

"And?" I repeat.

"Are you sure in doing that you're not signing their death sentence?"

I curl my fingers into fists. "If anyone touches them, they touch me."

He pats my shoulder. "Just make sure everyone knows that." He heads for the archway and pauses at the threshold. "You coming? I thought you'd be excited for a chance to see Earth."

I throw him a crude sign, which only makes him chuckle.

When Kian walks into the hallway, I go after him. Like all Alit children, I'd been curious about Earth when I was younger. But after Elsie's alleged death, my curiosity diminished. I lost interest in just about everything. It took all my energy to cling to sanity and be the ruler Zerra needs. Not a day went by that I didn't fight the numbness that had been steadily twisting around my soul like a vine, choking off the emotions I had left.

But now I feel again, and I want to know everything, especially if it concerns Elsie. I want to see the home in which she grew up and meet her adoptive parents. And that's exactly what I will do shortly.

I'm only a few stairs and a portal away from Earth, but before I go, there's something I need to do.

Catching up with Kian, I order, "You're going to give me the ability to speak English."

CHAPTER 19
ELSIE

Eucabeth clings to me. "No." Her whisper is frantic. "I don't want my memory wiped."

The king, the queen, Kian, Aruan, and the group of ex-slaves look on with expressions varying from concern to unease. The king's narrow-eyed scrutiny worries me the most. Thankfully, Vitai hasn't come to see the humans off. His presence would've only made the situation worse for Eucabeth.

I grip her shoulders and try to reason with her, keeping my voice down. "I know why you're fighting so hard against the inevitable, but there's no other way."

She stills. "I can't forget him, Elsie. I don't want to."

I understand why she needs to remember Vitai. However, the queen was clear about the conditions of sending them home.

Rubbing Eucabeth's arms, I ask gently, "Won't it be better like this?"

She purses her lips. "I'd rather live with the pain than without the memory."

Yes, I get that too. I would've felt the same. But if Kian doesn't delete her memories of Zerra, she can't go home. And she can't stay here. Which will leave the king and queen with only one option, one I don't want to think about.

"You don't have a choice." I emphasize the statement with a gentle shake. "Please, Eucabeth. Don't throw away a chance at a new life. You haven't come this far and survived everything you have just to…" I swallow the rest of my sentence, unable to say it out loud.

Even as she lifts her chin with determination, reality settles in her eyes. Eucabeth is a fighter. She's not going to sacrifice her life for the sake of a memory, no matter how strong her attraction to Vitai is. I'm hoping it's just a fixation because he healed her. I want nothing more for her than to move on and find someone else.

"It's time," the queen says for a second time, her tone insistent.

I take Eucabeth's hand and wipe away the tears that roll over her cheeks. "You have to be strong. Let the last thing they see be your smile."

She squares her shoulders and takes a shaky breath.

"That's better." I lead her toward the group. "I'm going to miss you."

Irina comes up and puts an arm around Eucabeth's shoulders.

I shoot Irina a grateful look. "I'll miss all of you."

"Even me?" Sandy asks, walking to my side.

I take in her glowing complexion. "I should've told you."

"I understand why you didn't." She pulls me in for a quick hug. "I overreacted, hun. It just came as a shock."

"I know," I say. "I hope you'll always be happy. I have no doubt you'll make a success of whatever you decide to do."

"Hell, yes." She juts out a hip. "That sounds just about right."

"I'm not going to miss these memories for a second," Alexa says. "I'm only too grateful to forget this part of my life."

"What happens when we arrive on Earth?" Karl asks. "Where will we be? Can we pick a destination, or will you drop us somewhere randomly? How much will we remember of our history on Earth?"

I repeat what Aruan's mother explained to me. "You'll be left where you were taken, and you'll remember everything up to that point, minus the abduction. It'll be like selective amnesia. But you'll remember your name, where you live, who your family is, and everything stored in your memory before you came here."

"What will we tell people?" Alexa asks.

"You won't know what to tell them," Kian says. "You won't know what happened to you, and you won't understand why you've lost a part of your memory. It'll be just as big a mystery to you as to everyone else."

Karl looks at Kian from under his eyebrows. "So we're just supposed to pick up the pieces and carry on?"

"How you live your life is up to you," Kian says with a flat smile.

"We'd better get going," the queen tells me.

"Wait." Karl holds up a hand. "How will your queen know where we were taken from?"

"I'll show her," Kian says. "I already know the places where the Phaelix snatched you from reading your minds."

Alexa shivers visibly. "That's so freaky. Can we just get this over with?"

We hug each other, wiping away tears as we say goodbye. Alexa volunteers to go first. The queen calls up a portal. Kian is at her side, presumably planting the location in her mind.

Alexa steps through the portal, and then she's gone.

One by one, they vanish into thin air, and then it's our turn.

Aruan takes my hand and gives me a warm smile. "Ready?"

I nod even though nerves are twisting my insides. "How do we get back to Lona?"

"I'll open a portal for you by sunset," the queen says. "Be ready at exactly the same place where you'll arrive."

I take a deep breath, remembering how unpleasant the journey to Zerra was—not that a little discomfort, or anything else for that matter, will stop me from seeing my parents.

Kian pats Aruan's shoulder. "Don't make me come look for you."

"Let's hope that won't be necessary," the king says with a look of warning directed at Aruan.

The queen opens the portal. The swirling lights run in a circle. Aruan pulls me forward. I hold my breath as I follow him into the portal, hardly able to contain my excitement.

A burst of light blinds me. I tighten my hold on Aruan's hand as we're sucked into a vortex. It feels as if my body is being pulled apart. In that moment, the thought that goes through my mind isn't life-altering or philosophical but a mundane question.

What day of the week is it? What is the date? I've lost track of time since landing on Zerra—if time even flows the same on Earth as it does there. Where will my parents be?

As it turns out, they're at home, preparing lunch in the kitchen when I wake up on the floor in my living room. Pans clang together, and the fridge door squeaks familiarly as someone opens it.

"Hold on," a man says—my dad. "Did you hear something?"

"It sounded like a thump," my mom replies, her tone apprehensive.

Aruan is crouching next to me, stroking my cheek while peering into my eyes.

"All right?" he asks in a soft voice.

I let him help me sit up, mumbling under my breath, "I think so."

I look around. The living room is exactly as I remember it. The painting of an Italian summer scene hangs slightly askew on the wall. The beige sofa with the brown-and-red throw cushions still has a dent in the seat on the right where Dad likes to sit and read. A pile of books is stacked on the coffee table. The cozy mystery on the top will be Mom's. The *Twenty-first Century Cosmic Science* lying on one side will be Dad's.

Footsteps fall on the floor of the kitchen. My heart starts thumping, threatening to burst out of my chest. Aruan takes my elbow and helps me to my feet. I blink, afraid that the room will vanish and I'll wake up from a dream, but the space remains unchanged.

Dad appears in the doorframe of the kitchen, carrying Mom's carving knife in one hand. He looks the same and simultaneously different. He's grown thinner. His hair is the same brown that's graying at the temples, but the shadows under his eyes are new.

Emotions crash into me, compassion, elation, relief, and trepidation warring inside me. Instinctively, I reach for Aruan's hand. He squeezes my fingers, reminding me that he's right here… that he'll always be there for me when I need him.

"Dad?" I croak.

The knife drops from his hand and falls soundlessly on the carpet. He's frozen in place, his face as white as if he's staring at a ghost.

"What is it?" Mom asks in alarm, appearing behind him with her phone in her hand.

She stills too, her lips parting but no sound leaving

her mouth. She's grayer than I remember. Her face is gaunt, and her cheeks are hollow. It looks as if she's aged ten years in a few weeks.

"Mom? Dad?" I inch closer. "It's me, Elsie."

"Is this real?" Mom's eyes are wide with shock. "Am I looking at a spirit?"

"It's me," I repeat, smiling through the tears that spring to my eyes. "I'm very much alive."

My dad opens and closes his mouth. "How is this possible?" He looks at Aruan, his shoulders tensing. "Who's this man?"

"I can explain." I hold up a hand when my mom starts swiping a finger over her phone. "Please, Mom. Put the phone down. No one can know we're here, or I'll have to leave."

At "leave," my mom lowers her phone with a shaky hand. Her lips tremble as she looks between me and Aruan. "Elsie? Is it really you?"

"In the flesh." I smile at Aruan. "And this is Aruan, my… boyfriend."

Dad's face is a mask of confusion. "You ran away?"

"No." I edge closer. "It's a lot more complicated than that."

"I don't understand," Mom says, her voice close to breaking. She looks me up and down. "You look so… healthy."

Dad takes in my shirt, pants, and boots before turning a gaze on Aruan's tunic. "Why are you dressed like that?"

"I'd like to explain," I say, "but I think you need to sit down."

Dad gives in first, overcoming his disbelief to rush forward and wrap me up in a fierce hug. He sets me free and holds me at arm's length. "Elsie? Is it *really* you?"

"Yes," I whisper, blinking away my tears.

Mom lets out a sob and clamps a hand over her mouth.

"It's okay, Mom. I'm okay. Everything is going to be okay."

She crosses the floor like a sleepwalker and stops in front of me. Emotions wash over her features as she tilts her face and studies me. She shakes her head in disbelief, and then she pulls me in for a hug too, sobs racking her frail shoulders.

We hold each other for a long moment as I try to soothe her. Aruan looks on from a distance, considerately giving us space.

Mom pulls away first, wiping her eyes and sniffing as she says again, "I don't understand."

I take her hand and lead her to the sofa. She sits down with her phone clutched in her lap. Dad comes over and plops down next to her, not taking his eyes off of me. I take the sofa facing theirs and pat the seat next to me.

When Aruan has taken a seat, I tell them more or less everything, minus the fact that I'm still Aruan's captive of sorts. I start at the beginning and end with how we got here. They listen quietly, letting me tell my incredible tale without interrupting me once. All the while, they stare at me as if I'm an apparition. It's only when I'm done that they look at each other.

"I'm sorry." Dad faces me slowly again. "The story you told is hard to believe."

"Ask me anything," I say. "I'll do my best to clarify it for you."

They have a ton of questions, which I answer as honestly as I can. Mom wants to know where Zerra is because the concept of a parallel world sounds too fantastical to her. Dad wants to know how the so-called Alit powers work, so I tell him about my theories about AI and the advanced ancient civilization on Zerra.

When Mom starts wondering out loud if I could be an alien clone of her daughter, I remind them of childhood incidents that only I can know about, such as the time during that camping trip when Mom doused me in mosquito repellent to which I developed an allergic reaction.

By the time the clock on the wall says we've spoken for over an hour and they're still frightened and confused, Aruan cups my nape to draw my attention. "I think your parents need a demonstration."

Mom and Dad watch him with tense shoulders and pale faces.

He turns his gaze on the curtains. They dissolve and reassemble in a snazzy coat on Mom's body. She jumps to her feet, dropping her phone in the process. Dad stares open-mouthed at the floral curtains she's wearing.

"I-I don't know—" She presses her fingertips on her mouth, trembling as she looks down at herself. "How—?"

"Good heavens," Dad mutters.

I go to the window and open it. A white-throated sparrow sits in the tree on the front lawn. "Do you see that bird over there?" I point in that direction. "What would you like it to do?"

Dad bounces his leg. He thinks for a moment before saying, "I want it to bring two leaves to me."

"Two, huh?" I laugh. "You've always been a stickler for leaving absolutely no cause for doubt."

The bird does what I command it to do, bringing first one leaf and then a second one that it drops on Dad's lap.

"Do you need more proof?" I ask gently.

They look at each other again. After a moment, Dad jerks his head sideways, which I take as a no.

Mom falls into her seat again, covering her mouth with a shaky hand. "It's true. You're not from Earth. Dear god, Elsie… you were never from Earth."

"But she's alive," Dad says, having a hard time keeping his voice from breaking. "Alive and well."

"I am. And I'm so sorry, Mom, Dad. I'm really sorry for making you worry."

"It…" Mom lets out a sniffle. "It's not your fault."

Dad remains the logical one, even in the midst of

the unreal situation. "The important thing is, you're here now. Does this mean you're coming home?"

I inhale deeply, bracing myself for telling a white lie. "I love you very much. You know that. But on Zerra, I'm strong and healthy."

"Not dying," Dad says.

"Exactly." I hold out my arms, displaying my new body. "Feeling better than ever. I can run and climb stairs without getting tired. I even have an appetite."

Mom gives me a teary-eyed look. "We'd never deny you that, Elsie. That's all we've ever wanted for you."

"I know," I whisper, biting my cheek on the inside not to cry.

She shrugs out of the coat and turns her face to Aruan with a lifted chin. "If you don't mind, I'd like my curtains back."

He obliges with a smile. "Of course."

In no time, the curtains are back in front of the windows.

"You have to keep everything I've told you to yourself," I say. "You understand why, right?"

Mom bobs her head up and down. Dad makes a sound of agreement.

Mom's question wavers. "Are you happy?"

My smile freezes in place, becoming stilted. "Very." I'm not going to put them through more pain by telling them Aruan will never let me leave. That there *is* no choice but to stay.

Dad glances at Aruan. "This is what you want?"

Aruan puts a hand on my knee. The touch is light but the warning it carries is clear.

"Yes," I lie.

It's so much more complicated than what I want. I've decided to stay because I don't know what will happen to Zerra if I leave, and I don't want to hurt Aruan. I can't stand the thought of him suffering. A voice in the back of my head says those are good reasons but not necessarily the right reasons.

"Well." Mom sniffles some more as she looks at Dad again. "That's all we want for you, honey."

Dad adjusts his glasses. "I have to admit, it's a lot to take in. It's so…"

Aruan's smile is friendly. "Farfetched?"

Despite the fact that Aruan is a giant compared to my dad, Dad nails him with a look as he poses a question at me. "Is he treating you well?"

"The way you deserve to be treated?" Mom pipes in.

"I wouldn't be here with you if it weren't for Aruan," I say. "He convinced his mother to make an exception to their no-contact policy and open a portal for us."

Mom gets up and walks to Aruan. Like a gentleman, he stands.

"Thank you." Her voice is tremulous. "Thank you for bringing our daughter home."

Before he knows what's hit him, Mom drags him into one of her smothering hugs. He stands there helplessly with his arms hanging at his sides as she tries to squeeze the air from his lungs. After a moment, he returns her hug awkwardly with a gentle pat on her back.

"Where are my manners?" Mom exclaims, looking flustered as she finally lets him go. "Are you hungry? Would you like something to drink? We were just making lunch."

Aruan's smile is all smooth politeness. "We don't want to inconvenience you."

"Nonsense." Mom bustles toward the kitchen. "You could never put us out. Why don't you come through to the kitchen while I throw something together?"

"What day is it?" I ask.

Mom stops and frowns. "It's Wednesday."

"Why aren't you at work?"

She fluffs out her hair, glancing at Dad. "We took some time off after… you know."

"I'm so sorry." I can't say that enough.

Continuing on her way, she says in a bright voice, "Let's focus on the moment. We don't want to miss out on a second of having you here." She spins around on the doorstep. "How long are you staying?"

"Only for the day," I say, hating how disappointed she looks.

She pulls her back straight. "Then we'd better make the most of it."

Dad stands and wipes his palms on his trousers. "I can grill a few steaks on the barbecue."

"That's a great idea." Mom beams. "I'll make the potato salad you like so much, Elsie."

"Care to give me a hand, Aruan?" Dad asks.

Uh-oh. I feel a lecture coming.

Aruan raises a brow in my direction.

I shrug, grinning as I watch him follow Dad to the patio like someone walking into a lion's den.

We spend a congenial afternoon together. Mom tells me about all the news I've missed out on, and Dad peppers Aruan with questions about his family and home. I soak up every minute of my parents' presence, basking in how Mom tries to show her gratitude and love by feeding us until we can't take another bite.

Aruan skillfully skirts around the questions my mom and dad ask about Zerra and its fauna and flora, not giving away more than necessary. I'm loving every second, but the closer it gets to sunset, the tenser I grow.

"Mom." I cup her hand where she sits next to me.

She cuts short her blabbering about a new season of a television series I used to love.

When I have her attention, I say carefully, "We have to go soon."

She shoots Aruan a panicked look. "Already?"

Dad remains stoically quiet, but I don't miss the strain that sets in around his mouth.

"We only have until sunset," I say, hating that I have to hurt them again when I leave.

Dad looks at Aruan. "Take good care of our daughter."

"I will." Aruan nods at my parents. "I give you my word."

"Will you come visit us again?" Mom asks in a hopeful tone.

Biting my lip, I admit, "I don't know if that will be possible. Aruan's mother is the only Alit who can create portals to Earth for us, but as I told you, it's forbidden. She made a huge concession for us today."

At my mom's dejected expression and the way my father's face drops, Aruan says, "But I'll ask her."

I look at him quickly. He'll do that for me?

"Though I can't promise anything," he says.

Gratitude warms my heart. I know how much it will mean to my parents if he manages to convince his mother to let us see them again.

He stretches his arm along the back of the sofa and draws circles with a finger over my shoulder, a touch that's meant to comfort me for the goodbyes I'm about to say.

The moment arrives too soon. Mom tries hard not to cry. Even Dad has to wipe something from his eye as he shakes Aruan's hand—after explaining how the greeting is done on Earth—and makes Aruan swear again that he'll take care of me. Mom is her usual selfless self, telling me that she's happy for me.

The lights appear in the living room before I'm ready. Mom and Dad put their arms around one another's waists, supporting each other as Aruan takes my hand and leads me to the portal.

I hang back, tears burning behind my eyes. I promised myself I wasn't going to cry. Saying goodbye is hard enough for my parents. I don't want to make this more difficult for them.

"It's okay," Mom says bravely, smiling through her tears. "We love you, honey."

"I love you too." I look between them. "I hope you'll always remember that."

Dad's nod is jerky, his Adam's apple bobbing as he swallows.

"Come, my sweet." Aruan ushers me forward with a hand on my lower back. "It was a pleasure to meet you," he says with a last tilt of his head.

My tears fall freely when we enter the portal. I burn every second of our visit into my memory so that I can revisit the time we spent together when I miss Mom and Dad too much.

The light disperses around us. Just before the vacuum sucks us in, another circle appears within our circle, the two spheres colliding.

Panic gets the better of me. What's going on? Is the portal malfunctioning?

Next to me, Aruan tenses.

And then I see it, a form taking shape in front of us.

I blink. I must be mistaken. It's impossible. But the Phaelix that materializes is very much real. His red eyes bulge as he notices us. He tries to backtrack, but it's too late. Aruan has already locked his fingers around the wrist of the Phaelix, pulling the screaming lizard with us back to Zerra.

CHAPTER 20
ARUAN

The Phaelix kicks and claws as we arrive in my mother's quarters. I'm holding Elsie's hand on one side, and on the other, my fingers are locked in an iron grip around his thin, scaly wrist.

My mother, who sits on her dragon chair, gives a start. My father stands next to her. He takes a menacing step toward us, his dagger already pulled.

My mother's knuckles turn white where she grips the armrests, her face pale with shock. "What in the name of the dragons…? You've come from Earth. Through my portal."

The implication hangs thick in the air. A Phaelix somehow crossed paths with us in an open portal to Earth.

I confirm their wildest guess. "We ran into a visitor on our way back."

My father bares his teeth.

"All right?" I ask Elsie.

I only let her go when she nods.

The Phaelix screams as I drag him to the center of the floor.

"What's the meaning of this?" my father asks.

I force the Phaelix to his knees by the back of his neck. He stares up at me with hatred simmering in his blood-red eyes.

My mother stands, her back straight and stiff. "What happened?"

"Our portals collided." I give the vermin a shake. "He was on his way in just as we were leaving."

"How is this possible?" my father asks.

"Portals bend toward one another," my mother says. "If they're created close enough to each another, one vortex will pull the other one in and vice versa."

"Like magnets," Elsie muses.

My father stares at me. "Who in the dragon created a portal for him? The Phaelix don't have powers. He couldn't have done it himself."

I grin at the Phaelix. "That's what I'm going to find out."

The Phaelix glowers at me.

I switch to his language. "What's your business on Earth?" I already have a good idea, but I want confirmation.

He spits a guttural curse at me.

My mother and father are fluent in the Phaelix tongue. They understand what I'm saying. Elsie doesn't. I repeat the question in our language.

The Phaelix pulls his lips away from his sharp teeth, offering me a sneer for an answer.

I let his nape go with a shove and catch his wrist in another bruising grip. "This is what's going to happen. You're going to tell me everything I want to know, or I'm going to melt you bit by bit, starting with your fingers and your toes."

He snaps his teeth at me like a rabid dragon.

"Fine." I lift his arm and squeeze hard enough to break his bones. "We'll do this your way."

The pain forces him to splay his fingers. He swallows the agony down, his throat rippling and his teeth clacking with the effort.

He's a tough one. Let's see how long he lasts.

I focus my power on his little finger. His scaly flesh bubbles, his sharp claw dropping with a glob of goo and a clunk on the ground. His chilling scream pierces the air as he grabs my fingers and tries to dislodge my hold on his wrist. When that doesn't work, he simply clings to his arm, holding it up in the air as he whines and wheezes.

"Don't make me ask you twice, Phaelix. For every breath I have to waste, I'll take another finger."

He heaves, sucking air through his teeth.

"Did you go to Earth to bring back a human slave?" I ask.

"Yes," he hisses. "Yesss."

"For whom?"

"For me." He snaps at me again, seemingly unable to resist biting like an animal. "For me."

My father crosses the floor and stops short of the Phaelix, forcing him to crane his neck to look at my father. "To do what with?"

"To sell," he says, writhing in my hold.

"Where?" I ask. "I destroyed the market."

"A new market." He spits at my feet. "New."

"Where?" I ask again, melting the first digit of his index finger for making me repeat myself.

He howls in agony, twisting and throwing back his head.

"You'd better answer him," my father says. "Before you run out of fingers."

"An island on the lake." He rocks himself while shooting daggers at me with his eyes. "The lake."

"What did he say?" Elsie asks.

I tell her.

"The barge," she cries out. "That's where Sandy and the others came from when you found me on that shore!"

"I know where it is." My mother gets up and walks to us. "There's only one island big enough on a lake to house a slave market."

"I'll send Kian and a team of guards." My father pushes a fist under the Phaelix's chin, forcing the Phaelix to meet his gaze. "How many slaves are still on Zerra?"

"Not a lot." The Phaelix bends his neck from side to side when my father lets him go. "Not a lot."

"How many?" I bite out.

The Phaelix quickly lifts his free hand, showing three clawed fingers.

My father translates for Elsie.

"What are you selling them for?" she asks.

My mother tears her gaze from the Phaelix to face Elsie. "Is that important?"

"It could be," Elsie says.

I translate the question and shake the Phaelix again. "Answer her."

"For opals." He pulls his eyes into slits. "Opals."

I tell her what he said.

Elsie considers that for a moment. "To do what with?"

I ask him in his language.

"For war." He utters a high-pitched laugh. "To buy weapons. For war."

My father nudges him with the tip of his boot. "Against whom?"

I already know the answer. "Us." I squeeze harder, making him mewl. "Isn't that so?"

His silence says everything.

My father's curse is quiet but lethal. He tightens his grip on the shaft of his dagger and curls the fingers of his other hand into a fist. His muscles tense as he prepares to pounce.

My mother touches my father's arm. "Don't kill him. We still need information." Contempt radiates from her as she comes to stand in front of the Phaelix. "Who created that portal for you?"

He looks between us, grinning through his cooked teeth.

"Was it someone from Lona?" My mother's upper lip curls. "Or from another kingdom?"

The moment seems to suspend in time as the silence stretches. For the first time, the Phaelix looks truly scared.

I melt another finger.

He howls and swears at me, spitting out curses with saliva.

"He's of no use to us," I say. "I'll take him to the cell where I can melt him slowly over days."

"No melting," he whines. "No more melting."

I put my face in his and melt a thumb. "That's for the repetition."

"It was Arix," he screams. "Arix! Arix makes the portals. Arix!"

My mother and I look at each other.

"There's no Arix in Lona," my mother says. "That's not even a name."

"Yes," the Phaelix cries. "Arix!" He resorts to sobbing. "Arix."

It hits me at the same time as my father slowly says, "Tarix?"

"Yes!" The Phaelix bounces on his knees. "Arix. Arix." He points a finger at my father. "Arix."

My mother stumbles back a step, her cheeks deathly pale.

"Tarix?" Elsie says as if she has to push the name from her lips.

My father wipes a hand over his brow. My mother walks with stilted steps to the table. She trips over her own feet but rightens herself and carries on. She's like a dead person, mechanically lifting a carafe and pouring wine into a goblet before downing the drink in one go.

"That son of a dragon," my father says through clenched teeth.

Cold fury pushes up inside me. "Where is he?"

My mother whirls around. "Why would he do that? What could he get out of such an act of treason except a painful execution?" She looks at my father. "Do you believe him?"

Anger draws stark lines over my father's face. "Why would he lie?"

I drag the Phaelix to his feet. "I'll throw him in the cell, and then I'm going to get some answers. Where is he—Tarix?"

"I don't know," my mother says. "We finished our official business this afternoon. He could be anywhere in the palace."

I exchange a look with my father. "Don't let anyone leave."

He sheathes his dagger. "I'll tell Kian, Vitai, and Gaia."

I don't bother dragging the sack of shit through the hallways. I hold out a hand to Elsie and open a portal. We enter it, dragging the Phaelix along, and exit on the underground level where the cells are located. We haven't used them in many moon cycles. There was never any need.

I throw the Phaelix into one of the cells. He kneels on the floor, cradling his injured hand against his chest while spitting and snapping his teeth. Not sparing him another glance, I close the archway and place a seal on the cell to prevent him from leaving and anyone else from getting in. We don't want a rescue party—such as Tarix—to free him.

My heart is like ice in my chest as I lead Elsie upstairs. My mother trusted Tarix. I didn't like him, but I never suspected a thing. He hid his talents well.

Once we exit on the level of the Great Hall, I head straight to Tarix's quarters, only to find them empty.

I stop a servant who walks past with a pile of clean bath sheets in his arms. "Have you seen Tarix?"

"Your Highness." The servant bows. "He left earlier this evening to visit the sacred site."

Of course. With a free pass from my mother, Tarix is a regular there. He's one of the staunch believers.

Gaia comes running up, her face drawn and pale. "Mother just told me. She's pulling up portals, trying to find him. What can I do to help?"

"Search the palace." I turn Elsie to me with my hands on her shoulders. "Will you help her?"

She nods tersely. "Tomorrow, when it's light, I'll call Betty. It'll be easier to search from the sky."

"Let's hope that won't be necessary. I want that son of a dragon found before daylight." I kiss her on the lips before letting her go. "Be careful."

She wraps her fingers around my hand. "You too."

Gaia takes off in the direction of the banquet hall. Elsie holds on for a moment longer, our fingertips brushing as I finally break our contact.

When I pull up a portal to take me to the sacred site, I focus hard on keeping my power in check. Betrayal burns hot in my gut. When I get my hands on Tarix, I'll make him regret every act of treason he's committed against our people. Theories are forming in my head. Did he instigate the Phaelix attack? If so, why would he want to overthrow our rule? What, except for power, can he gain from killing his own flesh and blood? He can't be stupid enough to believe the Phaelix will let him rule once they've gotten rid of the rest of us. They'll crush him like the insect he is, wiping away his existence like a dirty stain.

The guard jumps at attention when I walk out from the portal at the site.

"Tarix," I say, not needing to explain.

The guard's chin trembles. "He left a short while ago, Your Highness."

I gnash my teeth. "Did he say where he was going?"

"No, Your Highness."

And his mind is too vague for Kian to find him.

I stomp up the path, heading for the village. He could be hiding out there. But after a long time of asking around, I know I'm not going to find him there.

In a rare act, I open my mind to Kian.

Nothing.

I reach out to Elsie via our bond and find the same—there's no sign of my cousin.

If my mother can't find him either, there's only one explanation. He's hiding, and he's hiding well. Somehow, he knows we're on to him. He must've seen us coming when his portal collided with ours.

It's almost the middle of the night, but I portal myself to the nearest Phaelix village.

I'll find that traitor if it's the last thing I do.

CHAPTER 21
ELSIE

Aruan hasn't returned all night. I've been pacing his quarters, waiting for daylight so I can start my own search. I have to keep busy, or I'll go out of my mind with worry. Gaia assured me her brother will be fine. I know he will be. Tarix is no match for him. Neither is an army of Phaelix. I've seen what Aruan does to them when they dare to attack. Still, it doesn't stop me from fretting about the man I've slowly but surely fallen for.

At dawn, Aruan sends word via a runner—a man with the power to run faster than a high-speed train—that he's searching the villages farther north. Kian and the royal guards return from the island with the rescued slaves at sunrise. The queen sends them back to their homes after Kian has wiped their memories. The king leaves with a squadron of guards to comb through the southern villages while the queen opens portals all over Zerra to find her rogue advisor.

I set out after breakfast, flying on Betty's back all the way to the Phaelix settlement where they captured me, but the village is deserted. I scout the surroundings until the sun sits high in the sky, giving Betty frequent breaks to rest.

When I finally return to the Water Palace in the late afternoon, I'm dusty and tired with nothing but a sunburned face to show for my efforts. I prod our bond, needing to reassure myself that Aruan is fine. As always, the connection is vague, but it assures me that he's safe and well.

I'm in the cleansing room, splashing cold water on my face when the archway dissolves and the queen appears in our room.

My heart jostles in my chest, my mind screeching to a halt as I realize I've just thought about the room as *ours*. Not just Aruan's.

"Your Highness," I say, drying my hands on a cloth and throwing it in the wicker basket before entering the room. "Is everything all right? Is there news from Aruan?"

She walks toward me, the skirt of her silver dress brushing her ankles with a soft swish of fabric. Taking both my hands, she says, "Aruan is fine."

I tense. She's never touched me like this—as if she needs to support me for bad news. "Then what is it?"

The light in her eyes is compassionate. Sympathetic. "Once a portal has been opened to Earth, it leaves a residual energy I can sense with my power. As there's no sign of Tarix in Lona, I've been following all the portals that have been opened to Earth recently in the hope of finding a trace of him."

"Yes?" I say, holding my breath.

Her features crumble. Her expression is pitiful as she says after a slight hesitation, "One of them led to where I left you and Aruan."

I go cold. My stomach tightens with a horrible foreboding. "My parents' house?"

She blows out a breath. "Yes."

I stare at her, frozen in place as my pulse runs wild. "What happened?"

"There's been an accident." She adds in a soft tone, "A car accident."

"What?" I pull my hands from hers, the action robotic, my breathing mechanical. "How bad is it?"

My heart hammers in my ears as I wait for the verdict, praying with everything I've got, making bargains with gods I don't know and deities I've never believed in.

"I'm afraid your mother is critical."

Critical.

The word registers in my mind, but my brain struggles to process it.

Critical.

That can't be right. I was the one who was supposed to die first. Not my mom.

No, please, not Mom.

"Elsie, I'm sorry."

I steel my spine and force myself to operate past the shock gluing me to the spot. "I have to see her."

"Of course," the queen says gently. "Aruan has to continue the search. He can't go with you, but I'll accompany you to protect you and bring you back."

Now that we know Tarix is the traitor, we have to stand together. The queen needs both Aruan and me more than ever. I don't think she'll harm me.

I grasp the offer with a grateful nod, swallowing down the tension that squeezes like a band around my throat.

She tightens her hold on my hands. "Ready?"

"Hurry," I whisper. "Please."

A portal appears. We're sucked inside, where I break apart with the same ferocity as always, but the emotional pain wreaking havoc inside me is much worse.

I wake up on the floor with Aruan's mother standing over me. Touching my temples, behind which a headache is building, I look around. I'm in a cabin with wooden walls and floors. A single shelf is stacked with cooking pots. A foldout sofa faces a cold fireplace. The windows are barred with shutters, just enough daylight spilling through the cracks to illuminate the space.

This isn't my parents' living room. I'm about to tell the queen so when, right in front of my eyes, she changes shape.

What the…?

I scurry backward like a crab on my palms and heels. She keeps on transforming like a snake shedding its skin until Tarix looms over me.

I pinch my eyes shut, but when I open them, the man in front of me isn't a vision or a trick of the light. It's truly him.

How did he do that? He dismantled and reassembled his organic matter as easily as if he were reprogramming himself.

My heart stutters, my breath catching in my throat. I dare a brief touch, poking his shin with the toe of my boot. Yep. He's definitely real and, sadly, not a figment of my imagination.

I stare up at his neutral expression, trying to sound brave and not as freaked out as I am. "What the hell is going on?"

"Sorry." He grins. "Did I forget to mention one of my many powers?"

"Your many powers?" I parrot, battling to wrap my mind around what's happening.

"The one I broadcast is my extraordinary ability to store information. Here on Earth, you'd call that a photographic memory. That's why Nia finds me so useful. I'm a walking library, to use your Earth terms liberally."

"Let me guess. Your other powers are creating portals and managing freaky impersonations."

"What can I say? As far as portals go, I learned from the best."

My statement comes out as an accusation. "You used your photographic memory to learn how to open portals to Earth from the queen."

He nods. "As for the rest, I improvised."

My heartbeat is a staccato rhythm in my chest. "My mom… She wasn't in an accident."

"No," he drawls. "Obviously not."

Relief crashes through me together with fear. "What do you want?"

"What's best for Zerra."

"Is that why you helped the Phaelix abduct slaves from Earth?" I ask with sarcasm.

Not a single emotion shows on his face. "I did what I had to do."

Using the wall behind me for support, I push to my feet. "To what end? What were you hoping to achieve with such a barbaric crime?"

"The Phaelix agreed to help me, but everything comes at a price."

I gape as the insight hits me. "You were the man Sandy saw negotiating with the Phaelix in the jungle." Loathing pushes up in my throat, leaving a bitter taste on my tongue. "What did they promise you in exchange for human slaves?"

"To help me overthrow the rule in Lona."

I point a finger at him. "It was you. You orchestrated the Phaelix attack." I go still as another thought burrows into my mind. "The poison and the bridge… That was you?"

"I tried so hard to get rid of you, but you kept on persevering like a pesky plague."

"Why?" I ask, breathless now. "Why would you want to get rid of me?"

"Come on, Elsie." He tilts his head. "Isn't it obvious? Everything was going so well until you showed up."

"You don't really want what's best for Zerra." I curl my upper lip. "You're just another power-hungry asshole who wants everything for yourself."

He clicks his tongue. "Now that's not true. Aruan is a non-believer. He disrespects the sacred prophecies of the scrolls. He was never fit to be a leader."

"So you took the task upon yourself." My smile is cold. "For purely selfless reasons."

"Think what you like. My only interest is in protecting Zerra."

The feverish light in his brown eyes is that of a lunatic, a man who believes in his own bullshit.

"Why didn't you just try to kill Aruan?" I utter a laugh. "Oh, yeah, that's right. He would've crushed you like a bug."

"With you out of the picture, my cousin was as good as gone. A stone. Dead to any feelings. I watched him turn into nothing but an empty, useless shell over the years." He says with conviction, "Now that you're gone, he'll go back to that."

"You have no idea." Another hollow laugh tears from my stomach. "You have no idea what you've done."

"I know exactly what I've done. I've saved my world from a pending disaster. I'm preventing a terrible prophecy from coming true." He closes the distance between us and puts a hand on my shoulder. "It's nothing personal. I like you, Elsie. I really do. No, don't look at me like that. It's true. I'm not a monster. It's going to hurt me to kill you, but it has to be done. Nia was on the right track when she got rid of you when you were a baby, but she didn't do a good enough job. She was too weak. She should've done what I'm doing now. If she had the courage it took, we'd never be in this situation. Do you see now? Nia isn't fit to be queen. Lona shouldn't be ruled by weak Alit."

I shake off his touch. "And you're so strong? A man who approves of slavery?"

He sighs. "A necessary evil. I was going to wipe it out once I was in power."

"Without expecting retaliation from the Phaelix? You can't be that dumb."

"The Phaelix need to be converted into believers." He sounds sure of himself. "They'll see the light, just like everyone else."

"So on top of betraying your own family, you're going to take away the Alits' freedom and impose your personal beliefs on them."

"The scrolls are the only way. I've studied them for years. That's how we came about. We have to trust the prophecy."

I chuckle. "The prophecies are subjective interpretations."

"That's your opinion." He frowns. "It's rather sad."

"Aruan will destroy Zerra if I'm gone."

He flashes me a disapproving smile. "Trying to save your own skin? That's very selfish."

"Even if Aruan is out of the picture, which will

never happen, his family will destroy you before you have a chance of taking over the throne."

"I'll just hide out here until the dust settles. The Phaelix don't have powers, but they vastly outnumber the Alit. I'll hit when your mate is at his weakest." He sighs. "Nia was eating right out of my hand. It's a pity you came and spoiled everything just when things were finally going my way."

"If you think about it, that's rather ironic. I would never have returned to Zerra if not for you." I add with a taunting smile, "If you hadn't opened a portal for the Phaelix who kidnapped me, I would've been dead by now. I guess I need to thank you."

He scoffs. "It doesn't matter. Your arrival merely delayed my plans. Yes, things were going so well. Nia is a believer too, thanks to me. Lorak was a tougher cookie, as the expression goes here on Earth." He smiles as if he's very proud of himself for knowing that saying. "But once his mate is dead, killing him will be an act of mercy."

"And Kian, Vitai, and Gaia? What's your plan with them?"

"I can't risk vengeance," he says earnestly.

"How will your mate ever live with you?" I look him up and down. "She'll hate and detest you. She'll be ashamed to be with a traitor."

"I've never claimed her. I've decided to wait until I've put my plan into action. She'll be proud then. She'll walk at the side of the new king of Lona with her head held high."

"You're delusional, Tarix."

"And you, Elsie"—he taps my nose—"are in denial."

I slap his hand away. "Keep your filthy paws off of me."

"I was just trying to lighten the mood." He drops his arm at his side. "Don't worry. I won't let you suffer. I'll make your death quick."

The finality in his statement is like barbed wire hooking into my brain. This is it. The end. He's going to do it now, off me and let my body rot here.

"Wait." I think fast. "I should get a last wish." I need time to think, to come up with a plan. "That's the custom on Earth."

"Yes, I'm familiar with your customs. Of course, the scrolls forbid contact with this world as each planet must evolve as nature intended and no interference should be allowed. I only studied Earth and its history, species, and cultures for informational purposes. It's important to understand the bigger picture if you want to be a good ruler." He sighs. "And good rulers know that customs are important. Rituals and sacred ceremonies are the cornerstones of society. I suppose a last wish is not too much to ask. What do you want?"

"A nice meal." I lick my dry lips. "Pancakes with bacon and syrup. And coffee. God, I miss coffee."

He wrinkles his nose. "I like Earth, to share a secret with you, but I've never understood your vulgar taste in food."

"That's what I grew up with."

"That's what you want?" He judges me openly with

a condescending look. "Not to say goodbye to the people who raised you?"

I lift my chin. "I already did that. It will devastate them if they know I'm about to die."

He rubs a finger over his chin. "I suppose that makes sense. I'll just portal to the nearest restaurant then."

"No," I say quickly. "You can't buy pancakes and bacon at just any restaurant. It has to be a diner. But the food will be cold by the time you get back. You'll have to get the ingredients from a supermarket." I wave at the makeshift kitchen. "I can cook food here."

"This is just my temporary hideout. I don't normally eat here. It's not well equipped."

"If you can make a fire in that fireplace over there, I can make do with what you have."

He considers that for a moment while I rack my brain for a way of getting out of here. A weapon. There must be knives in the drawers.

"Fine," he says after a moment. "Give me your—how do you say?—grocery list."

I tell him what I need.

When I'm done, he nods. Tapping his temple, he says, "Got it all stored up here."

"I don't know why I never thought to ask."

"Ask what?"

"What your power is, the one you show to Alit in Lona."

He smiles. "Don't blame yourself for the oversight. I made it my job to become invisible. If people didn't notice me or pay me much attention, it was by conscious design."

"What is it again?" He's already shared that information, and I don't really care. I'm just playing for time. Every second I gain is a second that Aruan may discover me gone. But the connection between us is no longer there. The bond obviously doesn't stretch across parallel worlds. He won't know where to find me. I have no one to rely on to save me but myself. "Just for curiosity's sake."

"I told you. It's my photographic memory. You're not very intelligent for a powerful Alit, Elsie."

With that reprimand, he opens a portal and leaves.

I sag against the wall, the strength leaving my body. The first thing I do is run for the door. It's locked. I try the windows and find the same. It's impossible to force them open. The wood is too thick to break. I focus on the wall, trying to dissolve it, but nothing happens. Tarix must've put a seal on the cabin.

Shit.

Concentrating hard, I imagine a portal opening in front of me, the space folding to accommodate my will.

No luck.

It's harder than it seems.

With no other options left, I search for a weapon. Unfortunately, Tarix isn't stupid. He's removed every utensil from the cabin except for the spoons. That leaves me with hitting him over the head with a pot or stabbing him with the blunt end of a spoon.

Despondent, I grab the pot and slide down the wall

until I'm sitting on the floor. I'm so scared, not only for myself but also for Aruan and what will happen if he finds I'm missing.

An ironic laugh bubbles from my lips. Ever since Aruan took me, I've tried to get away from him. Now I'd give anything for him to find me. I'd give anything to be back in his arms. To embrace him one last time. All I want is one more chance to tell him I—

I halt my thoughts, my mind stumbling over the word I was thinking.

Love.

Yes, there's no more hiding or denying it.

I love him. I've loved him for a long time. Since the day he saved me from the Phaelix. I just didn't realize it then. Maybe even from the day I was born.

Fuck.

Now it's too late. He may never know. And that's the notion that devastates me. Not dying. Not perishing at Tarix's hand. It's never having told Aruan what he deserves to know—that he means everything to me, and that I'll love him forever.

Until my dying day, which may be minutes away.

CHAPTER 22
ARUAN

I'm leaving another abandoned Phaelix settlement after one more fruitless search when it happens.

My connection with Elsie goes dead.

Like a crater tearing a hole in the ground, the place where I felt her in my chest becomes a gaping void.

I stop, the nothingness slamming reversely into me just as her presence had pumped through my veins when the Phaelix had brought her to Zerra.

Impossible.

I refuse to believe it.

But the bond doesn't lie.

It's gone.

She's dead.

A howl tears from my chest as impossible, scorching heat explodes from me, radiating far and wide before forming a mushroom shape far above me. Shockwaves ripple through the air, killing trees and shrubs all around me, as far as the eye can see.

It should kill me too—I wish it would—but it doesn't. Somehow, I'm protected from the destruction around me. A destruction that will linger for eons to come—because I know what this is, what will happen if any Alit, Phaelix, or animal crosses the area.

They'll die.

It's the terrible, poisonous explosion from my childhood all over again, but this time, I can't bring myself to care.

As I stand among the death and destruction I've caused, all I feel is rage. It consumes me, devours me. My vision unravels. I clench my hands, needing to kill. Wanting to kill. Everyone and everything, but especially whoever killed Elsie. The person who's been after her since the day she arrived at the palace. Maybe Tarix. Maybe not. I'm going to torture every Alit and Phaelix until I know the truth.

I hold on to that thought to maintain sanity, clinging to it like a drowning man to a piece of driftwood until it carries me back to lucidity.

When my sight clears, I'm on my knees. I don't know how I got to this position or when I hit the ground. I only know I'm on a path of annihilation, more dead than alive. It's worse than when she disappeared the first time, when I was just a child. Because this round? I had time to get to know her. To fall for her. To claim her and make her mine. To love her.

Now she's gone, ripped from me again, and the agony is unbearable. The pain makes me blind. The ache is a flame scorching my soul. Yet everything continues as normal when I walk through a portal into the Great Hall, everyone going about their day as if nothing is wrong.

The sound that leaves my lips rips the palace right down the middle, the cracks running like lightning down the walls. That's when they start running. The bridge collapses, preventing them from escaping. Windows explode, and the sky turns dark.

Somewhere on the horizon, a volcano burns red. The ground shakes beneath my feet. An earthquake uproots trees. The sea rolls closer in giant waves, washing through the lower levels of the palace.

I'm not aware of walking to my quarters. I simply find myself standing there, taking in the emptiness. Like a masochist, I let the cold claws of that suffocating notion strangle my heart. Like a stone sinking to the bottom of a lake, the emptiness settles inside me.

She's not here.

An ear-splitting cry pierces the sky. Betty. Even the dragon knows. Animals sense these terrible things.

"Aruan!" Something shakes me. "Aruan, please!"

I swat it away like a fly. It thumps against the wall.

"Aruan, stop!"

I can't. I can't control the rage eating me alive from the inside out.

"Think about Elsie!"

The name twists like a blade into my gut. It burns cold and hot. "Elsie."

"Yes, Elsie. Think about your mate."

My mate.

My senses clear enough to recognize Gaia. She keeps her distance, looking scared out of her wits as she rubs the back of her head.

I bite out every word. "Who did it? Who killed her?"

"Killed her? Is that—" She cuts herself short, trembling as she asks in a scratchy voice, "Why do you think that?"

"Because I feel it," I snarl, the darkness already creeping in again.

"Look at me." Gaia rushes over and grabs my arm. "Look at me!"

She's taking a huge risk, daring to get near me when I'm an explosion just waiting to happen. But her touch grounds me.

"What do you feel, Aruan?"

My voice is dead along with my heart. "Nothing." Only the rage lives and grows.

"If she were dead, there would've been a body."

Maybe there is. I wouldn't even know where to look. We're only connected as long as the bond is alive.

"Think about it." Gaia's command is more of a plea. "You thought she was dead once, and it wasn't the case."

Her words hook into my brain, clearing the fog of rage a tiny bit. "She was on Earth."

"Yes," she breathes. "It's a possibility."

A slight one, but still…

The rumbling of the walls stops. The ground ceases

to shake. The sun returns, casting light on the destruction visible through the windows.

I still don't give a dragon's ass about what I've done, the terrible emptiness battling with the fury inside me. Yet that possibility, that tiny sliver of hope… "Why would she be there?" The hollow voice barely sounds like my own. "How would she even have gotten there?"

"If Tarix is nowhere to be found on Zerra, maybe he's hiding on Earth."

I drag in a breath, the sliver of hope expanding before my fury rises again, along with the simmering power. "You think Tarix took Elsie?" With effort, I keep the power contained, the hope just enough to make me want to do so despite the rage burning me up inside.

"I don't know, but it's possible." Gaia squeezes my arm. "Think about it, Aruan. After someone tried to poison Elsie and tampered with the bridge, Kian read the minds of everyone in the palace. The only minds he couldn't read were yours and Elsie's because you blocked them from him. However, he never got an accurate reading on Tarix's mind. He thought the vagueness was just because Tarix is a little dumb."

"Except maybe he's not."

The more I think about it, the more I'm convinced that Tarix is the one who tried to kill Elsie. The mere idea feeds the dark power inside me. Moon cycles of lightning flash outside, raining down from the sky.

Gaia gives a start and worriedly eyes the flashes of light through the broken window. "We won't know for sure until we find him, and if he created portals for the Phaelix to bring slaves from Earth, he's capable of going to Earth himself. What better place to hide?"

I've considered that thought, that Tarix is on Earth, but I first wanted to be sure he's not on Zerra. Gritting my teeth, I tamp down my power as Gaia says, "Mother should be able to help. Let's go see her."

She pulls me toward the archway, and I let her drag me along, the ember of hope flaring brighter within me. If there's a chance that Elsie is still breathing, I need to stay in control.

I need to save her.

My mother is dabbing a cloth to a cut on my father's forearm when we enter her quarters. A big bruise blooms over her forehead. Kian is pouring a potion from a flacon into a goblet, presumably something for the pain. The room is a mess of fallen stones and broken glass. Their injuries are no doubt a result of that.

My parents stare at me, white-faced, neither of them asking the question on the tips of their tongues. What happened? Why did I lose control of my power? They're too scared that talking about it will set me off again.

Instead, I do the asking as I look at the deep slash on my father's arm. "Where's Vitai?" My voice is as emotionless as it is harsh.

"Tending to Incus," my mother answers. "A stone from the ceiling fell on his head."

I feel no guilt. Nothing. The numbness has set in at an alarmingly fast rate, much quicker than before.

"Elsie is gone," Gaia blurts before turning to Kian. "Can you tap into her mind?"

The gaze he trains on me says he knows I'm not using a protective barrier to prevent him from reading her thoughts. Averting his eyes, he gives a single shake of his head.

"Then she may be on Earth," Gaia says.

"What makes you think that?" my father asks.

"Mother sent her there once. What if Tarix has done the same?" She turns to me. "You should go look for her there." She pauses before adding in a pained whisper, "At least then you'll know."

The tension on my mother's face eases slightly. "Gaia is right. You should go."

So if my power flares out of control again, it'll be on Earth, not on Zerra. They don't say it, but I can see it in their eyes.

Nobody's even mentioning the council that would normally have to approve this. They're only too eager to get rid of me.

For all I know, it's a trap. Maybe I'm the one they're banishing to Earth this time, a plan they concocted while I went feral and my power ran rampant. If I go, it may very well be a one-way ride. There may not be a portal to bring me back.

And maybe it's better that way.

If Elsie is dead…

"Do it," I growl, barely able to hold back the surge of rage. "Give me a portal."

My mother nods, and the circle of lights appears in front of me. I don't look back as I step inside.

A dissolving sensation later, I'm spat out on the other end, finding myself on a green pasture in front of a house when I come to. It's a small pasture but a big house. Elsie's parents' house. I recognize the furniture through the window. But I also recognize something else—a vibration that hums through my body. Awareness hits me like a strike of lightning, firing through my veins.

Dragons.

Gaia was right.

Elsie is here.

The sensation grows inside me, filling every part of me until I'm on fire with it. That painfully sweet longing tugs at my heart again. It becomes unbearable, tormenting me until I think I'll go crazy, and then everything inside me clicks into place. Perfect peace descends on me. I've never felt such harmony. For the first time in my life, I'm whole and not broken. Not incomplete.

My heartbeat quickens, keeping time in my chest with a pleasant echo. It takes me a moment to figure out the echo doesn't mirror my pulse but is someone else's. I can't explain what's happening to me, but the longer I listen to those twin pulses beating in my ears, the more at home I feel in my own skin… as well as in a different skin.

Then it hits me. I'm no longer alone. Elsie is here, inside me, our bond complete. She's a part of me just like I'm a part of her, two people who've become one. And I know exactly where she is.

I take off toward the path, trying to get my bearings. She's not close but not so far that I can't reach her through a portal. If not for the miraculous completion of our bond, it would've taken a long time to find her. I would've needed to go back for Gaia or my mother, who would've had to do continuous portal work.

A contraption with windows like a house and wheels like a cart rounds the corner. It moves fast, heading right at me. A man sits inside what I presume is armor. I blink as he screeches to a halt right in front of me with a blaring noise that comes from his armor. He leans through the open window and shouts curses at me.

I don't have time for this. I bang a fist on the front of his armor. A huge dent appears in the shiny surface. The man shuts his mouth and closes his window. He moves around me and gets out of my way. I barely make it to the opposite side of the path before another contraption in a different color barrels past.

Closing my mind off to the surroundings, I focus on Elsie. Her feelings spear through my heart. Her pulse races in my chest, speeding up my own. The cold sweat that covers my body is a mirror-reflex of our bond.

She's scared. It's the kind of fear one feels when

one's life is in the balance. I feel her breath leave her lungs even as I call up a portal, letting her know I'm on my way, refusing to face what the bond is trying to tell me.

That I may have come this far only to be too late.

CHAPTER 23

ELSIE

Tarix is still out on his shopping errand, but it's been a while. He could return at any moment.

I refocus my efforts on finding animals around the cabin in which he has locked me. He was clever enough to make sure there are none except for birds and insects. I test my power on a few ants that pass through the kitchen. The ants change direction as I command them. However, they're of no use to me. I can't attack Tarix with a few sugar ants. If they were fire ants, it would've been a different story.

Where the hell am I? There's not even a bee or a wasp around, and it's freezing cold.

I stoke the fire I built in the fireplace so that it doesn't go out. I found a few pieces of wood, old newspapers, and a box of matches in the cupboard next to the fireplace. The warmth is welcome, but my main objective is boiling the water in the pot that hangs from a hook over the flames.

Rubbing my arms, I take stock of the space for a second time in case I've missed something that could be useful as a weapon, but the room is pretty much bare. It's not a very comfortable hideout.

Awareness of Aruan hits me just as I throw the last log onto the fire. The sensations changing inside me are both scary and beautiful. I've never felt anything like it. The vagueness of our bond is gone, and in its place is pure and certain clarity. My whole body trembles with cognizance while heat shoots up my veins. I swear every cell in my body is vibrating. Most of all, there's a deep-seated notion of being whole and complete. It's as if an open line of communication has been established between our souls. I don't know why or how it's happened. All I know is…

He's here!

The knowledge gives me strength. I want to cry with relief, but the fight is far from over, and there's no guarantee that Aruan will find me in time.

I've barely had a few seconds to enjoy my first experience of our fully formed bond when a portal appears. A part of me hopes it will be Aruan, but the bond tells me differently.

When Tarix appears with a brown shopping bag under each arm, I'm ready. I throw the boiling water in his face and hit him hard over the head with the pot. He drops the bags, covering his face with his arms as he fights to stay on his feet. I block out his horrible screams, trying not to think about the damage I'm doing as I hit him over and over again.

I swing the pot through the air, putting all my strength into it, but Tarix is strong. He deflects my blows without going down. I'm quickly tiring myself while his knees aren't even buckling.

I've got the pot firmly in my grasp, bringing it down for another hit when he knocks it from my hands. For a second, the sickening sight of his face—skin blistered and red, eyes puffy and swollen with the pupil of one a milky color, and brown hair caked with blood—catches me off-guard.

He grabs me in that moment's hesitation, locking his hands around my raised arms.

Snarling, he drags me closer. "You're going to regret this. I was going to end you painlessly."

I kick and twist. Even injured, he's as strong as a bear, easily wrapping his hands around my neck and cutting off my airflow. I scratch his arms, but my efforts have no effect on him. I aim for his eyes and the bubbly, angry-red skin of his cheeks, my nails not finding their target as he easily lifts me off my feet.

I land kicks on his stomach and chest. He doesn't even grunt. He's like a wall of bricks, the muscles beneath his clothes hard and unrelenting. I tear at his hair until my fingers come away with bloodied tufts sticking to them, but he only squeezes harder. Spots burst behind my eyes. My vision grows dark around the edges, unconsciousness starting to creep in.

"You're not dying that easily," he says through gritted teeth. "Not before I carve off your face."

He unlocks one hand from around my throat and plants a fist on my jaw at the same time as he releases me. The blow knocks my head sideways even as my body crumples to the ground. Air hits my lungs just as the wind is knocked out of my sails. I'm gasping like a guppy on dry ground, helpless to do anything but curl into myself before he plants a boot in my ribs.

Shit, that hurts.

He pulls back his leg and aims again. I scavenge the strength I have left, catching his ankle and yanking with all my might. He falls backward with flailing arms, hitting the floor on his ass and winning me a few precious seconds to push myself onto my hands and knees. But he's faster than I am.

I brace myself for the impact as he bends his knee. I can't die here. I have to fight. For Aruan, my new life, and most of all, for myself. I didn't escape death countless times only to give in now, to the likes of Tarix, no less.

Throwing myself at him, I tackle him with my arms around his thighs. We go down with me on top. He grabs a fistful of my hair and drags my head back. Before he can throw me off of him, I punch a fist between his legs. He wheezes and pulls up his knees, hitting me in the stomach in the process.

I elbow him in the nuts, making him howl. While he cups his crown jewels, I struggle to my feet. That's when I feel him.

Aruan.

A portal appears. I press the heel of my boot on Tarix's throat, applying just enough pressure not to crush his windpipe. He grabs my ankle and then goes still as the circle of lights turns brighter.

"That's right, Tarix," I spit out. "Your game is over."

He grins sardonically, holding my gaze as he changes into the queen again. Aruan exits the portal to find me pinning his mother down on the floor with a boot on her neck, her face horribly disfigured and her hair clotted with blood.

Aruan stops in his tracks. Rage contorts his features.

Tarix raises a pale hand to Aruan. "Aruan, help me," he pleads in the queen's voice. "Please. It's a trap. I came to help Elsie, but look what she's done to me."

Shit. I know how this must appear. But then I look into Aruan's eyes, and everything that's happened passes between us without him or me saying a word.

Aruan turns his gaze on Tarix, staring at him and seeing the truth.

"Look what she did to me," Tarix whines again. "Help me, my son."

The hand Tarix holds out to Aruan starts to bubble and boil.

Aruan's lips pull back from his teeth. "You dared to put your hands on my mate."

The scream that leaves Tarix's mouth is in his own voice. He can't hold up the act any longer. He changes back into himself, showing his true colors.

Aruan extends an arm toward me. "Come here, Elsie."

I don't hesitate. I stumble over to his side and let him pull me against him. He brushes a kiss over my temple without taking his eyes off of Tarix. "All right?" His power rages, I can feel it, but he's in control, our completed bond a steadying influence on him.

I smile through the pain. "You know perfectly well how I am."

"I just wanted to hear your voice." He kisses the top of my head. "Don't look."

"Don't do it." I place a hand over his heart. "Don't melt him."

A muscle ticks in Aruan's jaw. "He deserves nothing less."

"The people he betrayed deserve to hear his confession."

Cradling his arm against his chest, Tarix splutters through sobs, "I did what I did for Zerra."

Contempt distorts Aruan's features. "I've heard enough."

He looks over his shoulder at the open portal. "We have to get back to the portal my mother created."

If she's still holding it open.

I can read his thoughts, even though he doesn't say it.

I brush my palm over his chest and offer him a smile. "In the worst-case scenario, we'll stay close to my parents."

His expression darkens. "Zerra needs us."

Because I almost destroyed it. And I have to go back and fix what I can.

Before I can fully process that, he bends down and grabs Tarix's good arm. "Hold on to me, Elsie."

I cling to him as he takes us through the portal to the lawn in front of my parents' house. I'm only grateful their car isn't in the driveway, which means they must be out. I don't want them to see the blood and gore.

Dragging Tarix along, Aruan rounds the neatly trimmed hedge. His chest expands with a breath when the circle of lights comes into view.

This time, as he pulls me through, I go willingly. Wholeheartedly. Because the only place I want to be is at his side. No matter where that is.

The immediate royal family waits on the other side. The king and queen, as well as Gaia, Kian, and Vitai, are gathered in the queen's reception room.

Aruan shoves Tarix in front of his mother.

She clenches her hands. "You betrayed me."

"I did it for Zerra." Tarix repeats the same line over and over. "I did it for Zerra."

"I trusted you to advise me," the queen says. "Instead, you abused my trust."

"He'll destroy us," Tarix exclaims.

"You're wrong, Tarix." The queen's smile is grim. "Losing his mate would've destroyed us."

"That's not true." Tarix glances between the queen and the king. "You're believers. You know what the prophecy says."

"Look around you, Tarix," the queen says. "*You* almost destroyed Zerra by taking Elsie. If Aruan hadn't found her in time, that's what would've happened."

Tarix glances out the window and blanches. "But the prophecy—"

The king lunges forward to grip Tarix's nape. "The prophecy be cursed. I'll hear no more about it."

Tarix bares his teeth. "You're weak, all of you."

The king's smile is cold. "We wiped out your slave trade operation and put an end to your pitiful rebellion. Tomorrow, at first light, you'll be on trial for the crimes you've committed against the royal family and citizens of Zerra, whom you were supposed to serve."

Tarix breaks free. "I won't be judged for doing what's right."

The king's smile stretches into a dark grin. "We'll see about that." He turns to Kian. "Take him to the cells."

"We need to block the cell so he doesn't try to escape with a portal to Earth," Aruan says. "He can also change shape. He impersonated you, Mother. Don't let anyone near him lest he tries to trick them."

The queen reels at that.

"Now if you don't mind," Aruan continues. "I'd like to take care of Elsie."

He puts his arm around my waist, leading me to the archway, which I dissolve.

"You should save your strength until Vitai has healed you," he chastises as we enter the hallway.

"I need more practice. I want to open my own portals."

So I'll never be anyone's prisoner again.

Aruan's voice holds grim understanding. "I'll teach you to do it—or better yet, Gaia will. Anything you want to know, you will learn. Anything within my power is yours."

I swallow hard, thinking about what almost happened. "Thank you for finding me."

"Always." His tone softens. "You made it easy for me."

"With our bond." Stopping, I face him. "What do you think happened? How did it become complete?"

Aruan's gaze burns into me. "My mother said the bond couldn't be complete unless you loved me."

My heart lurches, then settles into a rhythm that mirrors his. "I'm… not going to say that's not true."

His heartbeat accelerates, even as his eyes drill steadily into mine. "Do you love me, Elsie from Cleveland?"

"You know I do."

"Say it," he demands. "Tell me to my face."

Threading my fingers through his hair, I press our bodies together. "I love you, mate."

Fierce joy and primal possessiveness glow in his silver eyes. "I love you too, Elsie. Always have. Always will."

His lips are on mine before I can ask him to repeat those precious words. But it doesn't matter. Because all the answers I can ever want are an eternal part of me now, locked deep inside, and no one can ever take that away.

I break the kiss not only because I need air but also because we're in the hallway. "Take me to our room."

He growls under his breath. "With pleasure."

Scooping me into his arms, he descends the stairs with a brisk pace. As he carries me, I can't help but shudder as I note the damage to the palace.

He did this.

Because I was gone.

From what I glimpsed through our bond, he almost destroyed all of Zerra. Judging by some of the repairs I see in progress, the royals have already started rebuilding what has been broken.

The man cradling me in his arms has a terrifying, godlike power, yet I'm not afraid of him. I see him for what he is: dangerous and beautiful, violent and imperfect. And mine. Above all, mine.

"And you are mine," he says roughly as the archway of our quarters dissolves and closes behind us. "Nothing and no one will ever tear us apart again."

It's a beautiful vow, one that's fitting for the start of a new life.

EPILOGUE

ELSIE

Dawn breaks over the horizon, illuminating our room with the first light falling through the window. A soft pink sash runs over the purple glow of the remnants of night. A few stars are still sprinkled across the sky.

Turning on my side in our bed, I stretch out and yawn. Aruan is awake in an instant, staring at me with that beautiful silver gaze I love so much.

He brushes a hand up my naked hip. "You're awake early."

I burrow closer with a smile. "Zinnia will come bouncing in here before the sun is up."

His lips curve seductively. "That gives us a few minutes."

"Is that so?" I raise an eyebrow. "And what do you intend to do with that time?"

"This," he says in a deep, low voice as he rolls me onto my back.

"You're insatiable," I murmur, but my belly heats and my skin breaks out in goosebumps from anticipation alone.

He moves down my body with soft kisses, and then he works his way up with gentle nips on my inner thighs. I gasp when he spreads my legs wider and buries his head between them. His mouth feels so good and his tongue even better. I thread my fingers through the thick strands of his hair, holding on as he brings me to the edge without mercy. Like an explosion. Fast and devastating.

I go over as he shifts up and enters me. He interweaves our fingers and lifts my arms above my head to press the backs of my hands to the bed. Our gazes remain locked as he rocks inside me with a lazy pace.

The pleasure builds again but not just in my core. My heart swells with emotions I can't contain. My soul threatens to burst with happiness. Our connection is perfect, our love complete. It goes so much further than lust, although the desire never diminishes. Sometimes, when I look into his eyes like this, I'm scared that it's too perfect, that someone or something will rip it away and that I may lose it all. But then I wrap my arms around his neck, like now, showing both of us I'm never letting go.

He kisses me with so much tenderness it makes me want to cry. As always, he knows what I'm thinking.

His promise feathers over my lips. "No one can take this from you, Elsie."

Yes. Because it will always be a part of me, no matter what happens.

He seals his oath with another kiss. "I'm not going to let anything happen to you."

"I know," I whisper, moving my hips to his rhythm, allowing myself to fall into the warmth and protection of his strong arms just as I'm falling apart for him.

Again.

His lips curve against mine, the smile audible in his husky words. "I love you, Elsie."

I give him the truth as I cling to him while aftershocks are the non-verbal proof of what he does to me. "I love you, Aruan."

He comes with me, a physical reflection of our complete harmony. Of his love and devotion. Foreheads pressed together, we catch our breaths.

And not a minute too soon.

A little girl's bubbly laughter sounds on the other side of the wall. Aruan grins before kissing me one last time, a languid kiss that makes my toes curl. He pulls away, always satisfying me while simultaneously leaving me craving just a little more. The bed sheet dissolves and turns into a nightdress on my body and pants riding low on his hips.

God, I love it when he does that. It still turns me on.

He lifts the seal he put on our quarters and dissolves the wall. Zinnia skips into the room, her strawberry-blond curls bouncing around her face. I'm glad she got Aruan's eyes. This way, she's a bit of both of us. And plenty of herself. Zinnia has a huge personality. She even gives the older royals a run for their money.

She carries a toy dragon carved from wood in one hand, making it fly through the air. Our little girl has never taken to dolls. She prefers animals and dinosaurs.

She jumps onto the bed, flying the dragon low over Aruan's head. A delighted shriek leaves her lips as he catches and tickles her.

"Got you," he says, planting a kiss on her curls.

"My dragon got you first," she says with a jut of her chin that dares him to defy her.

Of course he doesn't. Aruan gives her everything she wants.

"As I should," he says, in tune with my train of thought. "My daughter will always get everything she wants. I'll make sure of it."

"Careful. You'll spoil her."

"She's a good kid."

True. Which is the only reason I don't interfere when Aruan gives her everything her little heart desires. Zinnia knows the difference between right and wrong. On values, Aruan and I agree. We're strict when it comes to teaching her what matters.

"Can we go to the Sky Bridge, Daddy?" She sits up and bounces on her knees. "Please? I want to see the sun wake up."

"Then you have to change out of your nightdress, princess." He ruffles her curls. "How about breakfast at the lake?"

"A picnic?" she squeals. "Oh, yes! Can Betty come, Mommy? Please?"

I hug her and kiss her cheek. "Betty can come."

"Yes!" She plants a sloppy kiss on my shoulder. "Thank you, Mommy."

Her nanny and tutor, Prislia, sticks her head around the archway with a broad smile. "Sorry, Your Highnesses. I tried to catch her before she could wake you up."

"I was awake anyway," I say, managing not to sound too guilty.

Aruan arches an eyebrow. *I can wake up like that every day.*

I narrow my eyes playfully. *You do.*

He gives me a scorching look. *Maybe I'll wake you up tomorrow with my head between your thighs.*

I scoff internally. *You do that too.*

I can do better. He grins. *I can wake you up with my cock already buried inside you.*

Heat pushes up my neck and down into my belly. I barely pull off a chastising frown. *Not in front of Zinnia.*

His answering wink melts my insides.

Oblivious to the nuances of the mood, Zinnia jumps off the bed and sprints through the archway, flying her dragon down the hallway.

"I'll go help her get ready," Prislia says.

"Are you sure?" I ask. "She'll tire you before you've even had breakfast."

"It's no problem at all." Prislia smiles. "We can play

the alphabet game while she dresses. It's a good opportunity to learn through play."

"Thanks." I tame my short hair by combing it through with my fingers. "She's doing so well with her letters too."

When Prislia is gone, I utter a happy laugh. "Zinnia really is a handful."

Affection glows in Aruan's eyes. "She takes after you."

"Oh, I was never that busy."

"Only because circumstances didn't allow you to be." As always, when he talks about my history on Earth, an unsettling darkness seeps into our bond. "I'm sure you would've tired your parents."

I hardly think about those sickly days. I have so much to be grateful for right here, and I prefer to live in the present.

"It's sweet of you to spend so much time with her." My chest expands with a warm, fuzzy feeling. "I know you're too busy for a picnic."

The council is voting on new laws in a week, and Aruan has done a lot to advocate for those laws in political circles, not to mention all the diplomatic visits he's made to the other kingdoms.

"You and Zinnia come first." He pushes up onto one elbow. "The rest will happen when it happens."

He's so good with our baby girl, who, at six, is not such a baby anymore. We waited two years for Zinnia, which are twenty-four moon cycles in Zerran time.

The only sadness that comes with that thought is that she's never met my parents.

Since I was appointed as ambassador for all human and Earth-related matters, I've fought hard for contact between our worlds. Yet the king and queen still believe bringing Earth technology to Zerra and vice versa isn't what nature intended for the natural development of our planets, and they prefer to leave things as they are.

For that reason, I can't bring my parents here, not even for a brief visit, and I won't risk taking Zinnia through an interworld portal until she's an adult. If a visit will ever be granted.

Maybe one day, when Aruan is king, things may change. The queen did, however, approve my application for books to be created and for children to learn to read and write. You never know. If, one day, our civilization goes the way of the ancients, at least we'll leave records of our history behind.

Aruan and I go through our morning routine but skip the breakfast we habitually have with Zinnia in our quarters. Instead, Aruan requests a picnic basket. When we walk into Zinnia's room next to ours, she's dressed in her favorite pink dress and matching shoes.

She giggles when Aruan lifts her into the air. Her skirt billows out as he puts her on her feet.

"Ready, princess?"

She slips her small hand in his, staring up at him with an adoring smile. The picture of the two of them together makes me all teary-eyed and mushy inside.

A squadron of guards go ahead inconspicuously. I understand why Aruan never takes any risks. Zerra has only known peace since the nasty business with Tarix. He's long gone now. He escaped trial by changing himself into the king and overpowering the bewildered guard who delivered his meal in his cell. He profited from the open archway to escape with the Phaelix we intercepted in the portal on our way back from Earth.

Karma must be a bitch, though, because Tarix only got as far as the lake before a dinosaur got to him. He accidentally ran between a quetzalcoatlus and her nest, unknowingly cutting her off from her eggs. The mangled bodies of Tarix and the Phaelix were found on the shore. There've been no threats or unrest since. Still, my mate is always careful. Zinnia has the same necklace as me to eliminate any possibility of poisoning. Aruan sports a ring with the stone, one I gave him as a mating gift.

Pip pushes off a windowsill in the Great Hall and follows us onto the Sky Bridge. We stop on the circular platform in the center to take in the sunrise, which is Zinnia's favorite moment of the day. Pip lands on the rail next to me, eyeing the basket in Aruan's hands longingly. Betty arrives with a swoop of her giant wings to welcome us.

I breathe in the fresh air, enjoying how it immediately invigorates me. I never grow tired of not being tired.

Zinnia grabs the rope and swings herself over the platform like a little monkey.

Aruan drops the basket, grabs her around the waist, and hoists her back to safety. "What did I say about swinging on the ropes?"

I stifle a laugh. "She definitely takes after you."

He straightens the ribbon on her dress before letting her go. "I never told you about that."

My smile is smug. "You didn't have to." I can feel the excitement of swinging over the sheer drop in his childhood memories.

Betty dives down and turns toward the lake.

"Can I fly, Daddy?"

Aruan's voice is stern. "Not until you're older."

Zinnia's power made itself known early. She used to levitate as a baby, which is why we had to keep the windows in her room closed. Sometimes, when she gets excited, she floats a few steps above the ground instead of walking.

Kian reckons she'll be able to reach impressive heights when she's an adult, maybe as high as dragons, which is the only reason I'm not freaking out when she swings herself over the platform. I know she can hold herself in the air if necessary, and she's doing it for longer periods with every passing day.

Aruan pulls me under his arm and takes Zinnia's hand on the other side. Together, we watch the sky grow from pink to orange. The sun peeks over the sea, turning the black water into liquid gold.

Zinnia sucks in a breath. "That's so pretty."

"Yes," I say. "It is."

A few pterosaurs cut over the water in the distance,

their silhouettes black against the clear blue sky. It does make a pretty picture, but nowhere near as beautiful as the powerful man holding the little girl's small hand in his broad one as if she's made of paper-thin glass.

I've come a long way since I first landed in the middle of a strange jungle with giant insects and scary humanoid lizards. I never thought the happiness surging through me was possible or that such utter content existed.

In the dusky hue of the growing morning, in that special place where day and night meet, a comet with a blazing pink tail tears through the sky.

Somewhere on Earth, another couple is standing together, watching as a new day begins.

WHAT TO READ NEXT?

Elsie and Aruan's journey ends here. Thank you for following their epic love story!

To be notified about our upcoming books, sign up for our newsletters at www.annazaires.com and www.charmainepauls.com. All of our titles are available in print and audio as well.

Craving more edgy, suspenseful romance? Check out *Close Liaisons* by Anna Zaires and *Coerced Kiss* by Charmaine Pauls. And don't miss our action-packed mafia romance collaboration, *White Nights*!

Turn the page for sneak peeks and to learn more about our books.

EXCERPT FROM WHITE NIGHTS BY ANNA ZAIRES AND CHARMAINE PAULS

Power. That's what I think of when I spot him across the ER. Power and danger.

One of the wealthiest Russian oligarchs, Alex Volkov is as ruthless as he is magnetic. He always gets what he wants, and what he wants is me, in his bed.

He's the kind of trouble every woman should run from. The bullet his bodyguard took for him proves that.

I should stay far away, but for one night, I give in to temptation. Before I know it, he's pulling me deeper into his world of excess and violence, invading not only my life but my heart.

How much trust can I place in a man so dangerous? How much do I dare risk for his love?

Alex is strolling leisurely down the hallway, dressed in a pair of jeans and a gray sweater. The clothes hug his large frame, revealing wide shoulders and a muscular build. A pair of hard-looking men are walking a few yards behind him, their eyes sharp and vigilant. His bodyguards.

He's looking at the phone in his hand, and I speed up, hoping I'll be able to walk past him unnoticed.

No such luck.

As though sensing my gaze on him, he looks up, and his blue eyes narrow with recognition. Then a small smile curves his lips, softening them a bit.

A warm shiver snakes down my spine, heating my skin, even as some instinct tells me to run. The urge is so strong my leg muscles tighten with it, the needles of adrenaline sinking deeper into my skin and spiking my heart rate.

Don't be a coward, Kate.

Steeling my spine, I continue walking toward him, trying not to react to the way his eyes rake over my body and finally linger on my mouth. When he meets my gaze again, there's so much heat in the look he gives me I may burn on the spot. My core clenches, and liquid warmth dampens my underwear.

Dammit. This is insane.

He stops in front of me. I'm cognizant of his bodyguards a few yards away, but all my attention is focused on him. I'd forgotten how tall he is, how big his body is compared to mine. I have to crane my neck to meet his eyes, and I can't help but be conscious of his size, his strength, his sheer maleness.

His accented voice is soft and slightly mocking, as if he knows the effect he has on me. "Hello, Katerina."

I stare up at him, Joanne's words ringing in my ears. I've always approached my relationships the same way as everything else, with a calm, steady rationality. I've never been one to leap before I looked. That's my mom's way, not mine. I like to think, to apply the same logical reasoning to dating as I do to my career. Casual hookups weren't my thing in college, and I've never had a one-night stand. The risks have never been worth the benefits. Instead, I've dated men I've liked and respected, with whom I've connected on a mental and emotional level. A man's personality has always been far more important to me than his looks.

I have no idea what Alex's personality is like. I don't know him at all. There's nothing logical in the way he makes me feel, nothing rational in the way my body reacts to his. Something within me responds to him on a subconscious, instinctive level, and there's nothing I can do about it.

Worst yet, what little I do know about him is frightening. He's a wealthy man from a place where wealth and corruption go hand in hand, and he's pissed off someone enough that they want to kill him. How crazy would it be to get involved with someone like that?

Insane. Completely, totally, and utterly irresponsible.

Yet yesterday's thought about throwing caution to the wind keeps wiggling into my mind. What if Joanne is right? It's not as if I'm going to marry or even date the guy. All he wants is a brief sexual fling. I can sleep with him, get this strange craving out of my system, and go back to my normal life. I'm not ready for another relationship—the incident with Tony has left a sour taste in my mouth—and Alex isn't looking for one. Would it really be so terrible to do something impulsive for once and give in to this attraction? To hook up with an attractive man?

Before I can think better of it, I give Alex an answering smile. "Hi. How's Igor doing?"

Something dark flashes across his face before his expression smooths out and turns inscrutable. "He's much better, thanks."

His eyes travel down my body again, making me feel flushed all over. I've never felt so blatantly desired in my life, and it's incredibly seductive.

When he looks back at me, there's a cynical tilt to his lips. "What time does your shift end?" His voice is low and deep, his tone self-assured. Somehow, he's sensed my weakening resolve.

I swallow. "At ten."

I can't believe myself. Am I really going to do this? Agree to a purely sexual arrangement with a man I barely know?

He flashes me a darkly sensual smile that makes my core tighten with desire. "I'd like to see you tonight. How about we grab a bite to eat after your shift ends?"

I hesitate. Despite his animal magnetism, there's something unsettling about him, some hardness in the line of his mouth that makes me think he can be ruthless. How can I even think about getting involved with a man like that? Someone who's a total stranger? What if he's as corrupt and dangerous as Nadia portrayed the wealthy Russians to be?

As though sensing my reservations, he says quietly, "It will be just dinner, I promise. I won't force you to do anything you don't want."

I blink, surprised. "A dinner at ten?" I thought *grabbing a bite to eat* was a euphemism for sex, at least the way he said it.

"Won't you be hungry after your work is done?"

"Probably," I say slowly.

I was planning on grabbing a quick sandwich at home before plopping into bed, but dinner with Alex sounds much more appealing. True, he unnerves me, but he also fascinates me. Surely a dinner won't be a big deal.

"Then it's decided," he says, his tone brooking no argument. "I'll send a car to pick you up here after work. The restaurant is nearby, but I don't want you to walk alone. I'll meet you there."

Before I can reply, he heads down the hallway, his bodyguards trailing in his wake.

Order your copy of *White Nights* today at www.annazaires.com!

EXCERPT FROM CLOSE LIAISONS BY ANNA ZAIRES

In the near future, the Krinar rule the Earth. An advanced race from another galaxy, they are still a mystery to us—and we are completely at their mercy.

Shy and innocent, Mia Stalis is a college student in New York City who has led a very normal life. Like most people, she's never had any interactions with the invaders—until one fateful day in the park changes everything. Having caught Korum's eye, she must now contend with a powerful, dangerously seductive Krinar who wants to possess her and will stop at nothing to make her his own.

How far would you go to regain your freedom? How much would you sacrifice to help your people? What choice will you make when you begin to fall for your enemy?

The ride to her apartment was oddly uneventful, taking only a few minutes in the absence of traffic. He again held her hand, gently rubbing her palm in a soothing manner. Despite her initial nervousness, Mia closed her eyes, leaned back against the comfortable seat, and was just starting to drift off when they arrived at their destination.

He walked her up the five flights of stairs to her apartment, holding her arm as an apparent precaution against any alcohol-induced unsteadiness. She felt tired and sleepy, wanting nothing more than to collapse into her bed at home. At one point, she managed to stumble and nearly fall anyway, missing a step with her high-heeled shoe. Korum sighed and lifted her into his arms, carrying her up the remaining two flights despite her mumbled protestations.

Upon reaching her apartment, he carefully set her back on her feet, briefly keeping her pressed against his hard body before letting her pull away. His hands remained on her waist, holding her at a short distance. Mia stared at him, mesmerized. Her breathing picked up, and warm moisture pooled between her legs as she realized what the large bulge she'd felt in his jeans meant. His breathing was a little fast too, and she doubted that it had anything to do with carrying a hundred-pound human girl up two flights of stairs. He leaned toward her, eyes nearly yellow at this point, and

Mia froze as he cupped the back of her head and pressed his lips to hers.

He kissed her leisurely, his tongue exploring her mouth with exquisite gentleness, even as he held her against him in an unbreakable grip. Mia moaned, a wave of heat surging through her body and leaving an oddly pleasurable sense of lethargy in its wake. Somewhere in the back of her mind, a warning bell was going off, but all she could concentrate on was his mouth and the sensations spreading throughout her body. He brought her closer, pressing his groin against her belly, and she felt his hardness again, her sex clenching in response. He lightly sucked on her lower lip, pulling it into his mouth, and his hand slid down her back to cup her buttocks, lifting her off the ground so he could grind his erection directly against her clitoris through their layers of clothing.

The pressure building inside her was different and stronger than anything she'd ever experienced, and Mia groaned with frustration, wanting more. Her hands somehow found their way to his shoulders, kneading the heavy muscles through his shirt, and it was not enough. She wanted, needed the feel of his naked skin against her own, the slide of his heavy cock into her sex, quenching the empty pulsing sensation she felt there. She wrapped her legs around his waist, grinding against him, and the sensations built to a fever pitch. She hovered on the edge for a few delicious seconds, and then went over, climaxing with a muffled scream against his lips. He groaned as well, his other hand reaching under her skirt and tearing at her tights as he let go of her mouth to press burning kisses on her neck and collarbone.

"Mia? Is that you?" A familiar voice reached through her daze, and Mia realized with mortification that Jessie had opened the apartment door and was staring at them in shock. "Are you okay? Do you want me to call the police?" Her roommate clearly wasn't sure how to interpret what she was seeing.

Still wrapped around Korum, Mia felt a shudder go through his body as he visibly fought to regain control. Suddenly fearing for Jessie, Mia barked at her, "Yes, I'm fine! Go back inside and leave us alone!" A hurt look appeared on her roommate's face, and she vanished inside the apartment, slamming the door behind her.

Mia pushed at Korum, trying to put some distance between them. "Please let me go," she said quietly, wanting nothing more than to curl up into a little ball in her room and cry. He hesitated for a second, and then lowered her to her feet, still keeping her pressed against his body. His golden skin appeared flushed from within, and his eyes still had a strong yellow undertone. The bulge against her stomach showed no signs of abating, and Mia shivered, realizing that he was holding onto his self-control by a hair. "Please," she repeated, knowing that there was nothing she could do to make him release her until he was ready.

"You want me to let you go? After all that?" His voice was harsh and guttural, and the arms locked around her back tightened until she could barely breathe.

Mia nodded, trembling, the white-hot desire she'd felt earlier giving way to a confusing jumble of fear and acute embarrassment. He looked at her, his expression dark and unreadable, and then very deliberately removed his arms from around her waist and stepped away.

"All right," he said softly. "Have it your way. Go to your little room, and tell your roommate all about it. Have yourself a good cry about what a little slut you are, coming like that from a kiss right out in the hallway." His eyes glittered at the stricken expression on her face. "And then you better get used to the idea that you'll come a lot more, from everything I do to you—and I will literally do everything."

With that promise, he turned away and walked toward the stairs. Pausing before entering the stairwell, he looked back and said, "I will pick you up after class tomorrow. No more games, Mia."

EXCERPT FROM COERCED KISS BY CHARMAINE PAULS

I'm an alibi for a killer, but he demands so much more than my testimony.

I stumbled across something I wasn't supposed to discover. I saw something I wasn't meant to see, and now I'm an alibi for a killer.

He's the most feared and powerful man in the New York underworld. I don't have a choice but to do as he says.

But he commands so much more than just my testimony.

~

Grabbing her upper arm, I break her run. The momentum flings her sideways, slamming her back against the wall. A soft puff escapes her lips as the air is knocked from her lungs. The strap of the bag is caught between my palm and her bicep, the buckle pressing into my flesh. I'm on her in a blink, pinning her frame against the bricks while swinging the strap of her bag over my shoulder to free my hand. My weight alone is enough to keep her in place, but the fingers I wrap around her throat and the tip of the knife I push against her belly are automatic reflexes that come from years of street fighting.

Like earlier, she freezes, her chin tipped up and the back of her head resting against the wall as she stares at me with wide, whisky-colored eyes. The streetlight washes over her, illuminating her features. From up close, I can make out the freckles on her nose and cheeks. That waterfall of fiery curls frames a small oval face. She's a delicate, exotic creature, more beautiful than a fragile little winged fairy.

I catalog the visual clues with a quick, practiced glance. Her shift dress and cardigan are humble. The thread is cheap. The matching set reminds me of supermarket clothing, yet on her, it's pretty. Paired with ballerina style flats, she pulls off a cute look. The soft soles of her shoes explain why I didn't hear her coming. My senses are always sharp.

I home those senses in on her now, taking in every little detail. She smells fresh, like someone who just stepped out of the shower. Standing flush against her, the difference in our height is even more apparent. Her chin barely reaches my collarbone. Her body is small and her bones are fragile. Her life is vulnerable. I hold it in my hands.

The knowledge flows between us in a quiet stare, a myriad of emotions transmitted in the flash of a second without a single word spoken. The pulse in her throat flutters under my palm. The wild gallop of her heart penetrates my breastbone and echoes in my chest. In this moment, as I become the master of her fate, her heart beats only for me.

For the first time in my life, I know what it feels like to own a life. It's different than killing. Giving isn't the same as taking. The knowledge is intoxicating. It stalls me. The rush goes straight to my head, and as I lean closer, trapping the blade between us, all the blood that pumps with something other than adrenaline through my veins goes straight to my cock.

I grow hard against her soft belly. She feels it. Her big, stunning eyes grow even rounder with the knowledge.

Fuck me.

Who would've guessed I'd be into this? I never realized I was such a twisted, kinky son of a bitch. Then again, it's the first time I hold a woman at knife point. Although, it's not the knife kink. It's not the blade. And it's not her fear. Well, not only. It's the control. It's knowing that in this well-lit corner of a dark street I am her god. Whether she breathes or utters her last sound for me and for my ears alone is entirely at my whim. She's a clever girl. She reads me well. The realization dawns in her eyes as she watches me with terrified uncertainty.

I allow myself to indulge in the fantasy just for a moment, imagining how I'd make her kneel and worship her god. I won't have to wine and dine her. I won't have to indulge in fruitless conversations. I won't have to meet her family and make promises I never intend to keep. The best part is that I don't have to trust her, because for as long as I live, I'll never trust a woman again. All I have to do is command her.

That's when I know.

I'm not going to kill her.

ABOUT THE AUTHORS

Anna Zaires is a *New York Times, USA Today,* and #1 international bestselling author of sci-fi romance and contemporary dark erotic romance. She fell in love with books at the age of five, when her grandmother taught her to read. Since then, she has always lived partially in a fantasy world where the only limits were those of her imagination. Currently residing in Florida, Anna is happily married to Dima Zales (a science fiction and fantasy author) and closely collaborates with him on all their works. To learn more, please visit www.annazaires.com.

Charmaine Pauls loves to write dark and edgy romance that will melt both your e-reader and your heart. She's a mom of two teenagers, an adorable dog, and a dominant cat. Her country of birth is South Africa where many of her stories play off. Her French husband kidnapped her to the south of France where she currently lives with her family. When she's not writing, you'll find her in the kitchen baking cakes or in the gym lifting weights (because ... all those cakes!).

Printed in Dunstable, United Kingdom

71550444R10205